A NOTE ON THE AUTHOR

DAVID PARK has written eight books including *The Big Snow*, *Swallowing the Sun*, *The Truth Commissioner*, *The Light of Amsterdam* and, most recently, *The Poets' Wives*. He has won the Authors' Club First Novel Award, the Bass Ireland Arts Award for Literature, the Ewart-Biggs Memorial Prize, the American Ireland Fund Literary Award and the University of Ulster's McCrea Literary Award, three times. He has received a Major Individual Artist Award from the Arts Council of Northern Ireland and been shortlisted for the Irish Novel of the Year Award three times. He lives in County Down, Northern Ireland.

Stone
Kingdoms

DAVID PARK

B L O O M S B U R Y

LONDON · NEW DELHI · NEW YORK · SYDNEY

First published in Great Britain by Phoenix House in 1996
This paperback published 2015

Bloomsbury Publishing Plc
50 Bedford Square
London
WC1B 3DP

www.bloomsbury.com

Bloomsbury is a trademark of Bloomsbury Publishing Plc

Bloomsbury Publishing, London, New Delhi, New York and Sydney

A CIP catalogue record for this book is available
from the British Library

ISBN 978 1 4088 6615 3

10 9 8 7 6 5 4 3 2 1

Printed and bound in Great Britain by CPI Group (UK) Ltd,
Croydon CR0 4YY

MIX
Paper from
responsible sources
FSC® C020471

For Alberta, again

NADRA says the rains will break soon. I say nothing but hope she is wrong, then wonder what the world will sound like when we finally fade into the renewed heat of summer. Since they brought me here, high in the mountains, far from the coast and the sea, the rain has been constantly in my head. Now the whole world narrows into the tightening vibrations of its sound, the electric cackle of its static. I touch the padded gauze which covers my eyes and listen to it clatter on the tin roof, rattle against the slats of the shutters the nurses close each night. Sometimes it rushes and gusts like a burst of temper, and then the gullies sluice and seep into a lisping babble of speech.

Somewhere an overflowing gutter stutters, and I count the seconds between splashes until they coalesce into a continuous stream. Occasionally a cooler breeze sidles into the room like a pick-pocket, ruffles the net over the bed, then slips away again taking what it came for. From time to time the whirr of the fans goes dead and the air slumps heavy and motionless, but then Nadra comes and fans little eddies of coolness which drift against the raw pus of my face.

I like the rain; there is a comfort in its presence, a reminder of a power beyond the human. Nadra says it is a gift from Allah and she sings a song from her childhood, but when she tries to explain the words they don't make sense. She's always close. I know the cool feel of her hands on my skin, her fingers teasing out the tats in my hair. My own hands lie muffled and swathed and her touch replaces my own. I know the whorled and toughened skin of her fingertips, the palms of her hands smooth as stone. They let her sleep on matting in the open-sided corridor which faces into the courtyard. I ask Basif if she can bring it into the room beside my bed but he refuses and says she would be in the way. Sometimes he likes to play the doctor, and I will not please him by arguing.

I ask Nadra what Basif looks like and she giggles and goes coy as if I'm asking her something personal. She guesses he's probably in his late thirties, is quite tall with thick black hair already flecked with grey. She whispers that his face is handsome and laughs again. I know he has long thin fingers, and when he examines me they play over my skin like a woman testing a table for dust. I know too that he smokes and has a taste for garlic. He was the doctor on duty when they brought me here and his was the first voice I heard. When he examines my face he tells me I shall be pretty again. It's clear that prettiness in a woman is important to him, a prerequisite for a healthy future. He assumes it is what I want to hear. I listen to him flirt with the European nurses and know he is one of those men who believes he has a unique charm and so sprinkles it about like some holy incense, confident that those who inhale its scent will become devoted disciples. He believes it so surely that I have no heart to tell him I hear his words only as some far-off drip of water from a broken pipe, and anyway he would assure himself that my indifference is because of my injuries, because of what I have seen.

Nadra tells me that the room is small, that mine is the only bed. The walls are painted a lime-green colour and opposite my bed is a poster of a smiling woman with her child below a slogan warning about Aids. She says the sun slants into the room through the louvred slats and throws a griddle of shadows across the bed and far wall, that the ceiling fan has white blades turned at the end like the propeller of a plane. The hospital has its own generator; at night I lie and listen to its hum until the rain returns and drowns it out.

2

Piece by piece they have taken the shrapnel from my legs, and the pain lessens as the days pass. Basif has promised that in another week or so they will let me sit out in the courtyard for a short while. He says the sun will help my skin heal. I ask him about my eyes and he makes a joke and tells me everything is going to be all right. He says my eyes will be more beautiful than Sophia Loren's; he says she has the most beautiful eyes in the world. But as he talks I hear only the silences between his words, the stepping stones of his evasion.

A nurse dresses my burns twice a day. She tries to be gentle but it's always painful when the bandages are prised away from the raw blisters of skin, and sometimes I can't help crying out. Then Nadra comes and stands close, smoothes my hair and whispers in my ear. Once when the pain made me shout there was a hiss of words from her and an angry return from the nurse and I had to ask Nadra to wait outside. I try to ask the nurse about my eyes but she pretends she doesn't understand. Basif says the bandages over my eyes mustn't be disturbed for another week at least. There is another doctor – a Swiss specialist – who is due to fly in from the south and then there will be another examination. So for the meantime there is nothing to do but lie here and listen.

Voices volleying across the courtyard; the slop and drip of the rain; the choking caw of some night bird; the faint far-off gurgling of water disappearing down the throat of a drain. The splash of wheels in puddles. Sometimes Nadra curls at the foot of the bed and sings the songs her mother has taught her. I try to find a tune in them but they ripple outwards like a stone dropped in water and never return to any recognizable melody. I think of my own mother. Sometimes as the drugs take their effect and I start the slow slide to sleep I hear other noises and want to cry out to frighten them away but the sounds die in my throat and I fall helpless into a deep rift of unconsciousness.

I try not to worry about my eyes. The pain has eased and that in itself is a relief. Now I can tell the difference between night and day. Once when Basif examined them I felt the heat of the lamp on my face and I thought for a moment that I caught the light shining through the fine filament of his hair. Perhaps I only imagined it, but for a second it was as if he had a halo like an angel's. I should have told him – it would have appealed to his sense of humour. Sometimes, not seeing doesn't seem like the worst thing in the world. Sometimes it even seems like a release except that the absence of the physical world throws the mind back into memory, and then there is nothing to distract from the past.

Most days, when he has finished his rounds, Basif comes and talks to me – he calls it my therapy. When they brought me here and started slowly to separate the rags of my clothes from the scorched patches of my skin he talked to me as he worked, as if he feared that silence would help me slip beyond his reach. When I told him I came from the North of Ireland he paused and said, 'Ireland? Bang! Bang! Boom! Boom!', then laughed at his joke the way I've heard him do so many times. He tells me he will make me beautiful again. Perhaps it is his eyes which are damaged – I tell him I was never beautiful and he tells me all women are beautiful. He talks all the time, his voice accompanied by the cold click of scissors, the dab and patting of sterile swabs. Sometimes he speaks in French to one of the nurses and then the words flow in a fluent stream and make me think of the ocean and as I scream I want only to drown in the coolness of its depths. A needle pierces my skin, somewhere a baby begins to cry, while hands gloved in plastic move over my body like termites over some rotting piece of scrub wood. Before I pass out I hear his voice praying over me, a litany of names: 'U2, Jackie Charlton, Bono, Under a Blood Red Sky.'

I want to tell him that I'm from the north, that Jackie Charlton is English, but he goes on with what suddenly sounds like his version of the last rites and before I can speak I fall into a shadowy well of nothingness.

Now he sits on the edge of my bed and talks to me about

himself. When he tells me he's from the Lebanon I have to stop myself saying, 'Bang! Bang! Boom! Boom!' but there's little chance of interrupting. Obviously, my therapy is to listen. He tells me of his father's fine art export business, of the swimming pool, of the two racehorses they used to keep, of their holidays in Europe, how everything was lost. But soon his father will start again, rebuild the business, and when I ask him how, he explains it only by saying his father is a well-loved man and has contacts all over the Middle East. About a wheel that must turn. About fate. He tells me everything about himself except the one thing which might be of interest. Why he is here in Africa. It is a question which I do not ask because I have learnt already that it is rarely answered with the truth. The mutual embarrassment of a clumsily conceived response is to be avoided. It is also a question which must be thrown back on the asker.

Of course, even now I like to believe my own lies. I had different ones for different people – my friends, the school, the agency, even myself. Polished, professional performances, bright with the sheen of sincerity. Once here it makes no difference, you fade into the woodwork. Every nation under the sun and every faith, the secular and the divine, establishing bridge-heads through which to funnel their particular brand of aid. And everywhere you go, the Irish. In the hospitals and transit camps, in the schools and field missions. Doctors, nurses, priests, engineers, teachers. A nation still of wild geese. As Basif's voice drones on, I think of young men and women, driven by the old hunger, arriving in London and New York, clutching the names and addresses of those who have gone before. And, when distance and alcohol generate sentimentality, they talk of going home, but the dream fades into the morning light of a new day in a big city. I have no sentimentality, no dream of going home, and I am glad.

Basif asks me about Ireland but I pretend I'm tired and avoid his questions. I grow weary of his voice; it flutters round my head like some waxen moth. I long for Nadra's touch, the sound of rain. I turn my head away, then feel him lift himself off the bed and hear his footsteps fade as he goes to share his therapy with someone else. I beckon Nadra to come close and she lies on the bed and I feel the warmth of her body, smell the scent of her skin. I try to touch her but remember my muffled hands. She lifts and separates the caked strands of my hair, easing them out with her fingers. The only sounds are the light crinkle of my hair and the whirr of the ceiling fan.

It is very beautiful to be loved. Before, I had only guessed at how beautiful. The fan stutters and starts again and I know now that there is no such thing as love in the abstract. There is only this – the giving and receiving of small tendernesses. The only light in the darkness. I think men do not understand about love – or I have not met any who do. Some women do not understand either, because they live in the shadow of men. Perhaps it is not the men's fault, perhaps they are to be pitied, but I remember what I have seen and have no pity to give.

Nadra sponges my hair and tries to untangle the matted mess, sometimes taking scissors and snipping out some unsaveable piece. I think my mother would cry if she saw my hair. Suddenly Nadra stops and moves away from the bed. A visitor has arrived. Charles Stanfield introduces himself and I wonder if his appearance has changed from the first time we met. He was the one who greeted our arrival, a small man in a white linen jacket, shirt and tie, carrying a briefcase full of American dollars for paying off the faction which controlled the airport. Technical services is what they call it in the accounts. His only concession to the climate was a Panama hat. He looked as if he were heading off to umpire a cricket match in the Home Counties.

His voice at least remains how I remember it – plummy, superior, English. 'How are you, Naomi?'

I resist the temptation of a facetious reply. 'I'm not too bad.'

'Under the circumstances you've been quite lucky.'

'Lucky, Mr Stanfield? Yes, I suppose in some ways I have.'

'The doctor tells me the shrapnel wounds and burns will heal. I believe they're bringing in a specialist to look at your eyes.'

I hadn't noticed it before; he has a slight wheeze in his chest, a little heaviness in his breathing. Perhaps the altitude does not agree with him, perhaps I never heard it before because I was listening too intently to his words.

'They say he's Swiss and will make my eyes as beautiful as Sophia Loren's.'

'The Agency will take care of everything, Naomi. You're still our responsibility. Despite everything we'll make all the necessary arrangements and when the hospital gives the all-clear we'll get you flown home.'

'Responsibility? You make me sound like a child. . . . But I suppose you think I am. An embarrassment anyway.'

He hesitates, and for the first time I can smell the spicy cocktail of his sweat and after-shave. I offer him a seat but he prefers to stand. Perhaps he thinks I might contaminate him, infect him with some of my insanity.

'I think you've been foolish Naomi, very foolish, but you're still alive and that's something to be grateful for. We've used our influence to keep the lid on this and the sooner we get you home the better. The Consul has been very helpful, agreed to make it a priority.'

'And where is my home, Mr Stanfield?'

'Ireland, of course, Naomi.'

'And what if I don't want to go back to Ireland?'

I hear him clear his throat, the rustle of his clothes.

'I think perhaps we should talk at another time. What has happened has been a great strain, greater perhaps than the doctors have realized. When you're back with your family to look after you things will seem different.'

'Nadra looks after me. Nadra is my family.'

'Nadra?'

It's as if he hasn't noticed her presence before. 'This is Nadra,' I say, as I gesture to her with my bandaged hand. He says nothing and I have to hope that his inherent good breeding has at least caused him to nod.

'Do you get many like me, Mr Stanfield?'

'Like you, Naomi?'

'People who go off the rails, people who cause you embarrassment.'

'Africa affects people in different ways. We try to eliminate the unsuitable with our vetting system, but someone occasionally slips through the net.'

I feel him sit on the edge of the bed and know he is about to patronize me with some personal observation, bestow some pardon for my unsuitability.

'It's not easy here, and you're young. Nothing can ever prepare someone for the type of things you've seen. Sometimes it's just too much, and when that happens the only thing to do is get out.'

I say nothing and into the silence comes the sound of a baby crying, a full-throated squall rising like a startled bird. He speaks about arrangements, about the right thing, but I have stopped listening. Eventually I feel him stand up again, the thin thread of wheezing lacing his breathing and making the ends of his words lapse into little puffs. He sounds like a man who has climbed too many flights of stairs. He is about to go. I picture him clutching his hat, fastening his briefcase.

'We'll talk again, Naomi, perhaps when you're stronger. I am staying in the UN compound – I've left the number in the office and you can contact me there.'

As he says goodbye and begins to leave I call out to him, 'Mr Stanfield, I've never been stronger, never all my life.' I hear the momentary confused halt to his steps and then the fading wheeze of his breathing.

After he's gone Nadra feeds me a milky soup of mashed banana. When I've had enough I turn my head away and tighten my lips but she clucks and I feel the metal spoon prising them open once again. It is useless to argue and there is no respite until I hear the spoon scraping the sides of the dish and swallow the final soggy crumbs. She makes me drink the glucose mixture, rubbing the teat of the bottle across my bottom teeth until I suck, and when the feeding is finished I make her go to the kitchens to get some food for herself by telling her I want to sleep. I do not tell her the pain is coming back. I had assumed too soon that I was out of its grip. Perhaps the drugs have run their course. The burnt parts of my body slowly begin to tighten as little flurries of pain wash over me, gently at first and then in insistent surges until I want to clutch at my skin to stop the spreading fire. I try vainly to smother the flames that sear my flesh, but all I can do is squirm in the bed and try to stifle the screams. Then I can't hold them any longer and there are running footsteps and voices all around the bed, a moist palm on my forehead, the scuff of a swab on my arm and the sharp prick of a needle. As it punctures my skin I'm crying but my eyes have no tears and even my throat feels dried up, like some dusty river bed. I want something to flow out of me but there is nothing there. Suddenly I am aware the rain has stopped and I don't want it to stop. I never want it to stop. I try to cry but it is only words which come out of me. There are no tears.

It is the ocean which I think of now, the memory I cling to more than any other. As I begin to spin into the slow spiral of unconsciousness I see it, feel it, remember it. Half-remember, half-dream it as I fall backwards beneath the azure shift of its surface, gasp again at the coloured clumps of coral – blue, red, fiery pink. Come, come with me as I hold out my hand to you. Swim among the shoals of fish which dart and disappear into its craggy shelter. The tiny tentacles of coral tremble and shiver as we swim by. Nebulous, filmy, fern-like branches jut out towards me and I touch the delicate tracery with my fingers. See a burst of almost transparent fish shoot past, each marked only by a thin filament of electric blue. All around us feathery pinnate branches fan the water as gaudy neon fish I do not know the name of appear and disappear amongst the staghorn coral. A cloud of yellow-tailed fish, their mouths smeared drunkenly with blue lipstick, puff across our path then turn in a collective quiver before pulsing away again. My whole body feels liquid, alive, more fluent than I have ever known it.

I dream it, half-remember it, long to feel the cool water wash over my burnt and broken skin. And then the voices all around me grow faint before they finally merge into the steady surge of the surf against the shore.

I grew up in a house that faces the sea. A squat stone house whose bulbous windows stare out over the grey bucking swell of the Atlantic. A house my father doesn't own but which belongs to the Church, who allow us to live there while he ministers to the scattered congregations of north Donegal. A two-storey house with grey plastered walls, darker blotches on the gables where damp rucks have been replastered, and chimneys coped with sieved cowls. I sleep in a front bedroom and so I fall asleep each night and rise each morning to the shuffling ebb and flow of the sea, the white-frothed breakers which rasp the bevelled beach and tussocky dunes.

There should be some magic in growing up by the sea, but I never feel my life touched by it. Instead there is only the constant sense of being under siege, as if the house is trapped between the mountains, the valleys of bogland and the unrelenting encroachment of the sea. So whether it is the fine slant of grey rain which mists almost invisibly in from the Atlantic, or the squalls rattling the loose glass of my bedroom window, it feels as if we are outsiders, interlopers whom the elements conspire to evict. I think my father believes it too, because each night after the repetitive ritual of his supper he tears the day's date from the calendar, tours the whole house, his heavy steps squirming the floor-boards above our heads, and checks that every window and door is securely locked. Sometimes he goes outside and inspects the car, closes the little iron gate, as if in some public demonstration that our vigilance is eternal and not to be slackened by the advancement of night.

We are outsiders in the community we live in, part of the declining Protestant population. They cling to their scattered farms or small businesses, only to watch their children move away in search of new lives. Outwardly we are good neighbours to the Catholic community but inwardly we are cautious, even suspicious. And as storms smack in from the sea, and the gulls are tossed skyward like days'-old confetti, our light flickers and shivers as my father disparages their religion and their politics. There is always the unspoken feeling that our future existence is under some vague kind of threat, and so we watch the world from behind our walls, hug the assurance of our certainties, the conviction of our election.

I rarely play with the Catholic children of the village and am never allowed to join the pattern of their lives. An only child, I am often alone, shadowing my mother at her domestic chores, or thrown back on my imagination and the world of books and dreams. In the village huddle a post office, a general store, a garage, two pubs and a chapel. I do not go there without some express purpose and my play area is confined to the dunes and the beach. But they are too open, too exposed and wind-swept to allow even a hungry imagination to transform them into something better. So I crouch hidden amongst the sharp fluted grass and rabbit droppings, and spy on the occasional strollers who walk their dogs along the beach, or else I browse in the sea's detritus – bleached tins, shards of glass, the bones of sheep – hoping, I suppose, for some message in a bottle, some object that will inspire speculation about other lives, other places. And when sometimes I chance upon the blackened embers of a fire, a spray of beer cans, I try to read the scattered remains like a book, gently touching and turning them with my foot, trying to piece together the clues. But there are never enough, never enough to help me begin to understand what shapes or colours might infuse the lives of other people.

It is from the dunes that I watch my father swim in the sea. A strange lifetime habit. He swims three or four mornings a week, all year long. Maybe he believes it keeps him healthy. I squat in some little gulley or the crest of some dune and watch him cross the road in his towelling bath-robe and open-toed sandals. His white legs are bowed and blue-veined, his bald head shiny in the morning sun, and as the black-faced gulls swoop and cackle above him he kicks off his sandals, folds the dressing-gown carefully, and walks into the sea. He never runs, never tests the water with his foot but wades straight in, shoulders pushing like pistons, until the water reaches his waist. Then he swims out through the swell. Bald head bobbing like a seal, he rolls over on his back, stretches out his arms and floats, kicking up white spumes of water with his feet. From the dunes the water looks cold, but he never seems to be affected or deflected from his course. I wish he could have known what it was to swim amongst the coral. I think it could have healed him.

My father is always old. He was in his early forties when he married, almost fifty when I, his only child, was born. As a small child I am a little frightened of him – the bald bulb of his head, the rawness of his eyes, the strength of his body. And my father has two voices, one which he uses to speak to my mother and me, one which he uses when he speaks for God. Sometimes when I have done something wrong he uses this second voice. It is deeper and slower and has a cadence which rises at the start of each sentence then falls at the end. The words are polished beads strung on the sure line of his thought. It is this voice he uses in church when he stands in the pulpit above his tiny flock. A church that could have been built in any part of the British Isles with its font, polished pews, memorial tablets, and wreath of poppies. Sprinkled across the front pews sits an ageing congregation. I am the only child. When we sing, my mother playing the organ, the faltering voices fade into the vaulted roof.

I suppose this is when I form my first impression of God as someone who lives in lonely echoing places and who speaks in two voices, someone who has slipped into old age.

I hear my father preach twice every Sunday, the same message delivered in the same voice. After the early service in the village we drive inland, across the black seep of bog with its white wisps of bog cotton and purple heather, until we reach another congregation. Every other Sunday we drive up the coast and hold Communion for a small group of elderly parishioners. I come to know at an early age that my father is a disappointed man. Perhaps it is from snatches of overheard conversation, an expression glimpsed on his face, the set of his shoulders as he walks across the rippled sand towards the sea. I think he feels someone is punishing him, diverting his career into a forgotten backwater where he is destined to be passed over again and again. I know, too, there is never enough money, and in the house there is a constant scrimping and saving, an endless counting of pennies.

Three mornings a week, and sometimes during the evening, he goes to his study and shuts the door. I suppose he prepares his sermons or writes letters. Sometimes my mother sends me with tea and biscuits on a tray and then I knock on the door and wait until he calls me in. When I enter he is sitting behind his desk, his back to the window, but there are no open books or papers, only the dark polished grain of the wood and resting on it his large hands. I think I am another disappointment to him. Despite what Basif says, I was never pretty. Thin, pale-faced, freckled across the bridge of my nose and round my eyes, a frizzy shock of red hair, wiry and coarse to the touch. I always have it cut short in a kind of variation on a bob that only retains its shape for about a week before sparking and jetting into its own crackling life. There is a dresser with a mirror in my room, the glass full of shadows and sky. I stand in front of it and try to dream someone else.

My father is never consciously unkind to me, but because I never know him I never understand what it is he wants me to be. Our life together seems uncertain and fragmented. I scurry behind him on the beach, stretching my stride to step in his footprints, wondering why he always has to walk to the very end when the wind snaps my hair and stings my eyes. Sometimes he takes me with him when he plays golf. I pull the rusted trolley of mismatched clubs and he calls me his caddy and requests the clubs, calling out their numbers like announcing hymns in church. When a ball is sliced into the tundra bordering the narrow fairways we search until we find it or it is deemed irretrievably lost. He is pleased when I find a ball and he laughs and always says, 'That which was lost is now found.' I think he is happy when he plays golf or when he swims. Mostly he plays the course alone, never replacing a single divot or ever marking a score card. When he plays well or is in good spirits he stops on the way home at Lavery's and buys me a quarter of midget gems or clove rock. I always hope it will be midget gems as the clove rock is burny and sticks to the paper bag, but I never tell him this.

I haven't spoken yet of my mother. I find it harder to bring her into the open, to find the words which will draw her out of her world. Somehow it seems unkind, an intrusion into the privacy of her self, but I want to tell everything and she is a part of me that can't be left out, if you are to understand, if I am to tell what I have seen.

Eleanor Sarah Arnold is the only daughter of the Arnolds, who own a shoe shop in Dunglen. She is thirty-six when she marries my father, six years younger than him, and I do not know if she marries for love or because she knows that if she turns down his offer there will be little chance of any other. By sixteen she has left school and it seems that the parameters of her world are destined to be the same as her parents' – a future of measuring children's feet, selling slippers at Christmas, her life transmuted into a window display which changes with the seasons. She has a gift for music and can play the piano and sing. When he first comes to Donegal my father stays in a holiday home the Arnolds own. She meets him at church. She plays the organ in church and when the inevitable happens it is considered by all to be a good match, of mutual benefit, a prudent investment against the vagaries of the future. A congregation prefers its minister to be married. The wife has an important part to play in social functions, in administering those delicate aspects of pastoral care, where a woman's touch is considered desirable and gives an impression of stability to a man.

When I look at the few wedding photos she keeps in an old jigsaw box, I wonder what emotions hide behind the smiling faces, but there is no way of telling and it is a question I cannot ask. On that day I think she is beautiful, in the wedding dress made by her aunt which ripples round her feet like surf, and the white shoes that come from her father's shop. A slight woman, her face pale as her dress, with wild roses in her hair – the hair she always lets me brush and comb. When I finish she brushes mine and when I complain about its colour, its shape, she shushes me and tells me it is beautiful and that if I were a nun in a convent out on the Point I would have no hair at all and that would be something to cry about. I'm glad she cannot see it now.

She has a fine white seam of scar on her scalp, smooth to the touch, and I make her tell me over and over about the day she was knocked down by an American tourist, how he sent her dolls and presents every Christmas for years and years, and she laughs and says that every other child in the village hoped it would happen to them. But I remember too, the first time I find the whisper of grey filtering her hair and know that some day she will die. I hope she will not die before my father. And at night, as the sea gnaws hungrily at the shore, I torment myself with the fear of standing by her coffin, seeing her grey hair folded lightly below her like a pillow.

My mother loves music and to my father's irritation she has the radio in the kitchen going all day. Most evenings she plays the piano she has brought from her father's house and sings. Sometimes she sings in Gaelic and then the soft-vowelled ballads conjure up romantic mystery that nothing else in the house can emulate. I sit beside her on the stool and watch her white fingers skim over the yellow-edged keys that look like fingers stained by nicotine. I don't think my father likes her singing in Gaelic, but he never says anything and when he sits behind a book or a paper I know he is listening to her voice. If there is never any public display of emotion, they are always respectful and often kind to each other. They do not kiss or even hold hands in front of me – I am the only evidence of their physical intimacy – but I know they care for each other and, in their different ways, for me.

Within the limitations of our world, the narrowness of our alloted space, I suppose we are not a particularly unhappy family. There are no bitter arguments or recriminations, no displays of petulance or passion. But it is also true that there are too many moments of silence. We exist in a sober, often sombre, world and although I have little with which to compare the quality of our life, I come gradually to feel that it has been absorbed in the greyness of the steely sea, and bleached of any vivid colour or experience. As I grow older I remain close to my mother, share the few secrets I can muster. But as I stand in front of my mirror I dream another me, dream another life.

Only the summer months bring some respite, some unpredictable variety, as the coastline fills with holiday-makers and even our own stretch of beach spawns family clusters when the weather is good. Dour village shops suddenly hang out postcards and fluorescent buckets and spades, and the roads are full of caravans and camper vans. My father pretends to resent this sudden influx but I think he really enjoys it. His Sunday congregation swells to almost double its size and he delivers his sermon with greater gusto, performing for his audience with a fresher verve. It is in July too that he brings out his Orange sash and white gloves and marches with a black bowler covering the bald egg of his head. As he sets off down the road we watch from an upstairs window and press our hands to our mouths to suppress the rising giggles, and as his broad stride takes him further away we let the laughter come bursting out like air from a balloon. There is always something between us, an unarticulated conspiracy which strengthens as I grow older.

My mother is the kindest person I have ever known. Kindness is a word that the world has tainted with sentimentality, infected with weakness, but now I know its strength, the purity of its resolve. Her kindnesses were unobtrusive, undramatic, uncelebrated, an intrinsic part of her being. I shall not tell you of them because they were secret, quiet things and if told I am frightened the clumsiness of my words would make them brittle, the heaviness of my touch break them into pieces. Only this moment will I tell, because it is my first glimpse of a world I have never seen and because all these years later it comes back again.

My father had been taking part in some convention at the Guildhall in Derry. It is a Saturday afternoon, and when the meeting goes into private session I leave with my mother to do some shopping. Parked along a street is a line of taxis; the first one has its diesel engine purring, the musk of its fumes filtering into the air. The shiny black frieze of head-to-tail cars wears a transfer of the sky and buildings. A knot of men stands on the pavement, some leaning back against the first car, and as we walk towards them we hear their laughter and then the knot loosens and the men step back to form a circle. In the middle of the circle is a man. He is shouting, 'Give it back, give it back!' and I see the first glint of a yellow ring being thrown across the circle. It is a game which children play, but as we get closer I know it is not a game. The man clutches at air, his hand like a claw, and his voice splinters into swearwords like broken shards of glass. As it rises into a scream the mesh of laughter is a skein of hate falling over his head, tightening his loss of control. We are close enough to see the disturbed skitter of the man's eyes as he jerks round, like some animal goaded and prodded trying to break out of the ring of pain which encloses it. His flailing arms convulse in the black frieze of the doors, and flecks of spit stipple the edges of his mouth. The men laugh louder and I pull my mother's hand away but she walks on. One of the men sees her in the corner of his eye and for a second is distracted and the ring he is about to catch tinkles to the ground, then rolls towards us. I am frightened but I feel my mother's hand tighten on mine and then she puts her foot on the ring, trapping it under her sole. One of the circle steps towards her, bends down to retrieve it, but she doesn't move her foot. Doesn't move at all, only stares at the men and says nothing until one by one they move to the side of the pavement, turn back to their vehicles. The owner of the ring is kneeling now, sobbing, and she helps him to his feet, takes his hand and presses the ring into his palm, and then we walk on and never speak of what has happened.

As I grow I carry the moment with me but it is only now I begin to know its meaning. As I look back, there is very little I know about the world. The little I discover is pieced together from books or from the few fragments of my experience. When I bleed for the first time I am sick with fear and shame. I do not understand. And so I smuggle the stained knickers out of the house and bury them deep in the sand, placing a little pyre of stones on the burial place. Now I lie here, I want something to flow out of me, something that will tell me that everything is not dried up, tell me that I am alive inside and not that dusty, stony river bed. But I have no tears, no warm wetness to stir and course into life. All I have is words, more words than I have ever known.

The evening my parents tell me I am being sent to a girls' boarding school in Belfast, I say very little but am glad. School becomes like a journey into the future and I am grateful for the protective camouflage of a uniform; it affords me enough time to assimilate what I need to know, to simulate knowledge and experience where none exists. I listen and learn, absorb everything assiduously. I am a good pupil, conscious always of making up for lost time, cramming everything in. After formal lessons are over I learn what I really need to know from the other girls. I let my hair grow long and remember the nuns out on the Point.

When I go home in the holidays it feels as if I am returning to the edge of the world. Donegal's gaudily painted bungalows, the grotesque shrines at the side of the road, the unrelenting loneliness of the landscape. And if I instantly renew my friendship with my mother, it feels as if some permanent distance separates me from my father. He develops a stilted style of talking to me – 'What is Naomi going to do today?' 'What book is Naomi reading?' When I allow it to irritate me I respond in similar style, 'Naomi is thinking of going for a walk.' 'Naomi is reading. . . .' As the years pass he grows more morose, more disappointed. Only his swimming goes on the same. Sometimes I watch him from my bedroom window, his bald head bobbing in the water like a buoy, little flurries of white where his hands and feet slash the surface. I think he resents that I have broken away, discovered a life other than the one he presides over. Perhaps he is envious – I don't know. He is a strong swimmer but there is an ugliness about his movements in the water. Where others seem able to give themselves to it, become part of the element they move in, he seems to be fighting against it, forcing a path through an unyielding barrier. I am older now, but as I watch him I realize I understand him no better than I did as a child and for the first time it is no longer important to me.

Three months after he disappears, a fishing boat out of Burtonport nets his body with their catch. Even in death he cannot escape. We are not allowed to see him. They say half his face has been eaten away.

WE sit in the courtyard under the shade of a canopy strung from the branches of a tree which Nadra calls Boswellia. She says it produces frankincense, but the only scent which drifts around us is a hybrid of hospital smells and the pungent spicy strain from the kitchens. The word frankincense makes me think of the Magi, and I remember the church crib and the waxen-faced dolls. I stretch out my hand to feel the bark but it's out of reach. All the times I listened to the Bible story, I never really understood what frankincense or myrrh were. Nadra tries to explain but runs out of words. Her efforts are punctuated by the high cries and squeals of children. They are playing a game, their laughter bouncing round the courtyard like a ball. They scamper round the hospital like mice.

It is very hot again, but not the dry, baking heat of the plains or the moist humidity of the coast. It heightens the smell of my body, the salved and sterilized gauze of tissue, and I long to peel the burnt skin away and shed it like a snake. Only the gloved hands stop me scratching at the prickly itch which spreads everywhere. Nadra tries to distract me with a familiar refrain of conversation.

'And Ireland is green all the year?'

'Yes, all year long. People say there are forty different shades of green.'

'Even in summer, Naomi?'

'Yes, especially in summer. Sometimes in summer it rains a lot. Where I lived as a child it rained all the time.'

'Tell me about where you lived, Naomi.'

I have told her many times but I tell her again, going over the parts I know she likes – the heather, the mountains, the sea. To please her I make it all sound interesting, paint the colours more vividly, but the landscape my memory evokes remains dead to me, the husk of a former existence which has withered finally away.

'Tell me about the different seasons, Naomi.'

I am not sure for whose benefit she asks these questions but I tell her anyway; try to explain about winter, about the traditions of Christmas. She fans me and as she does she expresses her disapproval that people should cut down trees to decorate their homes. I try to explain about forestry but we get lost in the words, and then I stem the flow of her questions by asking about the voice I hear in the background. It is an old man reciting the Koran.

'Do you believe in God, Nadra?'

She laughs at first, and clucks as if she is listening to a child who has said something funny. 'Allah Akbar, God is great, Naomi.'

'You still believe in Allah after all that we have seen?'

'We have seen what men have done, not Allah.'

The old man's voice drops to a monotone.

'Allah did nothing to stop them, Nadra.'

'It is not for us to know the mind of Allah.'

From the other side of the courtyard comes the sound of children's laughter.

'And you do not believe in your God, Naomi?'

I hesitate, torn between the truth and a desire not to hurt her. 'I think God has grown old, tired, and his voice is no longer heard.'

'That is a bad thing. If God is not strong, how can he protect us from the evil that men do?'

'No, Nadra, maybe it is a good thing, maybe the time has come when we must protect ourselves.'

The children's laughter comes closer, blocking out the sound of the old man. I smell the dust kicked up by their feet. Nadra says something sharply to them in their own language and the laughter is silenced momentarily, and then tumbles away in a new direction. I try to tell her they were doing no harm, that it is better they should play, but she insists I must have peace, must not be disturbed. The old man finishes his prayers and for a few seconds his voice lingers in the silence.

'Perhaps you should organize some classes for them – a couple of hours a day. Maybe Basif could give you a room to use. It would be good practice for you, and I could sit at the back and listen to you teach.'

'But, Naomi, who will look after you when I teach the children?'

I listen to her slander the local nurses, criticize their incompetence, their lack of education, pour scorn on their primitive superstitions. Eventually I manage to persuade her, and will ask Basif when he next comes. I haven't seen him so often in the last few days – perhaps he avoids me, perhaps he is busy with the growing number of casualties from the coast. They come in trucks, and sometimes I hear the drone of helicopters, recognize the sound of American Cobras.

'And your father, Naomi, was he a holy man?'

'When I was young I thought my father spoke for God, but now I think he spoke only for himself. He wouldn't have believed it if someone had told him his daughter would be sitting under a tree in Africa.'

'What did you think Africa would be like before you came?'

'Jungles, lions, tigers, elephants.'

She laughs at the familiar joke and then says she will read to me. I hear the slap of her sandal heels as she goes to find a book. She likes to show off her reading, her sing-songy pronunciation, and while I wait I remember my first impressions of Africa.

It was Stanfield who met us at the airport and shepherded us through the bureaucracy with his briefcase of American dollars, led us through the swarm of freelance porters. We side-stepped the families of migrant workers who seemed to have set up camp on the concourse, their worldly possessions packed into striped canvas bags. The gangs of children begging. One of them had a gun made out of a wire coat-hanger, and he brandished it in front of my face then smiled at his own joke. The drive to the coastal capital was my first view of the continent, a scrawny, flat scrub disappointing in its absence of drama. From the modern main road spread a network of red dirt roads where a haze trembled to a buckling, warping horizon of heat and light. On either side of the road the monotony was broken only by the occasional banana planta-tion where the languid leaves of the trees hung heavy and wilting, or by spiked fields of sugar cane. And at intervals clumps of houses – breeze-blocked, tin-roofed, patched with rough-edged bits of wood. In front of these children played, their feet skipping up puffs of dust. Sometimes we had to slow almost to a halt to negotiate potholes or dumped oil drums, sometimes to avoid the few stringy cattle or old men herding goats. As we entered the city, it unravelled before us: shapeless, haphazard, a sprawl of shanty-town suburbs giving way to white European-style buildings set on broad avenues. In some places building sites were enclosed with cages of bamboo scaffolding. But nothing seemed to link or lead to any pattern, tumbling onwards and outwards. If there was mystery it was in the scenes half-glimpsed through latticed courtyards in the dusk, the incessant, indefinable activity of crowded alleyways: a young girl in a yellow dress vanishing into the dark frame of a doorway, an old man having his hair cut under a string of neon pearls, huddles of men squatting round some street vendor, a mother and her children carrying tyres balanced on their shoulders.

There were six of us in the bus: Veronica, a young nurse from

London; Martine, a not-long-qualified doctor from Paris; an older couple, both doctors; an engineer from Scotland and an agricultural student from Kent. We had joined up in London for our initial training, and a friendly team-spirit had developed. We were taken to an area of the city which held government buildings and foreign embassies. Our hotel complex consisted of a central building with a reception area, a dining room and bar, an outdoor swimming pool, and a collection of self-contained bungalows scattered through landscaped gardens which led down to the beach and the Indian Ocean. We were to spend three days there, acclimatizing, being given further health checks and receiving final briefings. I think we felt a little guilty at starting our work in Africa in such comfortable surroundings but there was, too, the feeling of a last supper, that we should enjoy it, make the most of it before our lives took different directions.

We had a talk from a girl who had been working with refugees in a transit camp close to the border, an update on the political situation from Stanfield, and a final session from Swenlenson, the local director of the Agency's operations. The briefing took place in the lounge of our hotel and from time to time various hotel staff would pause in the doorway and listen with curious faces. Behind the bar a young man polished glasses and stared at Swenlenson as he hammered away at what we had heard a hundred times. If we were to be effective in our different fields of work we had to protect ourselves emotionally, to keep a sense of, not indifference, but detachment, a distance from some of the things we would see. Otherwise we would be sucked down and finally destroyed by the sheer enormity of what was out there.

'This is not television,' he said, 'this is reality. To cope with reality you have to be strong. To be able to do some good for the collective, build something better for the future, you must be able at times to walk away from the individual, to turn your back on the present. When you cry, do it in private, do it quickly and then get on with what you have come to do. Personally, I stopped crying a long time ago. I find anger a stronger stimulus.' He paused to sip his drink. From behind the bar came the clink of glasses. Something buzzed round his head and he flicked it away with a dismissive wave of his hand.

'And finally, before I wish you luck, I want you to have a realistic expectation of what you will achieve. If you're the right person, and I've no reason to doubt your commitment to the work, you will do some good. Lives will be helped. Some will be saved by your coming here. But the good you will achieve is a drop in the ocean. There are no dramatic victories, no revolutionary changes, just a slow building to something better. And what you must guard most against is despair, a feeling of helplessness, of frustration. There is no easy way, and at any given time a political decision, even a rumour, a failure of a crop, the vagaries of the climate, may undo everything you have fought to build. But despair and self-pity go hand in hand, and neither of them is worth a damn. All that matters is that you get up and start again. And if the day comes when you can't get up you're no longer any use and you go back home.'

By the time he had finished, the earlier buoyancy had dissipated and been replaced by a more sombre and introspective mood. We sat around sipping beer for a while until the group gradually split up and we made our way back to the bungalows. I was sharing with Martine and Veronica. I had already decided I liked Martine. She was cheerful and quietly self-confident but didn't pry into personal background or try to share whatever philosophy she carried with her. Veronica talked too much, oblivious even when politeness slid into indifference, bubbling on about her family, her boyfriend, her reasons for giving up a year of her life to the Agency. No matter which way she approached it she never sounded like anything other than a little girl setting up a hospital for her friends' broken dolls. She had a tendency also to talk of children as if they were puppies, going on about their big sad eyes, how it broke her heart to see them suffering. Once I caught Martine's eye and we both smiled surreptitiously at this surfeit of sincerity. Her family had given her a video camera as a present, and it seemed likely that her year was going to turn into a video diary, destined to sit under some suburban television set beside the wedding videos and mail-order catalogues.

The hotel proved less luxurious than first impressions had suggested. The air conditioning coughed and choked a few times then gave up totally; flicking the television channels produced only static. An air-locked shower spurted great wheezes of dust and yellow water. There was in-house muzak which we couldn't find a way to switch off, and in the drained pool green quivers of lizards slithered over the blue tiles. But the staff were friendly and eager to please and to complain about anything seemed decadent, even immoral in the circumstances, and so we smiled and made a joke of it, heating water in a kettle for Veronica to wash her hair, spending our free time sitting in the gardens sipping the sugary lemonade. What the bar served on any one day seemed to vary with their current reading of the regime's fluctuating, erratic fundamentalism.

Stanfield had organized a boat trip out to the reef, but only Martine and I took up the offer. We were chaperoned by Oman, who worked in the hotel and was occasionally employed by the Agency. He guided us down a dirt path through the gardens and opened a locked gate. Then he led us across a narrow strip of scrub grass and down to the beach. It was about four in the afternoon and the intense heat of the day had not yet spent itself, with the cloudless sky – a perfect mirror of the sea – stretching into the haze of the distance. Far out at sea the shadowy shapes of tankers slunk nose to tail like a convoy in silhouette. Groups of men squatted along the beach, some playing a game in which they threw objects on to a square of green cloth, their cries of excitement sharp-edged against the soft stillness of the air. A woman and a young girl, the lower parts of their faces veiled, sat with a red blanket spread in front of them, its corners weighted with stones, and on it jewellery, shells, painted combs, trinkets. They held up their hands to us as we passed but we walked on, skirting a group of boys playing football with a yellow, misshapen ball, the goalposts empty oil cans. They followed the ball in a pack, their thin arms and legs angular rods, their white soles kicking up spurts of silvery sand. In the surf a man led a camel, slapping its neck with a thin stick as its feet splashed eddies of white. A boy tried to sell us what looked like watermelon, but Oman shooed him away and apologized for the nuisance, and as we walked the mile to the old harbour he talked of how he was going to get a job with the Ministry of Tourism, pass their exams and become a guide for modern tourists. He attempted to impress us with his knowledge of our countries, but he knew nothing about Ireland and very little about France. What he did know about was America and Michael Jackson and Rambo and Terminator. Some day he would go to America, be big in films. As we passed some broken ruins, with worked stones scattered in the sand, he told us they were the remains of the Arab slave stations where their catches were brought to be loaded and shipped away.

The old harbour was formed by a natural curve of shore, its white-walled breakwaters draped with many-coloured canvas sails and fishing nets. Small, flimsy boats, no more than hollowed shells, were tied up beside more solid craft. A group of boys dived off a raft of bobbing oil barrels, disappearing under the water before surfacing again, the sun glinting off their damp skin. I thought for a second of my father and tried to recall the beach I played on as a child but could not; it seemed a transitory, paltry thing that could not replace what enveloped me now.

We stopped at an open fire where two friends of Oman sat cooking fish. A dozen small white fish were skewered on a rod, their mouths open, their eyes black spots. One of the men lifted a chunk of fish from the fire and offered it to me on the end of a stick, and I reached out and took it, tumbling it from palm to palm to stop it burning my hands, then ate the crumbling fragments as the two men laughed at my clumsiness. They shared a joke with Oman and I suspected it was at my expense. As they talked, a gaggle of children flocked round us, tugging our clothes lightly and peering into our faces with undisguised curiosity until Oman waved them away.

We found Hanif, who turned out to be Oman's brother, stretched out in the shade of a beached rowing boat. By his head was a radio with its insides spewing out like a gutted fish. The necks of empty beer bottles jutted out of the sand. Hanif's white singlet was a colander of holes and a gold chain glistened at his throat. He greeted us with elaborate handshakes. A small amount of American dollars was exchanged. Within a few minutes we were making our way through the rush of surf and heading out of the narrow mouth of shore and breakwater. Hanif chatted brokenly about the giant fish he had caught, taking his arms off the rudder to give an estimate of the size, telling us that some day he would buy a glass-bottomed boat and take many tourists on trips like this.

Not far from the shore he cut the engine, dropped his makeshift anchor and asked us if we wanted to dive and see the reef. From his tiny cabin he produced a withered wet-suit, still emblazoned with a BP logo, and offered it to us for a few more dollars. I had dived before but I hesitated until Martine persuaded me to try it, and after the toss of a coin she laughed and made me go first. And that was how I found myself slipping into the water and swimming not far below the surface, to where a crusted crest of coral reef sloped down to the sea bed, strangely verdant, intensely and unexpectedly blossoming into rosaceous heads of what looked like crystallized lava. I touched its surface as if to test that it was real, frightened that it might crumble in my hands, then kicked upwards for air before turning to swim through the petrified porous galleries. I passed tessellated pink horn-heads that looked as if they were made from terracotta, glided past diaphanous waving branches, and felt more alive than I have ever felt. I dream it, remember it, stretch out my hand to feel the living colours, but my gloved hand falls back limp as somewhere far off I hear the ragged shouts of children, the voice of an old man praying.

THERE is a rim of rust under the metal clips which fasten the mirror to the dresser; the glass is mottled and marked in places I have forgotten about. As I look into it for the final time I feel no nostalgia for the past, no desire to touch the childhood years which lurk somewhere below its cold surface. Even though it is summer outside, the skies scud low and heavy and the sea itself seems inert and lifeless. I am eighteen years old, and when I stare into the mirror there is no flicker of recognition from it, no sense of homecoming. My life exists in another place with friends and secrets that this room has never shared. Only my father belongs in this place, lying below in the front room, the coffin lid locked and the morning sunlight splashing the brass handles and glistening the cut glass on the sideboard.

As my mother makes tea for yet another set of half-forgotten cousins, I quietly open the door of his study. It smells like the church used to when we opened it on a Sunday morning; sepulchral, waiting for some resurrection. I enter without knocking but feel furtive, and as I close the door behind me I half-expect to hear his footsteps. The desk top is bare apart from a pen and a few sheets of notepaper already beginning to yellow and curl. I sit for the first time in his chair with its worn green arm-rests and wonder why he sat with his back to the window, staring at nothing but the flock-papered wall and a couple of black-framed certificates. I try the two desk drawers and find them locked as my mother enters.

'There wasn't anything much in them,' she says. 'Church business, letters, that sort of thing.'

'He spent a lot of his time here, didn't he?'

'He needed peace to prepare his sermons. I suppose he couldn't concentrate with all our foolish chatter and the radio on.'

'You'll miss him, won't you?'

'Yes, I'll miss him.'

'He used to like your singing. Sometimes he pretended he wasn't listening but he liked to hear your voice.'

She smiles and smoothes her hair. Outside there are voices in the hall and the sound of the front door opening and closing.

'I don't think he was so keen on the Gaelic ones. He probably thought I'd joined the other side.'

'Where will you live?'

'I can stay here as long as I need to. They don't throw church widows out on the street. It'll take them some time to find someone new. There's a pension as well. And enough money to see you through university, so you don't need to worry.'

'Why don't you come with me to Belfast? We could share a flat.'

'I don't belong in Belfast, Naomi. I'd only be in the way. You've got your own life now. I've been thinking of moving in with your grandparents – they're both getting on now. And they could do with someone to help out in the shop.'

She stands on the other side of the desk in her black dress and cardigan and for some reason I remember her wedding photograph – the white dress, the wild roses in her hair. Now it feels as if time is arching round her, waiting to reclaim her, and I don't know what to do to help her, how to break through the accepted pieties which always governed our lives in that house.

'My father was a good swimmer. . . .'

The words tremble like motes in the dusty silence of the room as she stares over my shoulder through the window. A long grey hair curls on the collar of her cardigan.

'The currents can be treacherous.'

The front bell rings and she turns towards the door, then hesitates. 'Your father was tired, Naomi. Maybe he just couldn't struggle any more.'

As the door closes I sit on, let my hands brush the grain of the wood, and then I too go back to serving tea and receiving sympathy.

There are more people at the funeral than I could have imagined. People I don't know, representatives of different organizations and interests, a road of black-suited mourners following the cortège to the church between hedgerows flecked with white. It is the first time I have seen the church full – even the parish priest attends, and speaks kindly to my mother. But it is a relief when it's all over, the last cup and saucer dried and stored away in cupboards, the final mourner woken from his slumber and gone. My mother puts on the radio but she keeps the volume so low that it's almost inaudible, and we sit in the kitchen and talk only of small things. To my surprise she produces a bottle of what looks like communion wine and fills two glasses. We try to drink it, our faces mirroring each other's grimaces, and then we toss it in the sink, throw back our heads and laugh. The sound fountains up through the empty house and suddenly falls back silently about our heads.

That night as I lie in my bed and listen to the shuffle of the sea I hear her voice singing softly, and when I put on my dressing gown I go downstairs and find her sitting by the stove warming milk. The sink still wears its red stain like a birthmark. She makes us milky coffee and we sit cupping it in both hands. Her hair is down, the grey tresses coiled about her shoulders. She turns on the radio and there is the sound of a voice simmering into passion, but as I watch her sip from her cup it is not the voice I want to hear.

'Can I brush your hair?'

She smiles and sets the cup on the table, points to her bag on the sideboard. Taking the brush, I start to move it gently through the coarsening strands. I turn off the radio.

'Will you sing to me?'

'What would you like?'

'One of the old songs you used to sing.'

I half-remember the tune, the sound of words I do not understand, as it slowly fills the room. And then I see it again, the white sliver of scar on her scalp and when I touch it with the tip of my finger she laughs and jokes that I'll be wanting her to tell the story about getting knocked down and the presents from America.

'Sure, what use would I be in Belfast with all those cars racing about? I'm still not safe crossing the road.'

She jokes too about her grey hair, and says that you can buy bottles in Neeson's chemist's that promise you any colour under the sun. I go on brushing, lifting and separating the strands, and tell her not to be silly.

'That's good coming from you, Naomi – the number of nights I had to listen to you moaning about the colour of your hair and begging me to dye it for you. You used to really hate it.'

'I don't love it yet but I've got used to it.'

Suddenly her hand grips my wrist. 'Your hair is beautiful, Naomi.'

And then she takes the brush from my hand and makes me sit before starting to work. For a second there is only the soft rasp and stroke of the brush, and then I ask her.

'Do you ever think of worlds other than this one?'

'You mean like Heaven?'

'No, real worlds, other places, countries, cities, different from here.'

'I suppose I did when I was your age, I don't really remember.'

'You never wanted to live anywhere else?'

'Not really. I always thought this was where I belonged. It

could've been different, though, there was a rep who used to come to the shop who had a bit of an eye for me – it was before I met your father. Travelled all over Ireland in a company car. But it never came to anything.'

'And were you happy with my father?'

She stops brushing for a moment.

'Yes, I was happy. Your father was good to me, and in his own way he was good to you. I know. . . .'

I hold her hand, stop the brush from shaking. 'I know, it's all right, it's all right. It's late now.'

We turn back to our coffees but skins have formed on the surfaces. She gets a spoon and skims them off, then switches on the radio. 'You're right, let's get cleared up and go to bed,' she says, busying herself at the sink.

When we have finished I go to switch off the radio but she tells me to leave it, excusing the eccentricity with a smile and putting out the kitchen light as I begin to mount the stairs. I wait for her at the top and we hug, giggling like schoolgirls as we stand on each other's feet. As I turn to my room she calls after me, 'Sleep with me tonight.' I think she means in her room but I can't lie in my father's place, and so I take her hand and we climb into my bed and I fall asleep to the sound of her breathing, the break of the sea, and distant voices on the radio.

IT took a day and a half's journey by truck to reach the camp at Bakalla. As dusk fell, we pulled off the dirt road and pitched our tents in the shelter of the truck. We had already dropped people at various projects along the route. The husband and wife doctors were staying at the capital to work in the new Red Cross hospital and that left Haneen our driver, Veronica, Martine and myself. It had been breathlessly hot and stuffy in the back of the canvas-topped truck, the packing cases of supplies and equipment bouncing about on the bumpy road and sometimes sliding into our knees and shins. Haneen seemed determined to reach Bakalla as quickly as he could and the countryside unravelled in a veil of dust and exhaust fumes. Insects, mistaking the green of the canvas for vegetation, landed and sunned themselves and once after an undignified communal toilet stop we returned to find what looked like a locust settled on the top of a tool box. We sat, stiff-backed against the side of the truck, until I cupped it in my hands and threw it out, unable to disguise a shiver.

At night Haneen gathered some scrub wood and lit a fire, the wispy smoke flitting skywards between fireflies and moths, while around us stretched the softened shapes of acacia trees, some of them bent over on themselves like inverted question marks. But it is the sky I remember – thick, palpable, studded with stars. Sometimes a shooting star flickered briefly, and we chatted excitedly like Girl Guides at their first camp. Haneen sat on his hunkers, listening impassively, but although we tried to include him in our conversation we got the impression that he spoke little English. He stirred life into the fire with a stick and added the few gnarled pieces of rotten wood we had gathered, and I felt that he resented our presence somehow. Occasionally, the shadowy shapes of bats swooped into the penumbral light of the fire and were gone again.

After a while Haneen left to sleep in the cab of the truck, but we sat on until the smouldering fire had died almost to nothing. For the first time, but not for the last, I had a sudden sense of the immensity that stretched out around me. For someone who had grown up trapped in a cleft between mountains and sea it was a giddy feeling, of lightness, of drifting weightlessly in an unfamiliar space. While Veronica chatted, I was barely conscious of her words, as I tried frantically to tether myself with some anchor of memory, some weight of past experience. All around me spun the malleable expanse of night, silent but for the call of some night bird, and then Veronica too felt the spell of the moment and we sat in silence until the final ember had dwindled into ash.

We woke at dawn, the coldness taking us by surprise and making us dress quickly. Straggly white tongues of mist laced the ground and licked round the wheels of the truck. Haneen was tinkering with the engine, wiping parts with an oily rag and cleaning some of the dust and dirt from the windscreen. We splashed a little water from a canister over hands and faces, and shared a bottled drink and some bread hardened by the journey. When we set off, we stretched our legs across the supplies and tried to doze, but our heads would jerk awake as we bumped over some pothole.

At first, the landscape repeated itself, sporadic pieces of cultivated land growing tawdry crops of sorghum or maize, a few thin herds of cattle grazing on scrub. Once we passed a burnt-out car. Then, after we had journeyed some miles south, we began to meet groups of people walking along the side of the road, their possessions wrapped in blankets and balanced precariously on their heads, some of the women with babies strapped to their backs. They trudged in single file through the rising heat, separated from each other by the burden of their solitary toil. Small children chided goats, punishing their dilatory wanderings with sticks. A few called out to us and held up their hands but the truck's wheels showered them with dust as we passed and when we tried to ask Haneen who they were and where they were going, he shrugged his shoulders and ignored us, hunching over the steering wheel and wiping sweat from his face with a rag. Peering out from the shadow of the truck, we sat unable either to ignore them or to acknowledge them.

Suddenly the truck's brakes were slammed on and we screeched to the side of the road with a violent, bumping swerve. Bits of machinery and packing cases tumbled across the truck, and I squealed in pain as a sharp metal edge cut my leg. Haneen was wrestling with the wheel and shouting wildly as we bounced off the road and into scrub before finally grinding to a halt. A thick cloud of dust billowed into the back, choking and blinding us, and then within a few seconds the tailboard was covered with children's hands as they pulled themselves up to see into the back. They came no further in but held on with one hand, the other stretched towards us as they filled the truck with a chorus of voices. Then there was the sound of Haneen's voice and he was wielding a long thin cane above their heads, striking some of them on the back until they released their hold and dropped to the ground. By now my leg was bleeding steadily, and one of the sacks of flour was punctured and flowing round our feet like sand.

The truck had swerved to avoid a makeshift barrier manned by a group of children, the oldest of whom was probably no more than ten or twelve. When we got out there was a smell of petrol and rubber, and tyretracks where we had braked and skidded across the scrub. Haneen swung his cane wildly when he saw any of the children encroaching and they clung together, cowering before its swish and sting as it sliced the air.

Martine got out her medical kit and dressed my leg, thoroughly cleaning the cut with antiseptic. The children's eyes studied us curiously. One of them came forward, momentarily indifferent to the cane, and when Martine had finished, he touched her on the shoulder, pointed to the case and then gestured to where two or three adults sat in the little shade afforded by some box trees. As she stood up, Haneen shoved the boy away.

'Back in truck, back in truck,' he ordered. 'We must go now to camp.'

But Martine was pushing the boy gently and showing that she would follow him.

'Martine, be careful, it could be a trap,' called Veronica.

'Back in truck, back in truck!' Haneen screamed and for a second I thought he was going to turn the cane on us. 'These people very bad – they will take everything like locusts. We must go now, back in truck.'

But Martine was already halfway to the trees, and the other boys turned from the truck and were following a few footsteps behind. I went after them, slowed by the pain in my leg, and then Veronica came too, scurrying behind and expressing her growing disquiet. As I glanced over my shoulder, I saw Haneen strike the ground with the cane, beating up little puffs of dust. Under the tree, a woman lay on her side, curled up on a woollen blanket. She wore a coarse brown cloth like a shawl and a purple skirt that reached to her skinny knobs of ankles. Two other women sat beside her, fanning and brushing flies away from her face, and at first I didn't see it – it was so small and she hugged it so closely in the folds of her shawl that only the slight sheen of its bulbous head betrayed its presence. Martine knelt close by the woman, talking gently to her and lightly brushing her face, showing her the red cross on her case until eventually she could lift the baby away and hand it to Veronica. Then she examined the woman. Veronica and I looked at the shrivelled, emaciated baby, its distended and distorted head, the leathery contraction of its skin.

'Is it new-born?' I asked.

'It's six months old,' Martine said. 'The mother hasn't been able to feed it. She's dehydrated, exhausted, probably hasn't been able to feed herself properly.'

At Martine's request I ran back to the truck and got a canister of water. With it she bathed the woman's face and gave her a glucose mixture to drink, then examined the baby, holding its head in the palm of her hand and resting the body along her forearm. Veronica helped her open up the rags it was wrapped in, unpicking them slowly as if the tatters were part of the skin. It was a girl. It looked already dead until its eyes opened for a brief second then closed again, and as Martine examined the child its mother sat up on the cloth and began to cry out, holding her hands skyward and rocking her head slowly from side to side. As the other women tried to comfort her, Martine turned to us.

'I think it's too late for the child – she's barely alive. She needs to go on a drip, needs treatment I can't give. Even then I think it's too late.'

'We could take the mother and the baby with us to the camp. I think it's only a couple more hours,' I suggested.

Martine nodded her head but I don't think she held out much hope for the baby. Leaving the child with Veronica, we walked back to the truck to talk to Haneen, but it was obvious he wasn't going to help.

'Against rules, not permitted to carry people,' he insisted, shaking his head and spearing the cane in the ground between his feet. 'Whole family want to come – maybe ten, twelve others. No room, steal everything. Not permitted. Against rules. Very bad.'

He spat on the ground and ordered us to get back in the truck, breaking his English with bursts of his own language. Over his shoulder I could see some of the children edging closer to the truck. Some had found their own sticks and it seemed likely that if we stayed much longer they would take everything that could be carried. We walked back to the group under the trees, unsure of what we should do.

'We'd have to take the whole family,' Martine said. 'We can't split them up. Haneen's right – there are too many. They'd all have to come.'

'But the baby. . . .'

'The baby is going to die, Naomi. There's nothing we can do.'

When we reached the group the woman had fallen back on the cloth and Veronica was cradling the child, trying to hold her out of the sun. 'Give her back the child, Veronica – it's too late,' Martine said. But Veronica continued to hold on, reluctant to give her back until, taking the child, Martine gently placed her back in her mother's arms. Then, despite Haneen's protests we left them the canister of water and I scooped up a bucketful of the flour that had spilled on the floor of the truck. They knew we were leaving, but there was no anger in their faces, only what looked like an exhausted acceptance of their fate. Their silence made it easier. But as we walked away the mother suddenly called after us, her voice rising into a high wail, and as we kept on walking, frightened to turn round, it grew more desperate, more insistent, until I had to turn and face her. She had struggled to her feet and was staggering towards us. In her hands she held out the bundle of rags. At first I didn't understand.

'She wants us to take the child,' I said as I finally realized.

Martine hesitated as we both looked to her for a decision.

'Maybe there's just a chance we could reach the camp,' said Veronica.

'I don't think so,' Martine replied, 'but maybe we should try. Maybe we should try.'

She slowly circled round and took the child again as the woman bowed her head and touched our hands. I took a piece of paper from Martine's case and printed the name of the camp, then pressed it into her hand and joined the others in the truck. As we drove off she dropped to her knees in the dust and buried her face in the ground.

We held the baby in turns, swaddling it in a sweatshirt and bathing its face with water as we bumped along the road. Martine tried to dribble glucose into its mouth with a drip but most of it ran out again. It felt weightless, a dried up bundle of sticks. We passed it carefully, afraid that its brittle bones might crack under the pressure of our clumsy hands. It never opened its eyes. About an hour later I tried to pass it to Martine but she shook her head and stared in front of her, then took a cigarette out of her breast pocket and lit it carefully, her hand jerking with the motion of the truck. 'It died some time ago,' she said, taking a long drag of the cigarette, holding it for a few seconds then expelling it through the tight purse of her mouth. 'We should never have taken it.'

She pulled her legs tightly towards her on the seat and rested her chin on her knees. No one spoke. I covered the baby with the folds of the sweatshirt. It suddenly felt heavy in my arms, this dried up parcel of air and bones, and I wanted someone to take it but no one offered, and so I held it until Haneen pulled off the road and stopped the truck.

Martine took a knife from her case and sliced the throat of the spilt hessian sack and we wrapped the baby in it. Then, taking a spade from the truck, I carried the body into the brush. Haneen stayed hunched over the wheel as if not deigning to look at us. The earth was baked hard and Martine and Veronica made little headway in digging a grave, able only to scrape away the surface of the soil with the end of the spade. Their shirts darkened with spreading stains of sweat, and flies flickered about their heads. Then Haneen appeared and without speaking took the spade and dug a shallow grave, gouging out the ochre-coloured earth with a two-handed stabbing motion. When he spoke it was to tell us to gather stones to cover the body, to stop the jackals digging it up, and then I set it in, its face covered with the thin veil of hessian. After piling up our smattering of small stones we looked down at the grave. Suddenly it felt unreal, like children burying a dead pet in a shoebox at the bottom of the garden. With a shiver I remembered hiding my first blood beneath stones and into the moment seeped those same feelings of fear and shame. Then we turned away, blocking out the reality by speculating about how long it would take us to reach the camp.

As we drove, Martine checked my cut and then we sat in silence, separated by our own thoughts and the guilt of our sweat. The landscape bumped by, almost monotonous, an unrelenting stretch of scrub, broken only by the occasional oasis of greenness where some crop was being grown, a grassy spread of plain, or ragged villages glimpsed through breaks in the bush. There were more people on the road now but we sped on, leaving them behind us in a blur of dust and a new-found reluctance to meet their gaze. We were entering the hottest part of the day and inside the truck felt airless, the canvas canopy protecting us from the sun a suffocating lid baking the air stagnant, so it came as a relief when we reached the outskirts of the Bakalla camp. Haneen relaxed at the wheel and pointed it out to us as we approached down a rutted dirt track.

The word 'camp' suggests an organized, contained area of set boundaries, but Bakalla was a sprawling chaos, its outer suburbs consisting of makeshift dwellings cobbled together crudely from packing cases, bits of polythene, and anything that could afford protection from the elements. Beyond these were the circles of Agency-supplied tents. The camp had been set up a year before, originally as a transit station for refugees fleeing over the border from drought and the sporadic outbreaks of tribal fighting, but more and more people had poured in and fewer left as war and famine spread through the region. As we drove into the camp children seeped out of its secret places and ran alongside, patting the side of the truck in greeting and shouting excitedly. At the camp's core stood the collection of semi-permanent buildings which included a clinic, a feeding station and storage sheds. These had dirt floors, roughly plastered walls and tin roofs emblazoned with the Red Cross insignia. More children fanned out in front of the truck, slowing us to a snail's pace. I could see a new series of buildings had been started, a few rows of blocks laid along string lines.

Bakalla was the central and largest camp in the region but there were other smaller ones scattered around it like satellites, manned by local workers but without medical facilities. When the truck finally stopped in front of the clinic I could hear music playing somewhere in the background – it sounded like opera – but then it was drowned out by the clamour of the children. Standing on the veranda in purple T-shirt and shorts was a man in his late thirties who introduced himself as Dr Charlie Wanneker, the Camp Leader. His blond hair, receding at the front, was pulled back into a shaggy ponytail. A pair of mirrored wrap-around sunglasses hid his eyes.

'Hi guys!' he said, pumping our hands in turn. 'Good to see you, good trip up?'

We nodded our heads as we made our introductions and he welcomed us to the camp.

'We passed a lot of people on the road,' I said, staring at the reflection of sky in his eyes.

'There's been more fighting in the Mankela region, but we haven't got a clear report on the extent yet,' he said, flicking away a fly which had rested on the bleached hairs of his arm. 'But we'll talk later. Aduma here will show you to your penthouse suite – I'm sure you'll want to get freshened up. I'll see you soon – I'm in the middle of stitching a wound.'

As we followed Aduma I could see the truck being unloaded and the contents carefully carried into the compound behind the clinic. We carried our own possessions. The children flurried round us and I could feel hands lightly touching my arms and back as if they wanted to know if I were real. Sometimes the smaller ones got pushed in front of me as I walked and I almost tripped over them. Then Aduma would turn and scold them.

'It is your hair,' he said, smiling back at me.

'My hair?'

'They think your hair is on fire,' he laughed. 'They've never seen anyone with that colour hair before.'

Our penthouse suite was a large ex-army tent pitched in the little shade afforded by two dead-looking trees whose upper branches twisted into each other, their bark cracked and riven, peeling away in places. Inside there were three beds, a table, two chairs, a smaller table with two plastic basins, and a hurricane lamp hung from the junction of some metal poles. There was a rubbery, fetid smell, but it was cooler and we dropped our luggage at random and flopped on to the beds. Aduma left but returned a few minutes later with a metal bucket filled with water and poured it into the basins, then shooed away the faces that still stared at us through the opening of the tent. Veronica zipped it up and we washed. The journey had done much to remove any embarrassments about personal hygiene and we stripped to bras and knickers and splashed water over our bodies, trying to clean away the dust and grime which layered our skin and lingered in our mouths. As there were only two basins we let Veronica use one and I waited until Martine had finished. I was still washing when we heard a voice and the sound of the tent flap being unzipped and Charlie Wanneker entered. Veronica and Martine had already put on clean clothes and I stood in my underwear looking at him, conscious of my embarrassment but unwilling to show it by scampering like some schoolgirl for the clothes which hung over the end of my bed. He was still wearing sunglasses, which made it hard to read his expression, but he didn't apologize for his timing or display any kind of discomfort. He sat on my bed, removing the possibility of casually sidling towards it and my clothes. He placed his head on his hands and stared somewhere close to the hurricane lamp.

'You guys get a couple of hours' rest and then we'll eat together, meet the rest of the team. Tomorrow, first thing, I'll fill you in on what I need from you. I know you've heard it all before but don't eat or drink anything except what you're supposed to. Period. And take all the tabs, every day take those tabs – you're no use to anyone lying there out of the game because you haven't been sensible.'

As he turned his head towards me I pretended to dry myself with the towel. 'What happened to your leg?'

'I caught it on a packing case on the truck.'

'Come over here and let me look at it.'

'It's OK, Martine dressed it earlier.'

'It's not something I want to take a chance with – infections can start up very easily. Let me see it.'

He had given me an order, and as I walked towards him I felt conscious of the imperfections of my body. In his mirrored eyes I saw the smallness of my breasts and hips, the shapelessness of my legs, the shock of hair. A small girl again at a mirror, and beyond her only the merging of sea and sky. Dreaming another self, dreaming another life. He gestured me to the bed and I sat there in my grubby underwear which smelt of smoke and he didn't look like a doctor. Holding the back of my leg, his fingers pushed lightly into the muscle as he raised it towards him. He took off his glasses and I saw his blue eyes for the first time. They glanced up at me as he unwound the bandage and his fingers played slowly across the muscle.

'Looks pretty clean, but keep it salved and bandaged until it heals up. Can't have you striking out before you reach first base.'

As he stood up I reached for a top and slipped it on while he replaced his sunglasses.

'That's some head of hair, Naomi. With your colouring you'll need to be real careful with the sun. Always wear a hat or a headscarf and make sure your neck doesn't get burned. Irish, yeah?'

'That's right, Irish. And you're American?'

'Chicago. I'm taking a couple of years out before starting a teaching post in medical school.'

Then he talked briefly with Martine and Veronica. I slipped on shorts and began to brush my hair. After he left, Veronica zipped up the tent and we sat on the edges of the beds and bathed our feet in what was left of the water.

THEY slowly circle the cowering boy. They chant 'Kill the pig! Kill the pig!', building up to a rhythmic chorus. 'Kill the pig! Kill the pig!' Over and over, round and round, the spears and knives jerking and stabbing menacingly closer. The chanting grows louder until it seems to come from one throbbing throat. A chair gets knocked over, someone collides with a desk and the pig squeals as someone prods his rump with a ruler. Behind the paper masks and tribal war-paint eyes narrow and mouths tilt into leers. 'Kill the pig! Kill the pig!' A boy bends over him and makes a throat-slitting motion with a rolled jotter. A first former comes to the door with an announcement about dinner tickets and they turn on him and chant 'Kill the pig! Kill the pig!' until he runs from the room and, as the laughter peaks and then subsides, I clap my hands, help the pig dust his blazer and usher them back to their seats.

How did it feel? A laugh, Miss. We needed better spears, sharper knives. I let them spill out the silliness and then when we've had our laugh we start to talk. A bit scary, Miss. Why was it scary, Leona? Because you weren't really yourself any more, because like you could be anyone, someone different from yourself and no one would know. Another voice. It felt good, like we were all part of the same thing, like everyone was equal and there weren't any leaders. An argument. It was stupid – nobody can make you do anything you don't want. It's just a bunch of stupid kids pretending to be tough, egging each other on to do something they haven't the bottle for. But wait, let's ask how the pig felt. Funny, stupid answer first, then – On your own, Miss, different from everybody else and starting to think that maybe you'd done something really bad and deserved what was happening to you.

We talk about masks. Why did the boys paint their faces? Daniel understands. Because it helps them lose their inhibitions, because they're able to hide behind the mask, behave in a way that's maybe different from what they're normally like. Some don't understand. A joke about wearing a mask because it's an improvement on someone's face. Kerri understands – maybe you don't feel as guilty about what you do because you can put the blame on someone else. And when the talking's done we make a display. They work in groups, drawing and designing, cutting pictures out of magazines and, when they ask if they can play some music while they work, someone puts on a U2 tape and I pretend I like it. I've bought a poster of a desert island with palm trees and golden sands and we group their work around it. There are pictures from magazines of shadowy faces, painted sports fans, an African tribe performing a dance, the stone statues of Easter Island, a dark figure wearing a combat jacket and a balaclava silhouetted against some Belfast gable wall. We don't have a conch but someone brings in a large white shell and we hang it from the display board.

After school I stand and look at it all, read their words. 'This book provides an insight into good and evil in the world. It shows that there is good and evil in every person and in certain situations this evil escapes and takes control of the person. It was the boys' own evil which brought the images of beasts and their own fears which made it real to them.' Around me the school sounds quiet, only the occasional banging of a door or the sound of a cleaner intruding into the room. I look into the deserted playground where empty crisp bags and pages ripped from jotters skirmish with the wind. I turn to Daniel's group. 'The boys used masks to hide away from reality. By covering their faces they could turn into someone else, run away from responsibility and believe they will not be blamed for the violence they have used. The boys use rituals to unite them. When they come together they are not afraid of anything. The group gives them a power stronger than any individual.'

Some girls have written about how it would have been if it had been only girls on the island. The wind rattles and flaps at the corrugated roof of an outside store. 'We think it would be slightly different with girls. At the beginning they would all stay in one group but after a while would split into smaller ones and stay with their friends. Girls would be more careful about things like safety and not physically hurt each other. They would be more scared of any creatures living on the island like insects. They would keep themselves clean and keep the fire lit. They would miss their families and their mothers.' In the playground some released detainee speeds towards the escape gates, his schoolbag slithering and bucking across his shoulders. As he meets the road two army Land Rovers pass by, the soldiers standing at the back like charioteers, their eyes skittering across street corners.

I am a teacher. I stand in a room at the end of a lime-green corridor and talk of Yeats and his gyres, the blood-dimmed tide of innocence loosed upon the world, of rough beasts, of Golding and his island. They sit in groups and stare at my hair, the clumsy clothes I have chosen to wear, my shapeless legs. Some, mindful of their exams, take notes, others sit comatose, cocooned in an inviolable world. On the walls of my room I have posters of characters from Shakespeare, displays of work and a picture of James Joyce. Some afternoons when I play them music or Richard Burton reading *Under Milk Wood* they roll their eyes or draw the names of heavy metal groups on the covers of their notebooks. One day I make a fool of myself by finding a homework diary in the corridor and ask which class Axl Rose is in. Their laughter is better than their indifference. I laugh too, and the next day someone brings in a Guns 'n' Roses' tape and I pretend I like it.

I remember it as an ugly building, the corridors painted that lime-green colour – probably a left-over lot from some store. Most things in the school are second-hand, with books and equipment salvaged from earlier closures. It straddles the peace-line of North Belfast, plumped in the middle of a road where two communities rub raw against each other. It had been a Protestant school until its enrolment withered away through population drift. Then it had been involved in a series of amalgamations with similar schools, but continued to diminish in stages like some Babuska doll until it was too small to be viable. When it eventually re-opened, it was as an integrated school, where Catholic and Protestant are educated together. The children come from various parts of Belfast and for a variety of reasons; some are there because their parents think it is a step towards a better society, others as a compromise – the products of mixed marriage. A number are merely misfits or rejects from other institutions. I think Daniel was in this last group.

I am the headmaster's dream come true. I like the job more days than not, like the children, the people I work with, and before long I secretly think of the school as my family. Each day I go home just before the caretaker locks the door, and I get involved in every activity I can. I think I feel happy, begin to believe I do a job that is important. The past slowly seems to slip into the clouded and faded mirror of sky and sea and I turn my face to the future. Sometimes I even think the children like me.

Now they sit in a circle, the symbolism of equality, of an equal voice, pushing them into a self-conscious display of maturity. They are to tell of a time when they experienced fear, and already some squirm with embarrassment, try to push their chair behind someone else's. Some will pretend to play the game, some will bottle it – that is the phrase Daniel would use – side-stepping the short moment in the spotlight with a carefully calculated anecdote. Something safe, held up a long arm's length from their private selves. Each speaker holds the white shell, the token which entitles them to a hearing, the temporary respect of the listeners, and when finished they hand it to another speaker in the circle. Everyone plays the game, gives the obligatory grimace when the shell is placed in their hands but some, perhaps for the first time, really speak.

The shell is held by Sinead. She takes a deep gulp as if she's going to dive into deep water, her back straight and stiff, one foot sanding the floor backwards and forwards, trying to smoothe the rising knots of nervousness. Then the words start, slowly at first and then breaking into a rhythm both fragmented and eloquent. She is seven or eight years old and she sleeps in the bedroom at the front of the house – Shona has not yet been born so she has the room to herself. It is late, she can't sleep – she likes to wait for the sound of her father returning from his shift in the bakery. Likes to hear his key in the door, the kettle filling for his supper. There are only her mother and herself and she is half asleep when she is wakened by a knocking at the front door and the sound of a voice screaming. A woman screaming, screaming for help, her words lost in the scream. Sinead's mother is trying to calm her and then slowly words filter into her room. Men have come in the night and shot the woman's husband. He is lying in the hallway bleeding. She hears her mother go next door and then there is a silence which is worse than the screaming and it seems to last forever and she thinks the men will come back to kill her too, and she is frightened. She hides in the bed and after a while she hears footsteps on the stairs and she starts to scream and then her father is holding her and as blue lights spin around her room he tells her everything will be all right.

She is fighting back the tears as she tells it, and I want to stretch out my hand to her but am not brave enough. No one speaks, no one moves, as she tells us that sometimes it all comes back to her in a dream and then she stands up, flicks her hair with a shake of her head and hands the shell across the circle to

Daniel. I thank her and in the silence he looks at it, looks at Sinead, then looks at me and for a moment I think he is going to crush it between his hands, say he won't play my stupid game. I smile an encouragement and he stares again at the shell. I half-expect some story of brutality, some male posturing, a tale of gangs, of street cool, of survival.

'I was ten or eleven and there was me and Gerry Lavery – Lav, he was called. We used to hang about together before we moved away. One winter – it was coming up to Christmas and it was really cold – we were living in Ligoniel then and there was this quarry up behind us on the mountain.'

Daniel was the first pupil I met on my first day, met before I had even taught my first lesson. I had parked my car at some shops on the road about a mile from the school, intending to buy a paper to hide behind in the staff-room. As I headed towards the newsagent's I read the headlines on the billboards hanging from the wire grilles on the windows, the raw abbreviations of atrocity, a blackened shorthand of some far-off tribal war. As I looked away the traffic suddenly slewed to a halt in a whining lurch and jerk of brakes.

'We used to go up there a lot and sit on the diggers, or clod stones at cans. We had this stupid game we used to play where we climbed these mountains of loose stones and started landslides. And there was this pit which was always full of water – it was about waist deep and sometimes we used to float wood across it. Well, this Saturday afternoon when we went up it was frozen over, and when we threw stones the ice didn't break.'

Through the curse of horns ran a boy, his schoolbag slapping his back, his red hair an exclamation mark in the dullness of the morning. Weaving in and out of the cars and behind four or five other blazers of a different colour. Only then I realized it was a chase; saw that one of the pursuers, unrestricted by bag or uniform, was running parallel to the quarry on the pavement opposite and that soon he would cross over and cut off escape.

'So Lav dared me to walk across it and I wouldn't at first, and I dared him but he wouldn't either, and then he kept calling me chicken and flapping his arms like wings. So eventually I said I would if he did it after me.'

In that moment too I realized the quarry was wearing a blazer that marked him as one of mine and I ran too, mindful of the startled faces of passers-by and the renewed flow of the indifferent traffic. I could see them now, the boy with no uniform hanging on, trying to pull the other down, to hold him long enough for the rest of the pack to arrive. And as it did a welter of voices and kicks broke over the boy on the pavement. As I reached them, he had managed to roll himself into a ball in the urine-splashed doorway of a boarded-up shop, the narrowness of the entrance restricting them as they pushed and jostled each other to deliver their blows. Their voices were guttural, rabid, synchronized with the smack and slither of their feet.

'It was OK at the start and the ice seemed really thick, so I got a bit cocky and started like I was marching, and I was halfway across when there was this friggin' crack and I fell through. Lav was laughing and calling me the Titanic. My feet were on the bottom, but it wasn't flat and my feet were slipping, and when I tried to climb out the ice kept breaking and wasn't strong enough to take my weight and it was cold and then I cut my hand and I was really bricking it and Lav wasn't laughing any more. And I started to think that I'd fall – it was stupid, but I started to think that I'd get trapped under the ice. The more I got scared the more I panicked, and then Lav threw this bit of wood and I started to use it like a hammer and broke a path back to the edge. And when we got home me da scalped the arse off me for getting wet.'

And now I was close enough to smell the fear, the sweet stench of self-hate, and I felt my own fear tumbling over and over in the hollow of my stomach and I knew that what was happening was stronger than any voice my pathetic training had given me, stronger than any appeals. And then I screamed and thumped backs, pulling hair when that produced no response, and kept on screaming and suddenly there was another woman beside me shouting and pulling them off, until one by one they wheeled away, the whoop of victory in their throats. Only the boy with no uniform remained, trying desperately to inflict some final piece of damage with his feet. As I grabbed the back of his hair he spun round and knocked my hand away and for a second we looked into each other's eyes and I tried to hide my fear as I waited for his fist. But I was too far beneath his contempt even for that, and he gave me only his spit and a 'fucking Fenian bitch' and then he too was gone, his final curse still tainting the air after he had vanished.

In the doorway the boy hugged himself, his head clamped in the tight vice of his arms, as if unwilling to risk a return of his attackers or perhaps because movement brought too much pain. As I turned towards the other woman – small, older, a pink roller peeping out from under a headscarf – she patted me on the wrist, swore her own orison of despair and wiped away the spittle from my jacket with a shredded tissue, and then she was gone before I'd time to thank her properly. I touched the boy on the back with a shaking hand and felt his muscles tighten, and then as I knelt beside him amidst the silver shards of take-away cartons, he looked up at me through his fingers and smiled. Smiled like he'd been playing a game all along and was pleased that he'd fooled me. Only the blood coming from his nose and the side of his mouth told the truth. I watched him feel his nose first, delicately pinching it to check it wasn't broken, then spitting out gobs of blood.

It was a smile I was to become familiar with over the next year, a public message that no matter what the world did to him he was immune to even its most malevolent efforts. As I drove him to school that morning he laughed off my concern for his injuries and when I tried to discover the reason for the attack he merely pointed to the shamrock and Celtic F.C. emblem on his bag. He was embarrassed to be in the car with me and clearly glad to reach the school and escape the patronage of a teacher. Everything he said and the way he spoke suggested that what had happened was just a trivial, run-of-the-mill occurrence. He didn't thank me but as I locked the car and watched him stroll away he stopped for a moment and called back, 'You aren't going to scream like that in class, are you, Miss?' and then he smiled again but this time there was no defiance, just a simulated innocence which made me smile too.

A few minutes before I faced my first assembly, I hurried into the staff toilets and emptied the contents of my stomach. While the pupils laboured through the first hymn of the year I heard only the smack and slither of feet on a pavement. As a fidget of boredom rippled through the rows of standing children I remembered another pavement, another time, saw again a shiny black frieze of city and sky, a man's hand clutching the air like a claw, a voice splintering into swearwords sharp as glass, flailing arms in a black mirror. And then I thought of the boy's smile, and I looked for him in the body of the hall. Eventually I picked out his red hair – he was close to the back, leaning against the side wall sharing jokes with his companions, his hand occasionally raised to his nose as if to reassure himself that his earlier diagnosis had been correct.

The next time I saw him was in my fifth period English class. That was also the moment he said his thanks. He said it by not giving me a hard time and by unsubtly ensuring that no one else attempted to. At first he didn't participate, but sometimes I would look up and catch his curious stare. Sometimes, too, he looked at me as if he couldn't believe I was true, as if I were some creature from an alien world, but it only made me try the harder, sending me scurrying off to find something new, some newspaper article or story that might connect with his world and that of the other children. Driven by the unbearable zeal of the missionary and the naive enthusiasm of the newly apprenticed, I clutched the spurious belief that I could alter what I conceived then as the narrow limits of their existence. And not even the collective wall of apathy or their studied, practised cynicism could deter my frantic outpouring of energy. I just kept on trying, stubbornly seeking out the chinks in their indifference, offering myself again and again and nursing no hurt or resentment when rejected. Perhaps in the end they took pity on me. Perhaps it was easier to humour me. Just maybe, some of them let themselves like me a little.

I think Daniel liked me. Gradually he relaxed his pose and allowed himself to participate, and through some of the things he said and did I realized he was smart. Not as smart about the world as he thought he was, but smart enough to be interested in books and curious about the things he didn't know. He borrowed books, sometimes by asking, sometimes surreptitiously slipping them into his schoolbag like a shop-lifter. One wet lunchtime he strolled into my room as I sat marking at my desk.

'Working hard, Miss?'

'Just a few homeworks I want to return after lunch. You'll not kill me, Daniel, with the amount of homework you produce for me.'

'That's because I'm a kind person, Miss, and I don't want to see you overworked.'

'The last piece you wrote was very good – you could do even better if you worked at it.'

He shuffled his feet in embarrassment and looked at the rain streaming the windows. 'Do you like being a teacher?'

'Most days I like it. Some days I feel I'm making a bit of a mess of it.'

He smiled and flexed a plastic ruler he had lifted from my desk. 'What was it like living in Donegal? I stayed in a caravan in Bundoran once. It was the pits. Never stopped raining.'

'I didn't like it much. I was glad when I left.'

'A bit like living in West Belfast, then. I'll be glad when I leave too.'

'Where is it you want to go, Daniel?'

'America, maybe London, don't really care. I've a brother in Boston, does painting and decorating, has his own business – might go there, work for him. I've a brother in the Kesh as well.'

He twanged the ruler then lifted his head to watch my reaction.

'That must be hard for your family.'

'Not really. Me ma says he's safer where he is and me da's never had so many free drinks in his life.'

'What did your brother do?'

'That's a question you're not supposed to ask.'

In the corridor there was the sound of laughter.

'I'm sorry, I didn't mean to. . . .'

'You're from Donegal, Miss, you don't know any better,' he said, his smile breaking across his face. He dropped the ruler on the desk and turned to go. I watched him rest his hand on the door. Someone was bouncing a ball against a wall.

'They said he drove the get-away car after a hit on a policeman. They missed the peeler and killed an oul lad coming out of a bookie's.' He turned away again and I couldn't see his face. I wanted to say something but I didn't know what.

'Daniel,' I called after him. 'Do you miss him?'

'Miss him? Why would I miss him? Killing oul lads was about his limit. All it means is I don't have to share a bedroom any more.' And then he gave me one of his smiles but as I struggled to read it he was gone, his voice shouting loudly after someone in the corridor.

His face is smiling now, teasing, challenging, but there is nowhere for me to hide. As I take the shell in both hands they stare at me with a collective curiosity and for perhaps the first time I feel the sharp focus of their concentration burrowing into me. Moments fall open in my memory as if someone is flicking the pages of my life – a young girl hiding her blood in the sand; the cold brush of the mirror on my lips as I kiss my loneliness, wonder if anyone will ever love me; my father drifting still through some salted sea of tears. They wait patiently for me to speak.

A chair scrapes across the floor. Someone coughs. I hold the shell tightly and begin.

BASIF sits smoking a cigar. He tells me his father sends them for his birthdays. I joke that at least the smoke will discourage mosquitoes, but he insists that they are of the finest quality and offers to let me smoke one. I decline his offer but thank him genuinely for providing a room to let Nadra set up a school. It is a good idea – it gives her less time to worry about me and keeps the growing number of children occupied and out of trouble.

'You are a teacher, Naomi?' he asks.

'Yes, I was a teacher in Ireland.'

'And what did you teach?'

'English, literature, books. Do you read, Basif?'

'When I was a student, but not very often now.'

'Will I ever read books again, Basif?'

I smell the cigar smoke drifting past my face, listen for the silences between his words.

'Of course you will read again. Have you forgotten that I told you your eyes will be beautiful as Sophia Loren's? Soon the Swiss doctor will come and everything will be fine.'

I try to press him but he fobs me off and eventually I give up. 'You're a big fan of Sophia Loren – do you watch her films?'

'Films? No. I am a friend of Miss Loren.'

I laugh. I can't help it. I laugh, compliment him on his sense of humour, try not to hurt his feelings.

'You don't believe me?' he says, his voice like a hurt little boy's. I apologize for my rudeness, trying to think of some escape, but before I find the right words he continues.

' "Thank-you, Basif, for the good work you do here", that was what she said as she shook my hand. Later we have a meal together.'

He sounds almost convincing but I can't believe him. 'Where did you meet Miss Loren?'

'She came last year, touring the camps along the border – she represents the United Nations High Commissioner for Refugees. "Thank you, Dr Basif, for the good work you do here." That was what she said, and when we have our meal we talk just the way we do now.'

'And what did she do when she came to the camps?'

'She cry a little, feed some children, talk to the staff and have her picture taken by a camera crew from *Hello* magazine.'

We both laugh, and again he offers me a smoke of his cigar.

'And was she beautiful?'

'Miss Loren is not such a young woman now, but I think she is still very beautiful – all women are beautiful.'

'Even women with burnt skin and red hair?'

'Soon everything will heal, even sooner than you think, and then you can go back to Ireland.'

I don't tell him that I do not want to go back. I do not want to talk of Ireland but I know he has waited patiently for this moment. Over our head the branches of the frankincense tree stretch and creak a little like the stiffening of old bones. All its scent seems dried up and forgotten, but I feel the sun fleck and dapple my face through the slowly moving branches and wonder what I shall say when he asks his question.

'Are you happy, Miss?'

'I'd be happier if you worked a bit harder, Daniel.'

I go on painting the notice boards at the back of the class, trying not to let the paint run. My feet shuffle across pages from the *Belfast Telegraph*, green blobs of paint splatting the black print. I have to stand on a chair to reach the top parts.

'And what'll working harder do for me?'

'It'll get you a ticket out of here. You're always saying how much you hate it.'

'But you worked hard and got your qualifications and you're still here.'

'I'm here because I want to be,' I say, as the brush strokes a hair across the painted surface. I try to pick it off and the paint slimes and coats my fingers.

'Why do you want to be here?'

It's difficult when he talks to me like this. Part of me wants to answer openly but part tells me that I am a teacher and should only say what will be good for him to hear. As I hesitate, he rescues me with a joke.

'I suppose after Donegal anything seems good. You've got a drip over there. Miss, do you think you could write me a letter saying I'm a victim of social deprivation and get me a cross-community holiday in America?'

I laugh and stretch too far, almost falling off the chair.

'I'm serious, Miss, half our estate's on one. You get shacked up with some rich family who treat you like the golden child. Only if I get one I'm not coming back. I'll tell them a good story about the bullets whistling through my windows every night and the Brits breaking down the door every five minutes. What do you say, Miss? You're an English teacher – you could write a good letter, have them gurning their eyes out.'

'I think you could probably write a better letter than me, Daniel. And what do I know about anything?'

'That's true, Miss – do you remember the day you were looking for Axl Rose?' We both laugh at the memory and then I get down off the chair and hand him the brush. He takes off his blazer and starts to paint the bits I've missed with deft, sweeping strokes, and as he works I tell him my mother's story about being knocked down by the American tourist. Then he tells me about a family he knows who go around looking for cracked pavements so they can fall over them and sue the council. Before long the boards are almost finished; sudden sunlight rakes the room, lighting up the brush strokes and the glint of staples I wasn't able to pull out, the redness of his hair.

'Why did your parents send you to this school, Daniel?'

He stands with his back to me, surveying the finished work.

'To spite the priest. Me da did it to spite the priest,' he says as he turns to look at me. He hesitates, then finger-prints green paint across the headlines of one of the papers. 'I told you I'd a brother in the Kesh; well, I've another brother in Milltown. He was shot by the Brits. I was ten when he died. He was called Sean. The priest wouldn't let the coffin come in the chapel grounds with the flag and gloves and stuff on it. He and me da stood arguing on the steps for about five minutes. I thought me da was going to deck him. Afterwards he never went back, even though me ma begs him every other day. So he sent me here because he knew it would get up their noses.'

'Your family's had a hard time.'

'Not as bad as some,' and the sudden defensiveness in his voice tells me he doesn't want my sympathy. In my confusion I reach out to touch the boards as if to see if the paint is dry, and leave an imprint of my fingertips. He shakes his head in pretend exasperation and brushes out the marks.

'What's the point, anyway, of painting these boards when you're only going to stick things all over them and in the end you won't even be able to see them?'

I smile and push hair out of my eyes. 'Maybe life won't always be like this, Daniel. Maybe there's good things waiting out there in the future.'

He looks at me as if I'm a child who's just said something incredibly stupid, goes to say something in reply then stops himself.

'When you're a big-shot businessman in America, would you give me a job as a painter?'

'No way,' he says. 'You've got more paint on your hair than the boards.'

As he stretches out to touch my hair I start away a little. His hand drops, he shakes his head with a smile and then he is gone. I look at the mark of his hand on the newspaper. I kneel down in the empty room and match my hand with its print.

'Why did you come to Africa, Naomi?'

How can I start to explain? How can he understand? I would have to begin with a feeling, a feeling which belongs in a city I once thought of as home. It is a sense that we are slipping closer to the abyss, that with each new atrocity comes the frightened knowledge that all semblance of restraint, of the accepted parameters of barbarity, has gone, and that there is nothing to stop us slipping over the edge.

Two days after Michael Stone attacks the mourners at the funeral of the IRA unit shot in Gibraltar I pass a paint-daubed wall. 'It only takes one Stone to kill three Taigs', it says. Soon the same celebratory slogan is everywhere and suddenly it feels as if we are spiralling out of control, no longer just some monotonous side-show, each new burst of savagery reaching out to taint any life it chooses. The whole city tenses, the tight little lines of streets I pass each day, spokes on a wheel which rolls inexorably towards its fate. As always it is unspoken, but you feel it in your stomach, see it in the eyes of the policeman who checks your licence, hear it in the staff-room conversations which avoid its every mention. And always the hovering helicopter, watching, waiting, the sound of its engine throbbing at first like a migraine, then gradually absorbed into the consciousness until it is no longer heard.

It is three days after the Milltown attack and Kevin Brady, an IRA man killed by Stone, is to be buried in the same cemetery. The IRA is wary of a repeat attack and from early morning their men patrol and search the cemetery, look under cars on the funeral route, guard the streets around St Agnes' church on the Andersontown Road. Young men huddle on street corners, shelter in shop doorways, their eyes spearing each passing car with suspicion. Stewards, puffed up with self-importance, talk into two-way radios. Women and children are conspicuous by their absence. Veiled faces peer from behind curtains, others watch from their doorsteps. Soon the shops will close as cars and vans unload the world's press to join the crowds making their way to the church. When the coffin comes out, the leather gloves and beret are placed on top and the cortège moves slowly to Milltown, thousands of mourners behind, and in front a phalanx of black taxis. Above, the helicopter treads air. Can you see it, Basif? Can you hear the throb and whirr of its engine? I feel the sun stir the burnt parts of my skin and I move my head to find new shade. The chanting of the children grows shrill as Nadra's voice urges them to ever greater efforts.

Suddenly a silver-coloured car appears as if from nowhere, heading at first towards the cortège. It brakes, turns, ricocheting from blocked-off exits, desperately seeking an escape. As it reverses, it finds itself hemmed in by black taxis and as it slithers to a stop the crowd breaks forward and surrounds it, pulling at the locked doors. There are two men in the car. I sit in my flat, the week's shopping spilling out of plastic bags round my feet, and watch it on television. All across the country we sit at home over lunch, in bars and clubs, watch as the crowd round the car grows. Twenty, thirty, forty men, kicking at the doors, banging at the windows with wheel braces. And as they swarm over it a man climbs on the roof and swings an iron bar again and again at the windscreen. You feel the terror of the two men inside as the car is engulfed by screaming, contorted faces and you want to shout, to try to stop what you know has already happened, but there is only the silent, sickening fascination, and so I sit with bags of groceries slouching their contents across the floor and watch.

The crowd is driven by its own collective fenzy; hungry, atavistic, each man outdoing the other, and suddenly I think it is a film and everything will be all right. But then one of the men is twisting himself out of a window and firing a warning shot in the air but all the fear is in the car and it is too late to stop what you always knew was going to happen, as the two men are trailed out of the car and vanish in a flail of fists and feet. They don't show any more on television. Only the helicopter sees it all, its cameras flicking the image on to screens in darkened rooms where uniformed men huddle together, watching as the IRA take over and drag the two men towards Casement Park. Watch the screens, Basif, push your way into the huddle. Come, stand beside me and watch as the men are beaten again, interrogated and stripped. See the crowd milling outside the closed gate as only the chosen few are admitted to watch, to lend a fist or a boot. Come with me, Basif, as we hover in the sky, become the unblinking eye of the camera.

See the semi-conscious bodies thrown over the wall of Casement Park and taken in a black taxi where they are beaten again, follow it to waste ground close by where the summoned gunman appears and shoots one of the soldiers in the head, for yes, they are soldiers, and so required to die. See one of them struggle, for the final time, before he, too, is finished off. Hear the young man leaving the scene say to the arriving journalist, 'Short and sweet, good enough for him.' Look too, Basif, as a priest arrives and kneels beside the stripped body and gives the last rites, tries to administer the kiss of life to a bloody mouth. An old woman appears and places her coat over the head of one of the dead soldiers. Listen to what she says: 'He's somebody's son. God have mercy on him.'

But there is no mercy, and they show it again and again until it runs silently and perpetually in the head. I kneel on the kitchen floor and pack groceries on to fridge shelves, a feeling of sickness adding its own score to the images. Later we will distance ourselves with ritual condemnation, try to expiate our communal guilt with explanation, but for the moment there is no absolution. I take an empty polythene bag and clear out the half-used, wasted food that always litters the fridge, mop out the spreading puddle of water which forms on the bottom shelf. My hand shakes a little, Basif, for there is something else I have seen, something which I would have to tell you if I were to answer your question.

It is a face, Basif. It is a face I love. The first time I watched, I saw only the crowd. The second time I see the faces, but even then I tell myself I am mistaken. Something makes me flick to another channel and I record the news on video, play it back, freeze-frame, then release to the moment when the camera angles into three men breaking the glass at the back of the car. But one of them is not a man. One of them is a boy. A boy whose face I know. He is climbing on the boot of the car and his hand holds something I can't see but as his arm becomes a swinging arc the camera moves to another focus and he is gone again. I turn the pictures off, listen to the hum of the fridge, the sound of traffic outside, as an emptiness opens up inside me, and then into the emptiness flows an overwhelming sense of my own futility. I do not cry for the soldiers, Basif, I do not even cry for Daniel, I cry for myself and in self-pity I hug my own misery, force myself to finger each of my coldest memories like the bitter beads of some rosary. I stand once more in front of the frosted surface of glass and scan the unbroken band of sky and sea, see the future seep once again into its grey grasp. I try to break free by summoning the memory of my mother standing straight and strong on a pavement, her foot pressed on a ring, but as another crowd of men surges in my head she is powerless to prevent their course, and the glint of gold disappears inside a fist.

Suddenly puffing into my head comes the smell of the church when my father opened it on a Sunday morning. I step inside, look up at the vaulting roof above me as my father's tread scatters the thick layers of silence. Dust paints itself in the trembling light of the stained glass as we walk through the filtering eddies of damp and I feel the coldness brush my skin. And then I see a boy's hand stretched out in the silence to touch the paint in my hair, and he is smiling. But I turn my face away and hurry out onto a Belfast street where life flows around me and I melt inconspicuously into its indifference.

I walk quickly, without concern for destination but grateful for the distraction of physical activity. As people pass me I glance at their faces as if half expecting to see some shared acknowledgement of what has happened, but already the immediacy of living has taken precedence and anyway all that can be shared is limited to the common currency of soiled and meaningless words. Experts now at our parallel existence, where only personal loss joins the lines. As I walk I try to think, but everything is disjointed and as I look up, a shifting parabola of small birds comes pulsing over the roof tops of the houses in University Square. I walk through the grounds of the University, past the places where I used to study and know with certainty only that I know nothing. A couple of drunks sitting on the steps of the library turn their blown faces towards me as I approach, and then there is a splash of light in the green bottle which is raised in greeting and a broken, discordant attempt at a song.

Overhead a helicopter shreds the sky and I see what the hovering camera cannot see – little pyres of clothing sending up blackened flames of smoke, bruised and broken knuckles being anointed and salved, tissue removed from under fingernails, the clicking of scissors, and in some locked garage a taxi being sluiced out and scrubbed. I wonder where Daniel is and what he's doing. I stretch out my hand and touch the tightened torque of his spine, kneel down beside him in the shop doorway, then see the smile seep through his spreading fingers.

'I think you bottled it, Miss, when I handed you that shell. You looked scared – a bit the way you did that first day. Suppose that wasn't the best way to start a new job. Were you scared, right enough?'

'That first day, or when you handed me the shell?'

'I don't know – both.'

'Yes I was scared that first day, very scared. But maybe more scared when it was over than when it was happening. At the end I thought he was going to hit me – I'd've looked good walking into school with a black eye. It was the hate was scary. Did you not feel it?'

'All I felt was half a dozen Doc Martens kickin' the crap out of me – I didn't have time to think about anything else.'

'Why do you always pretend to be less than you are? What are you frightened of?'

'I'm not frightened, Miss, and didn't I take the shell and tell about the time I fell through the ice? It was a better story than yours.'

'Better than mine, Daniel, but not as true as Sinead's. She was braver than both of us that day.'

'Maybe, Miss, but so you did bottle it, then?'

'Yes, I bottled it. Right at the last moment I heard a voice telling me I was a teacher and if I said what was in my head you'd all think I'd cracked up and not trust me.'

He looks at me and when he turns and walks to the back of the room I know that when he turns again to face me it will be to hand me the shell. As I hold it in my hands I finger its ridged whiteness and know there is no escape from the moment, but I no longer want one.

'There've been many times in my life when I've been frightened – too many times, I think. I grew up in a place I didn't really like and sometimes I thought I would never get away from it, and when I was young I hated the way I looked – my hair especially – and that made it worse. It was like being trapped, and I know it sounds stupid but sometimes it felt as if the sky, the sea, the mountains, were all pressing down on me, suffocating me.' I pause to see if he's laughing but there's not even the trace of a smile and so I stumble on. 'I suppose, too, what frightened me was the fear that no one would ever love me, that my life would just wither away. And what really frightened me that first day was that it reminded me of something I'd seen when I was a child and it was as if it was all happening again.' I stop in sudden consciousness, embarrassed, and rotate the shell in my hands. I try to find an escape in a joke but I can't think of anything to say and only silence flows in the slipstream of my words. Then he stretches out his hand and takes the shell.

'I was ten when Sean was killed. I really liked Sean – he was dead-on, always looked after me when anyone was giving me a hard time. He even stood up to me Da once when he was knocking me about – took the belt out of his hand and threw it in the fire. I must've been a right pain but sometimes he took me places – football matches, things like that. Sometimes his mates gave him stick but he didn't take any heed. Well, there came a time when he wasn't around that much – he'd come and go, stay a night and not come back for a week or so. I thought he'd had some big row with me Da that no one was telling me about, and sometimes when I'd come in the room they'd stop talking. One night – it was coming up to Christmas – I was in bed reading when he came in, he always used to take the hand out of me when he saw me reading but he didn't this time. He just talked and asked me how things were going, but when I tried to ask him why he wasn't around he made a joke and that was the last time I ever saw him. The Friday before Christmas two men came to the door and said he'd been killed.'

He stops and moves the shell from hand to hand as if it's burning him. 'I really liked Sean – he was dead-on. When they brought the coffin to the house I wouldn't look at him. I didn't want to see him dead. Even though me Da said I had to see what the Brits had done I still wouldn't look. He'd left a Christmas present for me. Da said I didn't deserve it but me Ma made him give it to me. It was a book.'

As he finishes he angles his head so I can't see his full face but before I get a chance to say anything he returns the shell to the back of the room and stands for a few seconds, pretending to look at the display. As I start to walk towards him he turns with an imitation of a smile, out of synch with his eyes.

'Well, Miss, does that count as one of my GCSE oral assessments?'

'Yes, Daniel, I'll put it in my red book and tick off all the little boxes.'

'That's good, Miss,' he says, suddenly heading for the door but as he's about to leave he turns. 'As good as Sinead's?'

'As good as Sinead's.'

'Yours wasn't bad either, Miss.'

I call after him but the only reply is the rush and clack of his heels in the corridor.

The rush and clack of his heels. Startled, I turn my head to look behind me and as I do so, a boy on a skateboard leans and bends past me, all balance and friction. I watch him curve himself round one of the turnings in the park. Ahead, families make their way to the museum and on impulse I follow them, stumble round familiar exhibits but look only at the faces of the people. Sometimes I see someone look at me and I think they must know everything about me, as if the images running in my head are projected on my eyes, and then I turn my head away, stare myopically at some painting.

That night, as the sodium light of the street seeps into the shadows of my flat, I stand at the corner of the window and watch a young couple lilt along the pavement. Their voices spark the falling night, burning little holes in the stillness. I turn away, switch on the television and flick the channels to find something to divert thought, then sit in a daze, until slowly I begin to watch a programme, start to focus on the pictures.

It is about a reef, Basif. Somewhere there is a reef, stretching out into the languorous waters of the night, the coral bushes silhouettes against a running glaze of moonlight. Their horned branches jerk upwards to the light, each bush a ghost of polyps, fixed on the calcareous, peppered bones of their own skeleton.

There is a rhythm to the reef. It begins with a full moon, the stirring of warm currents and something we do not understand, as in the darkness each polyp contracts, puffs a little bead of egg into the water. They float upward like thistledown on the sea-wind to meet the pink slick of sperm. Then somewhere an egg fertilizes, and in the darkness an almost invisible ivory glint of coral larva starts silently through the waters. Drifting at first in the current, before a tiny filigree of hairs propels it into a gradual swim – a prey for protozoans and crustaceans, until it finds the safety of the reef and settles at last on its surface to grow and regenerate, replacing what has been destroyed. New generations of growth, living coral.

As I lie in my narrow bed in a city which sleeps fitfully in the rough cradle of mountain and sea, I dream of coral. But then the burning colours fade and I drift into colder seas. I see a shadowy shape carried by the will of the current and suddenly I am separated from it by a sheet of ice which forms over the moment. Now the face is pressed against the ice looking up at me, but I can't break through to it. I try to see who it is but the ice is too thick. I beat against it with my fists, I have to see if it's Daniel's face, the face of one of the soldiers, my father's face, but I cannot break the ice and then the current swirls the body away and I waken with a shout, touch my own face.

It is the sun slinking through the branches of the tree which touches my face now. The children have stopped chanting. I search for Nadra's voice, try to evade the probe of Basif's questions. How could I ever make him understand? But he persists.

'And so why did you come to Africa, Naomi?'

I move my head, shift slightly in the chair, try to ease into a little screen of shade.

WE stood in front of his makeshift desk like miscreants in the headmaster's study. He had already thrown down his shades, presumably to show the anger in his eyes, but they also revealed enjoyment as he berated us for our stupidity. I thought Veronica was about to cry and beg forgiveness, while at my other shoulder Martine stiffened and looked for an opportunity to stem his flow. But Haneen had told him everything and there was nothing we could say in our defence, nothing he would let us offer that might impede his performance.

'Rule number one – you do not play God. You're only here five minutes and on the strength of whatever lousy training they've given you, you decide to play Mother Teresa.' He stood up and paced the length of the desk. 'You knew that what was on that truck was needed here, and we're damn lucky they didn't strip it to the axles. Out here we play the percentage game, and one baby doesn't balance out the value to this camp of that cargo. I don't give a shit for your feelings – out here feelings are excess baggage. If you've brought feelings out here I advise you to go bury them in the nearest latrine.'

Over his shoulder, more and more children's heads compressed into the open window to watch our humiliation. He sat down again and waved his hand dismissively over the top of the table. 'Children, and especially babies, don't get separated from their mothers. One without the other is no use. Have you any idea how many kids there are out there without anyone to look after them? What do you think their long-term future is?'

As I tried to say something that would assuage his anger, convey contrition, Martine suddenly turned on her heels and left. I wanted to join her but wasn't brave enough. Fired up again by her response, he poured out the remaining dregs of his anger. 'She needn't think she's going to come out here and swan around smelling of Chanel. If she can't do what she's told she can haul her tight ass out of here on the next plane home – and you can tell her that from me!' He sat down again, momentarily drained of words, and we took the opportunity to nod our heads, mutter a few pathetic expressions of remorse and leave.

When we stepped into the sharp strike of heat children flooded round our feet, patting our backs and touching our legs in gestures that felt like commiseration, and as we walked through the light brush of hands I heard a sudden burst of opera bruising the morning air. It seemed to follow me as I made my way across the compound to our tent. Martine stood with her back pushed against the tree-trunk; the rigidity of her body as she exhaled from a cigarette held her anger in a tight press. She didn't look at me and I felt included in that anger.

'Mais c'est un vrai salaud, cet homme-là!'

'Je crois que tu as raison.'

'He'd no right to speak to me in this way, no right. I am not a child to be bullied and shouted at. If he has a complaint he should handle it in a professional way, not like this. Pas devant tout le monde.'

'You're right, but maybe he has his own problems, things we don't know about yet. He shouldn't have spoken that way, but maybe there's less time for the niceties out here.'

She pushed her back harder into the tree, then stubbed out the cigarette on its riven bark. 'You're a great peace-maker, Naomi. I thought the Irish were supposed to be great fighters.'

'The Irish only fight themselves. Listen, Martine, why should we let him put us off? We can always disappoint him by being good at what we came to do.'

She relaxed a little and asked where Veronica was. 'I think she's slunk back to prostrate herself to Mr Wanneker.' At last she smiled and slowly ground the remains of her cigarette into the dust, and then we parted to find the work that waited for us.

I was there to develop an educational programme. It sounds grander than it was. I learnt later that to qualify for additional UN funding they needed to provide evidence of educational development. I was that evidence. I who had resigned at the end of my second year of teaching, then spent a couple of years in a variety of temporary posts. The Agency was not particular in many things. And so in Bakalla my job was to set up a school, utilizing whatever resources were available, share responsibility for the growing number of orphans in the camp, and construct a register to help establish family connections and possible locations.

On one of those first mornings when sleep hadn't slipped into any pattern or rhythm I walked in the camp, threading a random course through the tumbling clutter of makeshift dwellings, the possibility of making any impression on what stretched all around me seeming suddenly absurd. Wherever I stumbled a raw course of life flowed, focused solely on survival, that central impulse jettisoning the superfluous, the conventional constraints of the external world. Each day was measured not by hours or minutes, but by the wait to draw water, the trawling and scavenging in ever widening arcs for firewood, the wood that fuelled their lives. The constant collection and rationing of resources. The doling out of life's dregs.

All the dwellings I passed were different, a patchwork of ramshackle structures that bore witness to ingenuity, to the creative exploitation of what the world had discarded. Little shacks fashioned from packing cases and polythene, cardboard walls fastened to battens of spindly sticks, oil drums driven into the sand for corner stones and roofed with sacking and plastic.

Old tyres bound together with rope supporting woven matting or strips of corrugated tin. None of them more than three or four metres high, their frameworks caulked and cemented with dried dung or clay. Even the front half of a jeep, its gutted innards replaced by a parcel of possessions and bedding. As I walked I passed small children returning from the scrub carrying mean little bundles of bleached sticks that looked like bones. One of them trailed two stringy slithers of goats whose skins were blistered with sores. A boy holding the hand of a younger brother crossed my path but only one set of eyes turned to look at me; the other's were locked in a torpid white blindness. Women carried the first water of the day, the heads of babies swaddled in the folds of their clothes, and as I stepped aside to let them pass along the ridged and rutted path, I felt the weight of their gaze, assumed the guilt. And I knew for the first time that no matter how much or little you might do to help, our very physical presence subsumed us into the essence of their suffering and intensified the knowledge that they had no future happiness until we were no longer there.

Sometimes as I walked I caught glimpses of inner worlds – a mother feeding her baby, her breast flapping loose and thin like an empty envelope, around her the sleeping forms of her older children snuggled into each other's hollows; an old man naked from the waist up with a white stipple of beard, his skin hanging from his shoulder bones like an old shirt on a wire hanger; a young girl in a doorway combing her hair with a painted comb, one hand rubbing the sleep from her eyes. And as I walked and listened to the slow unfolding of life around me, the smell of cooking seeped into the other smells which I had tried to block out. Somewhere a baby cried in hunger and in response a voice set up a slow chanting, a rhythmic cadence that pleaded for patience.

'You're up early.'

The voice was American. It belonged to a big man in green fatigues which looked tired from the strain of stretching over his body. In his late fifties maybe, his bald head glazed with sun spots and a thin smear of hair that looked like daubs of charcoal. He was carrying a medical kit emblazoned with the Agency logo, and he wore gold-rimmed glasses with lenses which looked too small to cover his eyes. As he stretched out his hand towards me he snuffled the glasses into a tighter focus. 'Dr Rollins, James Rollins – we didn't get a chance to meet. Welcome to Bakalla.' We shook hands, observed social refinements, my concentration momentarily distracted by a small child defecating in a little hollow then surreptitiously kicking up a concealing layer of dirt. 'You're Irish, aren't you? I hear Ireland's a very beautiful country, I'm going to take a vacation there some day, going to visit the Burren. I'm a plant man. Orchids mostly. There's wild orchids on the Burren.'

For a few moments we made small talk, and then as the words dried up he asked me if I wanted to come with him, and so I followed down alleyways where it felt as if the clumsy collision of his case or the brush of his elbow against the fragile frameworks might topple them into the dirt. Sometimes as he walked he raised his hand in a silent warning, and we stretched our legs over a coagulated trail of dysentery or side-stepped some indecipherable detritus which littered and stained the fissured path. At a slight distance from the huts we passed a score of children sleeping under a thin wrinkle of polythene, each linked to the other by silver beads of condensation. The crinkled shapes of their bedded bodies lay frozen like fossils in stone, only a whimpering or a mumbled snatch of dream words testifying to life. An old woman, bent over with the burden of her deformed body, shuffled towards the daily dug ditches that served for latrines, cursing us as we crossed her path. Through a gap in the shacks I saw a glimpse of the plain which stretched beyond the camp and in it disembodied trees and some young boys, their lower legs lost in the white mist which lapped around them. They carried thin curves of cane as they guarded the few slivers of stock which were the vestiges of a way of life they had never known.

Stuttering, slow smoke was beginning to limp skywards throughout the camp, spiralling tendrils of blue which faded into the low grey louring of sky. It was quite cold still and the sweep of the horizon was smudged by a blurred bevel of mist. Occasionally Rollins would turn to reassure himself that I was following and then we would smile and nod our heads, until eventually he paused at the doorway of a hut, a kind of wigwam of layered banana leaves and cardboard packing stamped 'Urgent Medical Supplies'. Across the entrance hung a tattered cloth, a towel with a picture of a surfer on it. 'Take a deep breath,' he ordered and then with a shout of greeting he bent down and entered, holding up the cloth so I could follow.

Inside we crouched in the flecked sprinkling of light which seeped through the colander of roof and sides, slowly absorbing the world we had entered. In one corner a man and two children huddled together, at their feet a couple of metal buckets and small bundles of clothing, a few cooking pots and little else. In the middle of the earth floor there was an older child – maybe eight or nine years old – curled on a strip of matting and covered by a coarse orange blanket. A girl. Her mother cradled her head on her lap, lightly brushing her face with the back of a hand. I listened as Rollins talked softly and reassuringly to them, and then he slowly removed the orange blanket. The girl cried out and tried to hold on to it but he coaxed it out of her hand. On one of her legs was a suppurating wound where the yellowing and pus-filled purple flesh thickened like lard. Her feet were swollen and livid with sores and as he examined her he pointed to the watery blister of guinea worm. 'She got separated from her family on the way here. Only arrived here last night. She's been walking in the bush for three days, been badly bitten by mosquitoes.'

He gave her a couple of shots, the smell of a different world puffing out of his open case into the fetid air of the shelter. As he cleaned and dressed her wounds he talked all the time, rhymes, songs, nonsense, but all delivered in the same reassuring tone, and when he had finished he told her parents to bring her to the compound later in the day. He left a supply of protein-filled BP5 biscuits, some maize-based porridge, and a supply of high energy milk. In the shadowed corner of the shelter sat the father, watching and listening with spiritless eyes, little leaves of light splashing his face, his silent stillness pulled around him as if a movement or sound might make him visible to the outer world, and vulnerable. As his wife bowed her face to the dust and grasped Rollins' hand in hers I saw him lock himself further into his own world, remote from the family which had left the shelter of his protection to beg their share of a stranger's bounty.

'Will she be all right?' I asked as we headed back towards the compound.

'Sure, she'll be OK in a week or so if they let her rest that long, don't have her out scavenging in the bush. The young nearly all have a chance if we reach them in time. With high energy feeding and the right drugs you can see big changes in a short time. Nature culls the rest. Out here one in three infants don't reach the age of five – but you know that already, I guess.'

'I know the figures but it makes it different when the figures have faces.' With a sudden wither of shame I remembered the baby we had buried in the dirt, its striated skin hidden in hessian; heard again the mother's cries breaking from her parched and broken throat.

'A lot of the children can make it. Older people are slower to recover, seem to collapse in on themselves. Weighed an old woman a couple of days ago – twenty-five kilos, Jeez, twenty-five kilos of nothing but memories. She died, didn't want to live any more I guess.' Children ran past us carrying empty jerry cans which were scabbed and oil stained. 'We've got everything here – malnutrition, dysentery, TB, malaria, AIDS – you name it, we've got it. Starting to see a lot of cases of blindness in kids from vitamin deficiency. A lot of the last influx brought their own disease with them. Did you see many on the road as you came?'

'Lines of people. . . . We stopped once, had some trouble . . .' I hesitated, wondering if he already knew.

'I heard about it. Not the best way to start. But you won't be harbouring too many illusions about what you've come to. I'd be more worried if I were you about those people you passed.' He saw the confusion in my face. 'Trouble anywhere means trouble here. If the flow of refugees increases dramatically we'll be stretched beyond our limit. There's a kind of fragile balance here: when something tips that balance you're looking at disaster. Too many hands grabbing for too few resources.'

'How long have you been here?' I asked.

'I came two years ago to work in the camps across the border when the first famine broke. Stayed off and on ever since. Came out of retirement, from growing orchids and watching TV sport. What I saw then I don't ever want to see again. There were a hundred dying every day – had to bring in earth-digging machinery to bury them in the end. Six planes were flying a hundred and fifty tonnes of food per day and it wasn't enough.'

We threaded our way back past families who had emerged from the sullen shadows of their shelters, to squat on their haunches round cooking pots and fan a few paltry flames into limping legs of smoke. 'And you know what we learned from that disaster – nothing. Nothing, period. Just another patch-up job, and now the camera crews have moved on and the money's drying up and we're about five minutes away from it happening all over again, only this time we've used up our compassion quotient. You should go down there some time to the border camps, Naomi, see the machinery, the pumps and lorries with their guts clogged with sand and no one with a spare part or the know-how to get them going. See the sheds full of the wrong vaccines. I once met a guy, swore it was true, said he took a delivery of ten crates and when he opened them they were full of electric kettles.'

He laughed full-throatedly, the light gilding the gold fillings in his teeth, and his eyes blinking behind his glasses like the excited stutter of a camera. 'And you know what I'm going to do if it starts again? Hitch a lift to the coast, get the first plane out of here. Go back home, drink some slow cold beer in the afternoon, watch it on TV. Be as much use there as here. No one's going to make me a grave-digger again.' The bitterness of his voice seemed to seep into his movements, giving his lumbering walk a new urgency. It also created a distance between us, replacing his friendliness with a new formality. When he stopped in front of another dwelling, he announced his arrival with a shout of greeting. I didn't know whether to follow him or not. He turned to me as I hesitated. 'You don't want to come in here – not when you have a choice,' the sharpening light of the morning blanching out his eyes.

Later that morning, I found the school. It was located on the southern rim of the camp, its area defined only by the yellowed and flattened mat of grass which the children's feet had pummelled and bruised into submission. I heard the voices first, a dull rhythmic chant like the hollow rub of sea against shore. I watched from a distance as a tall figure in white orchestrated the chorus, its long cane swimming over the scores of seated children, occasionally diving into their midst to touch a shoulder or the side of a head. The thin white body seemed to twitch and stutter in synch with the chanting, the sticklike arms flailing and threshing above the black bobbing mesh of heads. They sat huddled tightly, squirming together to ensure their anonymity, protect themselves from the arbitrary fall of the cane. From time to time hands would jerk up in response to shouted questions and a child would stumble forward to recite some long litany and receive the soft blessing of the cane on its head.

I returned to the compound and found Wanneker in the clinic, making an inventory of drugs and vaccines. I had guessed already that the school was not of central importance to him, but I asked him anyway about the figure in the white robe.

'His name's Medulla. He appeared about a month ago, he's some sort of tribal holy man – a priest or something like that. He took it on himself to teach the children.'

'What's he teach them?'

He looked up from his ledger, impatience already evident on his face. 'I don't know, Naomi – the Koran, I guess. It keeps the kids under some kind of supervision for a couple of hours so I'm not complaining.'

'And how am I supposed to organize a school if this holy man is already running his idea of one?'

'You've got a problem there – maybe he could be part of whatever you set up.'

'Have you seen him swinging that cane, Charlie?'

'Yeah, I've seen him, looks like he's herding geese.' He smiled. 'I know it's not a good start for you but sometimes you have to accommodate people, avoid offence, respect local traditions. Sometimes we just need to go with the flow.'

The conversation was over. The resolution of the problem was entirely in my hands. As I started for the door Wanneker lifted his head. 'There's a girl called Nadra. Check her out. She might be able to help. Speaks real good English.'

I found her in mid-afternoon, when the sun seemed set to bake the earth and the air hung limp and flaccid. She was with a score of other women, close to the banks of the dried-up river bed where what remained from the UN World Food Programme was growing. Ripening sorghum rippled a tattered splurge of green against the bleached scurf of the plain, and beyond it a field of sunflowers stood in serried, wilting rows. There was too, a small harvested crop of corn in yellow-coloured humps. The women used wooden paddles to fling it into the air, separate the chaff. Their feet beat and shuffled in a rhythm which echoed the rise and fall of their voices. The paddles dipped into the piles and flicked the husks into a sudden puff of yellow against the blue swathe of sky, and the cadence of the song looped over on itself as flecks of gold rained about the women's heads. I saw her first through the fine veil of falling grain, her face veined with slants of seed. She was taller and younger than most of the other women, and wore a white blouse and a long red skirt patterned with yellow and blue. Her dark hair seemed even darker where it touched the white of the blouse, dark as her eyes, and her face had sharp, fine features which suggested Arab ancestry.

I stood watching for a while as they worked, unwilling to disturb the spell, and then she walked towards me and handed me the wooden paddle.

'Would you like to try?' she asked.

'Yes,' I said, taking it from her, 'but I don't know the song.'

'I can teach you. Do what I do.' And as the other women smiled and laughed encouragement I stumbled into the shuffling rhythm and let my voice imitate the loop and roll of theirs. 'You do it good. You are a teacher?' I nodded my head. 'Have you read George Orwell's *Selected Writing*?'

IT makes me nervous driving into territory which is foreign, paranoia generating a fear that I am clearly recognizable as an outsider, a member of another tribe. I reach over and lock the passenger door, lift my bag off the seat and drop it out of sight at my feet. I try to look confident, sure of where I'm going, as I glance up at the gable murals, listen to the slogans which scream into the silence of the car, making its sanctuary seem violable and exposed. A different world, one I know nothing about and am not part of. As rain begins to stipple the windscreen, I switch on the headlights in my nervousness, flick full beam at oncoming traffic. Past video shops and takeaways, bars with metal grilles and security cameras, past a police station bristling with aerials. I have only a general idea of where I'm heading. Along roads that look like any others. Stopped at red lights longer than I want to be, I read the peeling propaganda skimming across walls, try to find the names of roads whose signs have been removed. The words tell me that I don't belong here. Once again I question the wisdom of what I'm doing and think of turning the car round and going home, but something stronger makes me keep going.

I glance at the piece of paper on the dashboard on which I have written the address and the roads I must take before I reach the estate. I try to think of what I will say if I find him. By now, others have seen the television pictures a thousand times, enhanced and frozen the monochromed images, started a steady match of names and faces. Already the first arrests have been made and the search for atonement has begun. For some

84

reason, I think of the Sunday drives we made with my father as he headed towards some waiting congregation through the saddle of mountain and across the bogland. As the rain grows heavier I remember the white wisps of bog cotton, the sudden pools of brackish water holding hostage the trapped image of sky. People waiting for my father's voice. I try again to think of what I will say, search for words that will not make me sound as if I too am come to speak for God.

Others in the school have seen and recognized and soon everyone knows. For some it brings a smug self-satisfaction. Their judgement has been confirmed and a rebuff given to those who, through youth or inexperience, sought to blind themselves to his true nature. He has not been to school since it happened and I know I can't leave it like this. As I drive, the car windows begin to mist up. When I switch on the heater, it roars in the silence. On the pavement people shelter under the striped awning of a fruit shop, getting in the way as the owner tries to move his produce beyond the drips and splashes.

I get lost, but rather than ask the way I keep driving until eventually, by a process of elimination, I reach the estate. It is bigger than I had anticipated. Most of the street names have been removed and replaced with Irish ones. Children play in the streets, oblivious to the rain, and as I drive slowly, straining to see names and house numbers, they turn to look at me, their pale faces framed by the damp sheen of their hair. I raise a hand vaguely but no one responds. A group of older boys kick a ball about on a tussocky area of grass but without energy or enthusiasm, sometimes simulating aggression with exaggerated raising of legs and arms. I drive past a row of boarded-up shops where only the light squinting from an open doorway hints at life inside, then, as I turn blindly into another street, I am forced to stop. There is a black limousine in the road and, blocking my path, groups of women and children. A chauffeur with a peaked cap is holding a car door open and I think I have driven into a funeral. As I pull up some of the women turn and look at me and I feel suddenly frightened but then there is a cheer and the faces turn away again. A young woman has come out of one of the houses, a young woman in a white wedding dress. A few steps behind a man follows, holding a black umbrella over the bride's head. As she walks the wind billows her dress and she presses it down with the palms of her hands. I remember my mother's photograph, the day she was beautiful, her dress rippling round her feet like surf, wild roses in her hair. I watch the bride bend her head into the car, gathering her train carefully about her and then the women crowd round, knocking the glass and waving in to her. Children run behind, trying to keep up as the car moves off, purring into the distance. I get out of my car and ask one of the women if she can direct me to the address I read from the paper in my hand. She looks at the paper as rain begins to bleed the ink and then she looks at me, at my face, my hair, my clothes. She isn't sure. I lie and tell her I'm from the Health Centre and she relents and gives me the directions I need.

The house is no different from the others. There is a motorbike draped in an old waterproof propped against the front fence, rosettes of oil staining the pavement and the flagged path to the front door. A burst football slouches and sags on the grass and as I put my hand to the gate, a dog emerges from the side of the house and barks loudly. I hesitate, and as I stand at the gate a woman's face appears at a window. The dog comes closer, testing its own bravery, and then the front door opens and a man stands staring at me. He is about fifty years old, older than I had anticipated, and I can see nothing of Daniel in his face. His hair is grey and the greyness seems to have seeped into the pallor of his skin, settled in the hollows of his cheeks. He is a slight man with a thick neck and lean body. His eyes are dark, laced with suspicion, and he offers no encouragement. It is only when I open the gate and he sees my intention to enter that he speaks for the first time.

'Stop that noise! Get to bed!'

I watch the dog slink instantly out of sight and I step towards him and smile. But before I get a chance to speak he takes a look at me and turns away and I hear him call, 'Cora, there's some woman here for you.' I stand on the doorstep for a minute before she appears. She holds a drying cloth in her hand and the front of her jumper is splashed with water. She is younger than her husband but with the same slightness of frame, the same thinness of face. Her eyes are brown like Daniel's and she has a trace of his features, and when I tell her who I am she hesitates then brings me in.

The room is small but clean and neat, with a three-piece suite taking up most of the floor. There is a wall unit which contains ornaments and sports trophies, and on a shelf a series of family photographs. I stare at the pictures a little too long. She follows my gaze but says nothing. I wonder which of them is Sean. I try to think of something to say. Through the open doorway and beyond the kitchen I can see her husband working in the yard.

'I just wondered if it would be possible to speak to Daniel, Mrs McCarroll?' She says nothing. 'I'm one of his teachers and I was worried about him. It's not long now to his exams and I was wondering when he was coming back to school.' She asks me my name again and turns it over in her mouth, her lips silently copying the words. 'Did Daniel ever mention me? I'm his English teacher. Sometimes we used to talk.'

'No, I don't think so. Daniel doesn't talk much about school.' There is a vagueness about the way she talks. As she looks at me, it is as if she has trouble focusing on the moment, in understanding who I am or why we're talking.

'Do you think it might be possible to speak to him?'

She realizes then that she's still holding the drying cloth and drops it on the hearth, sending up a whisper of ash from an unemptied ash tray. She's wearing black leggings which accentuate the thinness of her legs and reveal a raised tributary of blue veins flowing down her instep. She reaches for a cigarette packet on the mantelpiece and her hand shakes as she fumbles to strike a match.

'Daniel isn't here.'

'Will he be coming back to school?'

She inhales deeply, holding it as long as she can. 'No he won't be coming back.' She has steadied herself a little, the weight of her words helping to fix her in the moment. 'Are you the teacher who lends him all the books?'

'That's right,' I say, grasping frantically at the opening. 'He's a great reader, Mrs McCarroll, and he's a smart boy – he could do really well if he put his mind to it.'

'Daniel was always a good reader, right from no age. Sometimes he'd sit and eat his meals and read at the same time, or stay up half the night with some book or other. None of the others was that way – just Daniel.' The memory hurts her – I see it in the sudden blink of her eyes and the slow scribble of her hand across her lap.

'I'm very sorry for your trouble, Mrs McCarroll.' The words hang there in a pocket of silence and then she nods her head. Now she is going to cry, and I stand up to go to her but stop as her husband appears in the doorway.

'Why have you come here?' he asks.

'I wanted to help, because I care about Daniel.'

'Why should you care?'

'He's one of my best pupils. I want him to come back to school.'

'He won't be coming back. He won't be coming back to his home, never mind school. They've seen to that.'

'Do the police have him?'

'No, and they never will either if I've anything to do with it. They've taken two of my sons, they'll not take another. Daniel's where they can't touch him and he'll stay there until this war is over and the last Brit's gone home. In a box, if need be.'

He makes himself taller, the angular body tightening into

88

aggression. The ash on his wife's cigarette lengthens then slowly crumples on to the floral carpet as she stares past us both at the rain.

'He won't be coming back to school?' I ask. 'It would be such a waste, Mr McCarroll.'

'Waste? How can you come here and talk to me about waste when I've one son in Milltown and one rotting in the Kesh? You think I'm going to start worrying about school? All that matters to me right now is that they don't get their bastard hands on the one son I've left.'

'Maybe if he came back everything could be sorted out. I could speak for him, tell them what he's really like. He didn't know what he was doing.'

'You'll not tell them anything because I'm proud of my son and proud of what he did.'

'You're proud of what happened to those two men?' I've said it before I can stop myself and all it does is provoke him into a tirade of bitterness, his head jerking forwards and his finger pointing out through the window to a world which I have made myself part of.

'Those two men were fuckin' Brits who got what they deserved, and I'm not going to start feeling sympathy or shame for the likes of you. As far as Daniel and those other men knew, they were two Loyalist gunmen come to kill people like that fucker Stone, and in my book that makes the ones who took them heroes.' He pauses for breath. 'So let them all cry their phony tears and call us savages if they like, but I don't give a shite what they think, for it's nothing to what they've done to us and our people.'

As he finishes she stands up and passes between us to leave the room. A little spiral of smoke hovers in the air above her seat. I hear her slow tread on the stairs, the sound of her footsteps in the room above. I get up to go.

'Is there somewhere I can write to Daniel?'

He shakes his head and laughs. 'No fuckin' way, no fuckin'

way.' When I am about to open the gate he calls after me. I think he has changed his mind and I stand as the rain sluices through my hair. But when he reappears it is to throw a clatter of books on the oil-smeared path, their white pages flicking open in the grimed hands of the wind, and as the dog comes to sniff amongst them he shouts, 'We don't need anything belonging to you!' and slams the door.

I look at the books. One of them isn't mine. It's the only one I pick up. As I leave I glance up at the bedroom window, see her watching. I look up at her for a moment until the rain slants across her face and then I go. In the car I look at the book. It's a collection of Irish legends. On the fly leaf it says: To Daniel from Sean, Christmas '82.

O'GRADY says do this. Thin arms point skywards like reeds in the water of the sky. O'Grady says do this. Yellow, crepe-soled feet splay apart in the dust, smiles linked across the lines like a filament of light. O'Grady says do that. Two arms mirror mine then disappear into the motionless anonymity of the scores of frozen bodies. Speeding up the commands, O'Grady says, O'Grady says do this. They laugh at my contorted face and try to copy it. O'Grady says do that. I peer into their faces, try to make them laugh, whittle away some more but there are always too many who want to be winners. It's what I taught them best – O'Grady says, then chain tig and hunt the hidden treasure, simple English and songs and rhymes. Nadra taught them geography and writing and maths and sometimes when they grew restless we played O'Grady some more and I gave little prizes to the winners, and sometimes when she wasn't looking to the losers as well. And at first there's only the two of us and almost more children than we can cope with.

They came early each morning to the space we had claimed just outside the perimeter – it had to be close to the compound so that we could bring stuff back and forth, for we knew that to leave it overnight would mean its absorption and adaptation into other functions. There was never much to take. We had eight metal poles, part of the skeleton of a tent, fitted each day into a frame from which we hung a tarpaulin roof. Open on all sides, it still afforded some protection from the sun for those who managed to squeeze beneath, and served to mark out the location of the school. There was little equipment available to us apart from what we improvised. A couple of rolls of computer paper, plastic bags of crayons and pens, the four sides of a flattened-out packing case which we used for a blackboard, a chair and a poor assortment of picture books. In the end it didn't matter because there were always going to be more children than we could provide for and so we had to design activities for this growing number. It depended on what else was going on in the camp but we had a core of about a hundred children, double on some days. Medulla proved not to be a problem. We gave the children food – milk and protein biscuits – and once every day Martine would come and check their health. Some days Medulla stood trying to stare us out, lancing the ground with his stick and uttering some curse.

We tried to establish a list of the children in the camp who were without families. There were about twenty in all, some whose parents were dead or had disappeared, some who had become separated on the journey to the camp and others who were dazed and confused about the whereabouts of their families. We took Polaroids of them with their names printed on a little board of wood which they held under their chin and when we toured the satellite camps we showed them round, trying to trace anyone who might know them. I carried the pictures in a little plastic wallet, flicking it open whenever we went somewhere new, hoping always for that sudden gleam of recognition. We tried to take special care of these children, finding them clothing and extra rations when possible. Some of them had retreated far into themselves, indifferent to what went on around them; others clung to our sides trying to make us the mothers they had lost. How they survived I never knew, disappearing each night after school to find some kind of shelter in the crevices and cracks of the camp. All you could hope was that they would survive another night and be there in the morning.

Every family had its own children, its own lives to support, and there was nothing, not even a crumb for the ones who belonged to someone else. I couldn't blame them – charity is the consolation of those who have. But sometimes, as I slept in the tent with Martine and Veronica, I thought of them, wondered where they were, and remembered the morning when I had wandered bewildered round the camp and stumbled across their frozen shapes under polythene. When I asked Wanneker if we could build some kind of shelter for them inside the fence, I knew already what the answer would be. That we didn't have the resources needed to assume that responsibility. For the interim at least they had to survive on their own, take their chances with what existed in the camp.

They ranged from about six to fifteen. Two of the older boys became our helpers and helped also to look after the younger ones. Ahmed was quite tall and wore a pair of olive shorts and a purple shirt with rips where the knobs of his shoulder bones poked through. He said his father had been killed by a rival clan and that his mother had died on the long walk to the camp. He had two sisters somewhere but he didn't know where. Iman was smaller, even thinner, and his legs were bowed with rickets. He had walked to Bakalla across the border. They met in the camp and seemed to find solace in one another's company. Each morning they were waiting outside the compound gate to help us carry the equipment to set up the school, and one day Iman told us about his family. They had been herdspeople but had lost their cattle in the years of drought and, encouraged by the Agency, had tried to grow millet on a plot of land they had been given. After the crop failed two years in a row, they lost everything. One day his father walked away and didn't come back. They found his body hanging from a tree. His mother took the rest of the family and set off to find relations in the South, but he set out on his own and eventually wound up in the camp.

They both displayed a determination to survive, a desire to claim some better inheritance, and if I could have given it to them I would have. But all I could do was share the little I had and occasionally slip them something as a payment for their help. Ahmed had a little reed flute and sometimes Iman would shuffle and scuff his feet in a dance. And sometimes, too, Ahmed would play and lead singing while they made me dance, a kind of shapeless sway but performed with something that almost felt like joy. Because sometimes in Bakalla I wanted to dance, because there, in the midst of hardship and human suffering, I experienced moments of happiness such as I have never known. Moments when it was possible for the smallest fragments of joy to magnify and illuminate the darkest parts of yourself. In the tenacious struggle for survival there was an awareness of the preciousness of life, a raw, fierce commitment to it. In the face of that struggle, nothing else mattered. There was only that life and those children, and my memories were only the ragged cast-offs of another place. I never healed anyone, never saved anyone or diagnosed an illness, but each day I felt as if my hand touched something real and was touched in return. What I did had no special virtue, probably no lasting value, but it seemed that it was right for me and those around me.

Nadra helped. She was a year younger than me and had been educated in the teacher training college set up by the Russians before they abandoned the country for more lucrative investments. She proudly showed me the medal she had won for being top student. She had read as many books as she could get hold of; her English was good and seemed to get better by the day. If sometimes she was a little fierce with the children, they respected her, and maybe it was needed to keep things in order and to see that no one got pushed aside or hurt. At first she was very quiet around me, deferring to my decisions even when she knew I was wrong, and although I tried to push her forward she seemed happier in my shadow. Each night she went home to a shack in the heart of the camp that she shared with her mother and sister. There she kept the four books she owned in a little box.

We studied each other surreptitiously and with curiosity. I would catch her looking at my hair and sometimes, when she stood in front of the children, I would admire the olive sheen of her skin and the dark wells of her eyes, the black shock of her hair and the slender strength of her body. Beside her, my own body felt pale, blotched with bites and scratches, the colour of my hair an affront to the azure sky. And in our moments of rest we pieced together the broken fragments of our lives. I kept some back, just as she did, giving only the bits which might make sense.

She came from a nomadic people whose lives were bound to the search for water and grazing, but as years of drought and hardship saw the slow decline of their herds they were forced to settle and become farmers. It was a common tale and she told it without drama or self-pity – a struggle against the encroachment of dust and sand, the wind scorching and displacing the work of human hands, eroding bit by bit the little vegetation, until the moving dunes threatened finally to suffocate everything. Unable to feed his family, her father had set off for the capital, but in a short while his letters stopped and there was only the silent silt of desert to compound their fate. When there was nothing left they threw themselves on the mercy of relations and were passed slowly round until their own shame brought them to Bakalla.

One night after school I went home with her. Unexpectedly invited to meet her mother and sister, I followed her through the narrow thoroughfares of the camp, carrying a little package of tea as a present. Her home was a wood- and hessian-walled construction, roofed with polythene and thin strips of tin. Outside it stood her younger sister Rula – of similar build and colouring, the same dark wells of eyes. She held open the entrance flap and I had to bend low to enter. Inside, her mother sat on a roll of matting. She was dressed in black and her face was covered by a mask of netting to protect her infected eyes from flies. Only her teeth gleamed through the mesh. Apart from the sleeping rolls, water containers and cooking utensils, there were only some bags of clothing and an upturned packing case which served for a table.

Without awkwardness or embarrassment, Nadra motioned me to sit beside her mother and, after we had drunk tea, she opened one of the canvas bags and took out some of the contents, handing things to me for my inspection. There was the painted wooden box and the four books she owned – yellowing, bruised paperback copies of *Hard Times*, *Tom Sawyer*, *Dead Souls*, and a blue-covered copy of George Orwell's *Selected Writing*. Also in the box were some jewellery and combs, beads for braiding her hair and a photograph of her college class. While I held each object in my hand, examining it for what I hoped was an appropriate time, she laughed at something her mother said, then hushed her. When I asked her what had been said she laughed again and told me that her mother wanted to touch my hair. As Nadra shook her head and clucked her disapproval, I knelt down and put my head close to the net, felt the old woman's hands move slowly on my hair then pull away as if frightened that she might be burnt. 'Would you like to touch it, Nadra?' She smiled at me and then giggled like a child whose secret has been discovered. 'You can touch it. It won't burn you,' I said, looking at her in the half-light of the shelter. I moved closer and she stretched out her hand, feeling it slowly with her fingers, plucking it lightly and teasing out some of the strands. She did this for a few minutes, exploring my hair with an open curiosity, going deeper until I felt the tip of her finger touch my scalp. And then she stopped and everyone giggled again.

I stayed a long time, longer than I had intended, but somehow as the old woman started to talk of the past and of the things that had happened in her life, I didn't want to leave. Through Nadra, she told tales of women whose infertility was cured by spells and anointings, of men whose greed and lust fell back on their heads. Tales of hunting and wedding feasts which lasted for days and the giving of bridal dowries which impoverished the giver and shamed the receiver. And as she slipped further into the past she sang the songs of her childhood, the songs the young girls sang as they washed clothes by the river, herded their cattle across the burning plains. The words and music sifted out through the mesh, filling the shelter.

It was almost dark when I left their hut; in the sky above, black clouds spumed up against great pink weals of light, all around me the smell of smoke, of cooking, the drunken babble of voices echoing against and through each other. I shook Nadra's hand, feeling her touch linger on my skin for a second after our hands had separated. She wanted to walk with me back to the compound but I wouldn't let her, not out of kindness but because I wanted to avoid that moment of shutting her out of my world, that peremptory and arbitrary exclusion of what she was. I wasn't supposed to be in the camp after dark – Wanneker had warned us against it – but I felt no sense of danger and even in the closing darkness I felt confident that I knew the way. My presence seemed to startle some of those I passed, as if I were a pale ghost, a spirit from another world; others just looked away or blinked their red-rimmed eyes behind veils of smoke. Most of the inhabitants were already inside their shelters.

As I walked I remembered the first morning with Rollins, and something made me turn and suddenly follow a different course. I came upon them more quickly than I anticipated, almost stumbling into their midst. They lay stretched out before me; I counted ten of the frozen embryo shapes inside the sack of polythene, their shapes pressed into the silvery surface. They huddled together for warmth, sometimes with an arm draped over a companion, or with a face turned upwards, wearing the polythene like a mask. I stood and listened to their broken breathing, the sudden whimper of some dream, and found myself kneeling by their heads. And then a memory stirred, something I thought I had forgotten. I remembered my room at home into which the sea and sky flowed every day and I am young and in my ears is the slow rasp of the sea and the distant scrake and squawk of some frantic bird. The door is partly open and through it fans the yellow landing light. I hear my father's tread upon the stairs and I close my eyes and pretend to sleep because it is late and I do not wish him to be cross and use the voice which speaks for God. I hear the creak of the door, feel through my closed eyelids more yellow light, then sense the darkness as he pauses in the doorway. With each of his steps I tighten my eyes and try to sleep, to please him. And then I feel his touch, his fingers laid gently on my temple. Mostly his hands are full of the sea, the black weight of the Bible, the fingers crusted like a starfish splayed on the surface of his desk, but now they are gentle and light and I think they are weighted only with love. And when he takes his touch away and walks towards the door I see the broadness of his back and the yellow wash of light splashing the whiteness of his head, and I want to call out to him but something stops me, and then for a second he blocks the light again before he is gone.

In a different place and a different time, I called out to him as I knelt at each of the children's heads and touched them lightly, moving slowly and silently along the link of bodies. As I walked away, I still carried the shiver of their bodies, the whimpering wandering of their dreams. I sought to retrace my steps but my mind was full of other thoughts, and in my faltering concentration I began to guess at directions, hurrying along with greater urgency. By then I had started to feel uneasy. I told myself that I was conjuring something from my imagination to punish myself, but as I quickened my step I heard the footsteps and, glancing over my shoulder, caught a glimpse of something flitting from shack to shack. I stopped and turned to stare into the dusk, then called out. But my voice vanished into the camp's incessant murmur. I moved on, trying to remember the direction that would take me to the compound, trying too to stop myself from running blindly into the maze of dwellings. And then I heard it, the low rise and fall of his voice, the rush of words half-sung like some incantation. And as I turned I caught a glimpse of his white cloak moving between two shelters and I knew it was Medulla.

Running over the rutted uneven ground, in a growing darkness broken only by the smouldering embers of ebbing fires, would have resulted sooner or later in disaster, and I tried to keep my head clear and keep moving in what I prayed was the right direction. But the voice grew louder, a constant drone in my ears, and glancing back I saw that he had moved into the open, the whiteness of his cloak making him seem closer than he was. In one hand was the cane and in the other some sort of basket. I started to jog, taking any entrance which presented itself, stumbling and tripping as I ran but too frightened to let myself fall. I thought of seeking shelter in one of the dwellings that lined my flight but each seemed closed to me, and to choose the wrong one was to be trapped without a route of escape. His voice grew louder now, contorting itself into a flailing scourge of a curse, the struggle of his breathing and spit of words beating against my senses.

On even ground I knew I could outrun him, but there in the twisting pathways my speed brought as great a prospect of danger as of safety, and suddenly into my fear flowed an even greater sense of anger and as I broke into a swathe of unclaimed land I stopped and, trying to strengthen my voice, stem the ragged flow of my breathing, called out his name. Over and over until my voice steadied and I shot out his name with all the force I could find. He stumbled out of the gloom, his own breathing rasping at the edges of his words and the cane probing the space between us. I kept my eyes fixed on him, wanting all the time to glance about me to see if there was any object which I could use or any person who might offer help.

But I didn't dare to break my gaze as he edged closer to me. He now brandished a woven basket, holding it up in front of his face like a casket bearing some holy relics. I had nothing to use but my voice and I started to fight his words with my own, scoring any word or phrase deep into the space between us.

Suddenly he dropped the cane and held the basket up to the sky, moving it above his head as if in some ritual, then holding it out to me. There were no more than ten metres between us, and as he shuffled closer I pushed my feet into the earth to steady myself. And then he pulled the lid off the basket and lifted something out. It was only when its dark shape squirmed across the whiteness of his cloak that I saw it clearly. Black, wet with its own slime, wriggling the length of his forearm. He held it in front of his face, edging forward, keeping its head jammed upright in the vice of his fist. I could see his face now, the twitch and stutter of his thin, elongated features, the rolling whiteness of his eyes. And as he came closer his voice dropped lower and lower until the words were consumed by the stream of his breathing and I no longer knew whether the sounds came from him or the convulsing head of the snake. Suddenly the snake became a spasm, a spring that almost jumped from his hand, and as he struggled to hold it I darted sideways and picked up the cane. As his voice screeched again with its former strength I slashed the air between us, cutting into it with fierce swinging arcs, my own voice shouting and screaming at him. He stepped back involuntarily, his eyes blinking and rolling. Then he tried to come forward again, using the snake to drive me back. But I stood my ground, for the first time swinging the cane to hit him, striking his shoulders and arms, deaf to the volley of curses and trying desperately to hold my balance and keep the cane moving in the air. His arm jerked when I hit it and he almost lost his hold of the snake as he stumbled out of range. But as I saw he was in retreat, he shrieked his final curse and flung the snake towards my face. It coiled in on itself then opened, a twisting vibration on the slipstream of the air, and I threw my arms across my face and felt the slime and scale of its skin as it brushed my hands before falling to the ground. Medulla had turned and vanished into the darkness. As the snake slithered away I pursued it, and beat and beat until the jumps and jerks of its movements were caused by nothing but the whip and smack of the cane.

WE were all seated round the office which doubled as a dining-room – Martine, Veronica, Rollins, the Olsons (due shortly to return to Norway), and Wanneker in centre stage.

'OK guys, listen up and I'll start by giving you an update on the latest news. As you're already aware, there's been more fighting in the North. I guess we always knew it was going to be like this with the vacuum caused by the collapse of the government, but the end result and the one which affects us most directly is what we've seen already, more people looking for safety and food, more families on the road. Some of them have already started to arrive here and we've got to be real careful things don't slide out of control.'

'And how do we do that?' asked Rollins, taking off his glasses and holding them up to the light to see where they were smeared.

'I've been in touch with the Agency and asked for more resources – more tents, food, medicine.'

'And will we get it?' Rollins asked, polishing the lenses now with a cloth, the glasses small and fragile in his hands.

'I would hope so, James. I've stressed the urgency of it as best I can, but things are starting to fall apart in a lot of places, and if the fighting spreads there won't be enough of anything to go round. You know that better than I do.'

'Yes I know it,' he said, replacing his glasses and carefully folding up the cloth and placing it in his breast pocket.

'In the meantime, until we get more news or hear a response

from the coast, we have to play tough, tighten our belts and be extra vigilant about rations and quantities of medicines being used.'

'What are you saying, Charlie?' Rollins asked. 'That if they're sick we don't give them enough to get well?'

'No, that's not what I'm saying, James. We have to go on treating people, but it's not a bottomless well we're drawing on here and sometimes we need to make hard decisions, direct resources where there's the best chance of them making a difference. I did an inventory a week ago and if we keep on at this rate and there's a big influx of refugees then we got trouble.'

'Seems to me trouble's already on its way, Charlie.'

'I'm just trying to tell you how it is, James. But there's talk too of international intervention, some kind of joint force to try and restore order, safeguard relief work.'

'International intervention is always something that's going to happen tomorrow. Going to happen any day but today. I heard it too many times,' Rollins said, shaking his head.

'Listen, James, I know you've got a lot of experience out here but we've got to keep positive, keep the wheels turning. We can't pre-judge what's going to happen.'

Rollins leaned back on his chair, his head still shaking slowly, and said nothing more. It was always the same at the weekly meeting, with Wanneker and Rollins jousting and no one else saying very much until called upon to give a report of the week's activities. Then we'd follow the requested format, outlining our positive achievements. Whatever Wanneker conceived as its purpose, it always felt like some self-help group where confession and self-revelation are considered therapy. The Olsons were quiet, self-contained people who drew strength from each other and whose minds were clearly focused on their imminent departure, and they rarely said much on such occasions. Martine was mostly sullen, smoking her cigarette and displaying an open indifference. Only Veronica believed in it, reciting the catalogue of her week's endeavours and declaiming with strident sincerity her determination to work with maximum efficiency in the coming week. I found them an embarrassment, and my reports inevitably sounded of less consequence than the others'.

Wanneker's enthusiasm for the sessions never seemed to wane. I think it provided him with an opportunity to display his leadership, to motivate us with the team-speak which made him sound like head coach. He also liked to play games with us, seek out weakness in personality, play people off against each other. Sometimes it felt as if he merely used the sessions to wind everyone a little tighter. 'Naomi,' he would smile, 'how have you made the world a better place since last we met?' And I would say, 'Well, first of all I taught the children a new song and how to play "The Farmer Wants a Wife".' Then, if he was in a good mood, he'd laugh or make a joke, but when I succeeded in irritating him he'd drop some comment that emphasized the lowliness of my status and the esteem in which he held my work. Only the knowledge that he was a skilled doctor who had probably saved many lives preserved some of my respect. Unpredictable in many ways, he was still capable of small acts of kindness out of concern for our welfare, which seemed genuine if short-lived. The one thing we argued about was Nadra. Despite my constant requests, he refused to put her on the Agency pay roll which would have entitled her to a range of benefits and privileges. He excused himself by saying unconvincingly that he didn't have the authority to make that decision. So she was paid a pittance, when the truth was that the school couldn't have functioned without her.

Once or twice he visited the school. It felt like a visit from an inspector, but he joked with the children and did his tired old party pieces – blowing his bubble-gum into a trembling pink balloon, magicking coins from someone's ear, using his hands to make animal shapes and sounds, and all the time his glasses mirrored the children's laughing faces. Only Nadra wasn't impressed, standing at the side, indifferent to his performance. When he'd finished she would drive the children back to their learning with even greater zeal. Once, Wanneker asked me if I knew what had happened to Medulla but I shrugged my shoulders.

'Suppose the guy knew when he was beaten,' he said, watching Nadra over my shoulder. 'Jeez, I used to have a teacher like her in high school – scared the hell out of me. Once she caught me out in a history assignment I'd copied out of a book. Sent for my old man and it ended up like a public court martial.'

'The school couldn't operate without her. She speaks good English and probably knows more than I ever will.'

'OK, Naomi, I get the picture, so before you start in again I'll send up to the capital and see if Stanfield will agree to put her on the roll. But no promises, things are tight right now. Maybe he'll be able to get his hands on some more resources for you – books, paper, that sort of stuff – but I can't promise anything.'

I thanked him and watched him amble back to the compound, his ponytail bunched out the back of his baseball cap. That same day, after school was over and Ahmed and Iman had helped us move everything back to the compound, I walked with Nadra on the outskirts of the camp. It was a day which seemed to exist outside the confines of time, where only the sun directed the what and when. I felt the intensity of it as I walked and looked in vain for shade, conscious of the growing scent of my sweat. We walked by the dried-up river bed where great fissures shot out across the cracking parchment of earth, passed the heavy, wilting heads of the sunflowers. In the distance a grove of blue trees glistened like a mirage and in the sky above our heads a hawk glided weightlessly on secret currents of air. Down on the plain we watched a man drive a pair of yoked bullocks, their humped and black-ribbed sides creasing and almost cracking with the strain of dragging the plough through the stubborn earth.

'Tell me about Ireland, Naomi. Tell me about the sea.'

'Our house was right beside the sea. Each morning I woke up I looked out and saw it stretch as far as the eye could see. As far as this horizon,' I answered, pointing to the distant wavering seam of sky and land.

'What colour was the sea, Naomi?'

'The sea is many colours – sometimes green, sometimes blue, but mostly it's grey and all the colours are hidden to the eye. My father used to swim in it even though the water was cold.'

'Why did he swim?'

'I don't know. Maybe he thought it would keep him well, keep his body healthy.'

'And was it the cold that killed your father?' she asked, hesitating a little in case she had asked too personal a question. Down below, the hunched figure at the plough glanced back at the thin dry gouge of earth.

'I don't know what killed my father, Nadra.'

There was silence for a few moments as we walked on. A file of children wearing zinc buckets on their heads was setting off to the wells. The sky was folding itself in layers of pink.

'Do you think of your father, Nadra?'

'Sometimes when my mother speaks of him, tells us he will return and take us from this place.'

'And do you think he will return?'

'I think he will come back if he is able, but it is a long time and so I am not sure. I think if he was able he would come back. Maybe something bad has happened to him. I do not know.' She glanced at me to see if she should say more and I nodded to her. 'Sometimes I think I hear his spirit calling my name, trying to speak to me, but when I look there is no one there.'

She turned her face away, frightened that she had discredited herself in my eyes, and I touched her arm to stop our walk and tried to tell her I understood but the words wouldn't come out right and we walked on in an uneasy silence. When it was time to part I shook her hand, holding it long enough to say that maybe her father would come back to take them to some better place, and she nodded and hurried away. I stood watching until she was hidden by the terraced layers of the camp.

A new group of arrivals were struggling into the camp. There might have been two or three families – it was difficult to establish the connections between the people who stumbled towards me. A couple of older children carried hens in bamboo cages while a man balanced a precarious bundle of possessions on the seat of a bicycle. Other objects dangled from the frame and handle bars, while behind the bike trailed a small wooden cart with rubber wheels in which sat a boy of five or six, and as they passed me I saw his stumps of legs. A woman carried blankets and a straw basket on her head and strapped to her back were two small children whose heads peeped out from the folds of her clothes. A small boy carried a cardboard box on his head, holding it carefully with one hand while he drank from a bottle. An older boy and a woman carried a wooden hoe on their shoulders and from it, like washing, hung the line of their possessions. Another boy trudged behind, struggling to keep up, the sleeves of the man's shirt he wore trailing the ground like two extra legs. Then came a woman smothered in black on a donkey, and at her back what I thought was a cloth-wrapped parcel of possessions. As they passed me a tiny gap opened at the neck of the bundle and an eye locked on me, never blinking as the donkey picked its sullen steps towards the rim of the camp.

I was joined by Ahmed and Iman, Ahmed striding out and Iman scuttling to keep up. They had developed into spivs, wheeling and dealing in anything that was tradeable or saleable. Sometimes they tried to sell me small objects which had been stolen from the compound. When I refused, they would offer to exchange them for something trivial or simply try to give them away. As the weary procession of new arrivals disappeared into the streets of the camp, Ahmed held up a watch for my inspection.

'Very good watch, Miss, very new watch. You buy, you buy, yes?'

'It's a very nice watch.'

'You buy, Miss, yes?'

'Where did you get it, Ahmed?'

'My watch, my watch, very good.'

'Yes, Ahmed, it's a very good watch but I already have a watch. See?'

They gave the watch to me at my birthday party. This was a genuine surprise. I had mentioned the date of my birthday casually to Martine a couple of weeks earlier and she had remembered and organized the whole thing. Everyone was there – Wanneker, Rollins, the Olsons, Martine and Veronica, Ahmed and Iman, Nadra and a sprinkling of children she considered to be the best students. There were small presents – a bar of scented soap, a wooden comb, a jar of moisturizer and even something that resembled a cake, made from meal and biscuit and decorated with seeds. I walked in the door to take my place for supper and they were all there. Wanneker played some aria on his machine and suddenly the room was filled with laughter and music. I was twenty-six years old and it was the first real party I'd ever had. Nadra handed me a small package wrapped in white drawing paper which she had decorated, and in it was a little mirror in an ebony frame.

Everyone performed, carried along by some inexplicable surfeit of well-being. The party seemed to assume a life of its own, not stimulated by drink or exotic food because there were only half a dozen bottles of beer, a bottle of wine and some small biscuits which Anna Olson had baked surreptitiously. But no one opted out. Martine even danced with Wanneker, a gliding, flamboyant Strauss waltz which the children clapped and sought to imitate. Veronica sang a sentimental song and then Rollins stepped up and gave his own crazy rendition of

'Danny Boy', accompanied by Ahmed on his flute but never quite in the same place at the same time. Wanneker did some conjuring tricks, even managing to produce some new and not totally obvious ones, and the Olsons did a little skit involving a young woman's visit to the doctor and sang a duet they explained had been done originally by Peter Sellers and Sophia Loren. Martine did an impersonation of Charlie Chaplin and recited a poem by Baudelaire which nobody understood. Nadra conducted the children in a rendition of 'Happy Birthday'. And then it was my turn and I didn't have a turn, but the children started to stamp their feet and clap their hands, bouncing the sound off the ceiling and vibrating the plates and glasses off the table. In my confusion I remembered my mother and the songs she used to sing, the sense of mystery they brought, but I couldn't remember the words or enough of the tune to carry it off and as the audience grew more demanding I stood up and recited the first poem that came into my head. When I was finished no one knew if that was it or if there was more to come, and so I had to bow elaborately to signal that my performance was over. As I sat down and felt the touch of the children's hands, I thought of the children I used to teach, thought too of Daniel and wondered where he was at that moment. His mother's face at the window, rain slanting across it like tears, the wind blindly flicking the pages of his books. But then the thin arms draped across my shoulders and hugging my neck pulled me back to the moment, and I heard once again the flow of opera and the chatter of voices, smelled the sweet scent of food and sweat.

I tried to thank as many people as possible, and when I spoke to Anna Olson I knew it was probably the last time we would talk. She looked thinner, older than I had noticed before, the secret pain of illness etched deeply about her eyes. 'Are you looking forward to going home?' I asked, sitting beside her on a narrow bench.

'Very much, Naomi – we've been in Africa a long time. Nearly twenty-five years, on and off.'

'That's a long time.'

'Too long, I think. Time to go home. We have grandchildren now. We're looking forward to seeing them, doing the things that retired people do.' She paused and clapped her hands to the music. 'We never got to know each other, Naomi, never really got a chance to talk. I'm sorry about that.' A tiny lime-green lizard scurried across the floor, miraculously evading the flailing feet of the dancers.

'When I first came, Peter and I weren't long married and just when I was getting used to being a wife I found myself living in Africa and working in a hospital which was barely entitled to call itself by that name. I used to go home at night and cry my eyes out and beg Peter to take me home, but he'd say we had a job to do and there'd always be another time to go home, and so we stayed and did what we had to do.'

Nadra had the children sitting on the floor and was leading them in a traditional song. Other children's heads crowded into the windows and open doorway. I held the little mirror Nadra had given me, anxious not to smear the glass with the sweat of my fingers.

'You must go home too, Naomi, when the time is right. Don't wait twenty-five years like I did.'

'How do you know when the time is right?'

'I think you'll know. You'll just wake up one morning and know that it's time. I knew but never listened. And make sure to go home while you've still a life to go to. It's very easy for Africa to become all there is, all there is of you.'

'Sometimes, here seems more real than home.'

'I understand that. In a place like this you feel closer to life because you're closer to death. And being close to death can make a lot of other things seem meaningless. But to make this all your life is to give yourself to something that will finally consume you, like it's almost consumed me.'

Rollins came over and asked her to dance, and she let go of my hand and giggled like a girl, then stood up with him, moving round the room with stately steps, her head barely reaching his chest, the whiteness of her hair floating like a lily on the green sea of his fatigues. I glanced down at my face in the glass, the red rims of my eyes, the dried-up furze of my hair.

'You're very serious on your birthday. Did you not get enough presents? I'm sorry I couldn't find balloons.'

'I was just thinking about home, Charlie.'

'Yeah, well, we all get homesick sometimes. You miss Ireland, then?'

'Yes, that's right, Charlie.'

'Another three months and you get six weeks' leave. You can go home, soak in a bath, eat real food.'

'Sounds good.'

'Can I have this waltz?'

He offered me his hand and I took it, my hand on his shoulder still holding the mirror. I felt the press of his hand on my back and his body push close to mine as he led me round the tiny space and I tried to follow his steps without entangling our feet. Round and round we went, more quickly than I wanted, my hand clutching the mirror, my head beginning to spin a little, and then I was aware of a noise beyond the music and a woman's voice crying and a man's voice shouting over her cries and slowly people's heads were turning from us to the compound outside. We stopped dancing even though the music played on and I felt dizzy and wanted to sit down but people were pushing past us and through the open door. Only Aduma was coming the other way, waving the children out of his path. He came to Wanneker and I knew it had been his voice shouting.

'There is a woman outside, she wants speak to girl with fire in her hair. She wants speak to Miss, she says to give you this.'

I took the dirty little scrap of paper from him and opened it and read where I had written the word Bakalla and I felt dizzy again. I stepped towards the open door, my hand slipped and there was the sharp tinkle of broken glass and a sudden surge of silence all about me. She was standing in front of the building. I stepped towards her and she stretched out her arms to me and the voice breaking from her throat was calling for her baby. As I stood silently looking at her, she sank to her knees in the dirt and held up her arms.

I asked only Nadra to come with me, thinking that I was sparing Martine and Veronica, but then realized the terrible thing that I was about to make her do, the words which I was to ask her to say, but there was no other way. We helped the woman from the ground, her flailing wail of pain evidence that she had already read the truth in our faces, and walked her slowly to where the darkness softened and blurred the thorns of the acacia. The words seemed to come from another world, but I had no others and so I passed them to Nadra and tried to hold the woman's hand, listening as they twisted into a different tongue. But she jerked her hand from mine and plucked at the dirt, showering the dust over herself and swaying back and forward as a shrill, ululating wail escaped her throat. Spiralling into the barren branches above our heads its shrillness punctured the calm of the night like a hole in a gourd. Then her family came round her and joined in the rising cry. Nadra took my arm and led me away.

Back in the clinic I asked Aduma to take them food and water, and watched as Martine and Veronica brushed away the broken glass and gathered up the little store of presents. As we walked to our tent the cries pierced the night and opened up everything that had been shut away – the hessian-shrouded bundle of leathery skin, the ochre-coloured earth, the tiny pile of stones. In the morning the family had gone, absorbed into the fraying, unravelling fabric of the camp, hidden from our sight by the weight of numbers and the growing spread of makeshift shelters.

WHEN Veronica told me the news it felt as if Wanneker was offering us a convalescence, a three-day restorative for our failing spirits. It seemed unfair that Martine had been left out, but as the Olsons had departed it probably wasn't possible for her to go too. The purpose of the trip to Mercu was for Wanneker and Stanfield to meet and plan the immediate needs of Bakalla and for Stanfield to hand over the American dollars that made the wheels turn. Mercu was on the coast and Stanfield would fly in to a nearby airstrip belonging to an American oil company. The journey would take us a day and a half by jeep. We were to go along too, just because a change of scenery would do us good. His promise of a couple of nights in a small hotel with clean beds and fresh food was enough to persuade us.

On the journey, we stayed overnight at an irrigation scheme organized by the Agency and met the two workers who had flown out with us, and slept in tents amidst a sweep of greenness – rice fields, a crop of millet, banana groves. That first night, the three of us sat round a fire and I listened as they talked of home and where they grew up and I was happy that there was little room for me to speak. The mood was suddenly light and foolish, like the first day of a holiday, and Veronica and Charlie's stories spilled over each other.

'Have you seen the film *Out of Africa*?' she asked, and we all laughed. 'Why are you laughing – it's a really great film. I've seen it twice, once in the cinema and once on video. No, three times – I saw it once on television as well. It was on one Christmas.'

'What's it about, Veronica? I can't quite remember it,' Charlie said, widening his eyes.

'It's about a woman, Meryl Streep, who has to choose between two men, Robert Redford and someone else. And she has this beautiful house and garden just like she's living in England.'

'Wow,' he said, 'and why is she in Africa?'

'I can't remember. She just is, and at one point she's nearly killed by a lion.'

'Jeez, Veronica, you're just telling us this to scare us. Do you think there might be lions out there somewhere in those groves?' And he growled his impersonation of a lion.

'Very funny, Charlie. All the lions in Africa are in game reserves.'

'I hope you're right, Veronica, but I'm not so sure. Once I talked to the head of a village, not a million miles from here, and he told me a lion made off with three people in three weeks. And you know, Veronica, lions get bored with the same diet all the time, sometimes they like a change – a bit of white meat maybe, know what I mean?'

We encountered no lions on our way to Mercu. It was a small town which had grown from an old Arab trading post, set up to facilitate the shipping of slaves, a sleepy little place with low white-walled buildings and narrow streets winding up from the shore. Cooler breezes blew in from the sea and the inhabitants made their living from fishing or working for the oil company, which had a refinery a couple of miles up the coast. The hotel was run by an Italian called Sandro who told us he was a second cousin to Luigi Riva as he showed us to our rooms. The dozen or so rooms were mostly occupied by Americans flown in to service some part of the refinery or search for new oil fields. We ate meals of pasta and fish in the small terrace restaurant, and I shared a room with Veronica. That night I slept in a bed with white sheets and a mosquito net that draped over it like a canopy. It felt so soft that I seemed to float into sleep the moment I lay down.

The Americans would sit in the tiny bar which formed the hotel's entrance and drink the local beer, mixed with shots of Southern Comfort, which they kept stashed in their bags or wrapped in beach towels. Wanneker would sit and talk sport with them, discussing the latest football news or else bad-mouthing government foreign policy, and sometimes they'd pull their chairs in tighter and talk and laugh in conspiratorial voices, then drink toasts to increasingly meaningless things. On a couple of occasions they asked Veronica and me to join them and then they'd slip into the role of Southern gentlemen, holding chairs and redirecting the fan on the bar so that it cooled us. Their boss was a man called Homer who wore shorts which struggled to hold the sag of his stomach and a Hawaiian shirt. It was soon clear that he claimed centre stage in every discussion and that the other men deferred to his wisdom. There was no sign of Stanfield. One slow afternoon, as the fishermen trailed their nets on to the beach to repair them, we sat in the dark little bar with its shrine to Luigi Riva and listened to Homer talk.

'The first and worst thing gonna' happen if the Fundamentals take over is that this country'll be as dry as a preacher's shoe. It'll be no different from Saudi or any of those states, so you guys savour that drink because the only thing you're likely to see in the bottom of your glass is Coca Cola.'

'Come to think of it, Homer, wouldn't surprise me at all if Coca Cola weren't behind everything's going on in this part of the world. Dry everywhere up, then open up your factories. You can bet your life that someone's making a buck out of it,' said his sidekick George.

'The people making the biggest bucks are the arms dealers. Everywhere you look, some kid with a hole in the ass of his pants is carrying a Kalashnikov or a rocket launcher, or some other piece of technology that costs an arm and a leg,' replied Homer, pouring more drinks for everybody. 'Excuse my language, ladies, we're not used to being around women too often. Six months out here either makes your marriage or breaks it. Either every homecoming is like a second honeymoon or it's another instalment in the divorce plan. Now me, I've got one of the loveliest ladies alive back home. Every time I come home she puts out the flag and ties a yellow ribbon round the front tree. Can you believe it? A yellow ribbon!'

They laughed and one of them called for more beer. In the doorway, transfigured in the intense block of light, stood two rags of boys. One of the men flicked coins at them and then Sandro came and shooed them away.

'It'll be a hard six months if this place goes dry,' continued Homer, as tiny rivulets of sweat licked his temples and vanished in the folds of flesh that swaddled his throat.

'Whatever the law, you can always get a drink,' said George, flicking flies away from the finger-smeared rim of his glass.

'Oh sure, you can get a drink and you can also get a lot of lashes as a chaser. Sure as Hell have to be a mighty fine drink to be worth that. You remember Danny Sullivan – the little Mick out of New Jersey? Got caught, took ten, ended up an embarrassment to the company and out of a job. Hell of a hangover that proved.' Some young girls tried to come into the bar to sell peanuts and plastic flowers, but Sandro chased them away, flapping a drying cloth at them like a matador's cape. 'You know, ladies, I sure admire the work you do out here. I know it can't be easy for you seeing all those little kids dying and not enough food to go round. Where exactly you from?'

When he learned I was from Ireland he asked me if I knew Danny Sullivan who had now become a 'Hell of a nice fellow'. He seemed surprised when I said I didn't.

'Now I'm no expert on Ireland, but it seems to me as if you've been killing each other over there for a mighty long time. It just doesn't seem to make much sense at all, going round killing people because of what religion they happen to be. I mean, back home most people don't give a hoot whether someone's a Jew, a Baptist, a Catholic or whatever – it just doesn't seem that important at the end of the day. You understand what I'm trying to say?'

'Yes, I understand,' I said, sipping beer from the bottle.

'Now if it was about colour, well, that's a whole different ball game,' he said, slapping the soft flabby flesh of his thigh and leading the laughter until the rucks of flesh on his face and neck quivered and his mouth cracked open in a contorted grin. 'You'll excuse us Miss, we all like our little joke around here. No offence meant.'

Wanneker winked over at me, and asked, 'Do you guys not think business could give some more to humanitarian aid?'

'Oh sure, sure,' replied Homer. 'I guess big business could cream off a little of their profits, sink the hand deeper in the pocket but you know, Charlie, there's kind of a problem with that, isn't there?'

'What's that, Homer?'

'Well, you know it seems to me that the more you lay out to someone the less inclined they are to do things for themselves. I saw this programme once back home. These panhandlers, these bums, were picking up more money on the streets than some folk with honest jobs. Don't seem right, does it? Where's the incentive to get off your butt and make things happen if you know someone's coming round handing out all the time?'

There was a murmur of assent round the group. Sandro came over and rested his arms on the top of the brush he had been using to scoot fag ends out into the street.

'But it's hard to get off your butt when some drought's wiped out all your crops or killed off your cattle and your kids haven't had anything to eat in a week,' said Wanneker, still smiling.

'Sure, Charlie, I take your point and don't get me wrong, I'm all for putting food in the hands of starving children, but you know what I'm saying. Sometimes it feels like we're pouring water into a bucket with a hole in it. And one thing you can't tell me, because I've been around these places too long to buy any bull, is that in every place where we bail them out some local bigshot's not taking a fat cut.'

The gang gargled its agreement and one of them formed a bull's eye with his thumb and finger, then there was a call to Sandro for more beer. 'Sure,' said Wanneker. 'But maybe that's the price that has to be paid.'

'But, Charlie, they're taking food out of the mouths of their own people and we're supposed to go on paying the bill. Back home, a lot of poor whites, poor blacks, without a job between them, maybe they're just gonna start saying that charity begins at home. Know what I mean, Charlie?'

'Maybe we're just trying to clear up a mess we helped make in the first place.'

'Now that's crazy talk, Charlie, and I don't think you believe that for even a second. Back home I have to listen to all this shit from these so-called African-Americans, and a lot of talk from people who ain't been closer to Africa than the Staten Island ferry about what a paradise this is and how us whites screwed it up, when the truth is that the only decent things they have we gave them. And every pathetic little state of theirs ends up with a flag like a bubble-gum card and a national debt the size of the Empire State.'

And so it went on into the afternoon, until Wanneker was called away to take a call from Stanfield. He couldn't make it due to operational difficulties and they arranged a new rendezvous later in the month. We left the oil men tanking up as if the state might go dry at any minute and walked round the narrow streets of the town, followed at every turn by little clouds of children who tugged our clothes and begged for money. We passed a mosque with blue enamelled doors and a police station where they invited us in to inspect our papers to help ease their boredom. As the crowd of children grew bigger we returned to the hotel and Charlie drove the jeep far out through the town and across a seam of scrub on to a deserted beach where we sat and fanned the sea breeze round our faces. There was no sign of any kind of life, and we drank some of the bottles of beer he had lifted from the bar.

'Weren't those guys something?' he said, slugging on the beer. 'What a bunch of assholes.' And then he did an impersonation of Homer and made us laugh. 'You guys want to go for a swim?'

Veronica giggled and joked about having no costume. 'Did you never go skinny-dipping, Veronica?' he asked, and she shook her head and said there wasn't much point because she couldn't swim, and then we started to laugh at things that weren't funny and he asked me if I wanted to go for a swim and he asked in a way that assumed I wouldn't. Getting out of the jeep I walked down to the water's edge, slipped out of my clothes, and without looking round walked out a little and started to swim. I felt the sweat and dust of my body washed away by the cool heave of foam as I let myself float, kneading the water with my fingers, kicking it up between my thighs. When the sun felt hot on my head I ducked below the surface and let the water rush through my hair. As I shook it out of my eyes I saw Charlie leave the jeep and, still holding the bottle, run to the water and shake off his shorts and top. His body was white and thin and as he held up the bottle to take one last drink the sun hit it and it looked as though he was drinking light. Then he was swimming out towards me, the colour of his hair and groin glinting in the sunlight before vanishing and reappearing.

'You're a hell of a swimmer, Naomi,' he said, gasping for breath and trying to steady himself in the swell.

'I grew up beside the sea – my father taught me when I was a child.'

On the shore, Veronica was paddling and waving out to us and as I waved he looked at my breasts lifting out of the water. I turned away and swam parallel to the shore and I could hear the slap and thrash of his arms as he tried to keep up. He was calling too but I couldn't make out the words and then after a while I turned and waited for one of the larger waves and followed it to the shore. As I started to wade in he caught up with me and I felt the hot dampness of his arm as he draped it across my shoulders.

'Wow, that was good,' he said. 'Did you enjoy it?'

I told him I felt cleaner, and when we reached our clothes we put them on straight away and lay down in the sand beside the jeep until the sun had dried us. As we drove back to the hotel the light was thickening and silencing the conversation, coating each of us with our own thoughts.

When we arrived back at the hotel, the oilmen were still in the bar but they had other companions now – four young girls, probably somewhere between the ages of seventeen and twenty. They were wearing Western skirts and blouses and had flowers in their hair. The oldest one sat smiling and joking but the eyes of the others flitted round like little birds unsure of where to land. They held their glasses tightly, the red polish on their nails and the white flowers in their hair the only bright points in the gloom of the bar.

'Got company then, Homer,' said Charlie as we passed them.

'That's right, Charlie. Six months is a long time, a man has to stay sane. Think of it as an investment, doing our bit for the economy,' he said, handing one of the girls a cigarette and lighting it for her.

Veronica and I walked on to the stairs but we could still hear his voice. 'Don't worry, Charlie – we're not stupid. Double rubbers all round!' There was the sound of laughter and the clink of glasses and a loud voice urging one of the girls to sing.

We reached our room and in a short time Veronica was asleep. I think she'd drunk too much and soon she was snoring gently, her arm lolling across my pillow. From the bar below I was conscious of a girl's voice singing and something took me back out into the corridor towards the sound, but before I reached the top of the stairs I was met by the American called George. He was unsteady and had to hold the rails as he came towards me, lurching in front of me as I tried to pass him and stretching out his arm to stop me, then angling me into the wall. I pushed him away but he came close again and I could smell the rancid mix of alcohol and sweat, the sour stream of his breath.

'You have beautiful hair,' he whispered, and touched it with the back of his hand. As I tried to move away he grabbed my hair suddenly, pinning back my head, and when I kicked out at him and shouted, he pressed me tightly into the wall so it was difficult to move. 'Come to my room and have a drink with me, forget the world's troubles for a little while.' I shouted at him again and started to lever myself off the wall with my feet. Then a hand grabbed his shoulder and spun him round and I thought Charlie was going to hit him but there were loud apologies and talk of a misunderstanding and then George stumbled back to the bar.

'Are you all right?' Charlie asked and I said yes and laughed, wanting all the time to be back in the sea, swimming slow and straight, feeling the waves sweep the ruck of my back and carry me forward with a will other than my own. And so I let him take me to his room and hold me in his arms, listened to him tell me I was beautiful, and it didn't matter that he lied because maybe there was no truth, and so I lay on the bed and held him while he kissed and nuzzled my body, tasted the salt of my skin on his lips. We didn't speak and the only sounds were the whirr of the fan and from the bar below a girl's song threading a melody through the clink of glasses and a babble of voices. My body felt a stranger to me under his touch and as he came into me my cry of pain shocked him, stopped him for a second, and then he stroked my hair and told me everything would be all right and as my hands fanned across his back, his need rose and fell inside me, breaking again and again in its hunger. And the fan turned, rippling and raising the net above our heads while through the sounds of his want filtered the high cadences of the girl's song before at last it was swallowed by the slap of hands on tables, the bounce and rattle of glasses and his final cry as he spent himself in me.

ON the journey back to Bakalla there was no sign from Veronica that she knew what had happened. There was nothing to be seen or sensed that was different from what had gone before. Charlie talked and acted the way he always did, and when I saw myself in his mirror shades I felt glad that he didn't feel the need to pretend. I think Martine might have guessed. She never said anything but maybe she heard something in my voice when I talked of Mercu, or read it in one of a dozen other ways known only to people who live close together as we did in the camp. A couple of times I almost told her, but as each day passed its meaning diminished and I knew it would seem a kind of betrayal. Some nights, we sat outside the tent that was our home and talked until the light died in a searing flush of riven sky, always different from the night before, and I listened to the pleasure in her voice when she was able to surprise or shock me.

'I've been to Ireland,' she said one evening.

'You never said before. When? Where?'

'When I was a student. I was with a boy on my course. We went to Dublin one summer and then we hired a car and toured different places.'

'Did you ever go to Donegal?'

'I don't think so. I suppose it was too far.'

'And did you like Ireland?'

'Yes, parts were very beautiful.'

'And was this boy someone special?' I asked, watching her pull her knees tightly to her chest, the way she liked to do.

'All boys are special, Naomi – at the time anyway. Henri was a very nice boy. We had a good time in Ireland. We stayed in a youth hostel in Dublin which wasn't good – they made us have separate rooms – but when we got the car we'd stay in a different place every night and nobody seemed to care. Maybe when they heard we were French they expected it. The only thing I didn't like was in the morning they'd try to make you eat these big breakfasts – big plates of food with bacon and sausages and everything piled up, and sometimes when they were serving you'd see them looking at you a little.'

'When I lived in Donegal I used to look at people like you. In the summers I'd see students, young people in cars or on bikes, sometimes hitching, and I used to wonder about the lives you led and how it felt to be as free as that. And it made it worse because I knew by September you'd all be gone and I'd still be living a life that never went anywhere.'

'But you're in Africa now.'

'Sometimes I think I'm dreaming it, dreaming it the way I used to dream different futures.'

She nodded her head and smoked her cigarette carefully, as if it were the last one she possessed.

'And this boy Henri, did you love him?'

'Of course,' she laughed. 'I love all my boys. Always, even now.'

'So what happened to him?'

'Nothing, after a while we both became bored, that's all. Time for a change.'

'Do you have many changes, Martine? Many boys?'

'I don't count,' she laughed, 'but I think quite a few.'

'And do you sleep with all of them?'

'Of course, Naomi – if it lasts long enough and I like them enough. Have you had many boyfriends?'

'A couple, just a couple.'

'And did you sleep with them?' she asked.

'Just once.'

'Just once? It wasn't good for you?'

'No, it wasn't good.'

And then she turned her face towards me, and when I felt the weight of her curiosity I joked, 'I'm a minister's daughter, I have to be a good girl.'

'Just because your father's a priest or a minister it doesn't mean you have to be a nun.'

I brushed something away from my face. 'When I used to moan to my mother about the colour of my hair she'd say I was lucky I wasn't a nun out in the convent on the Point or I'd have no hair at all.'

'I think my mother wanted to lock me in a convent once – she always disapproved of the things I did. When this is all over for us, you must come to Paris with me and I'll introduce you to many boys.'

'And how do your parents feel about you being in Africa?'

She shrugged her shoulders and stubbed out her cigarette. 'They don't like it very much, especially my mother. She worries, always she worries. My father . . . I think he worries too but he just tells me to be careful. He never interferes with my life. Even as a child he wanted me to discover things for myself.'

'And what is it like living in Paris, Martine?'

'Right now Paris seems very beautiful to me. If we were there now we'd be sitting in a little café I know in Montmartre, dressed in beautiful clothes and smelling nice, sipping our glasses of wine and watching the world pass by. When this is over, will you come and do it with me?'

'Yes I will,' I said, as from somewhere beyond the compound I recognized a tune filtering into the night from Ahmed's flute. We sat listening to it until it vanished into the distance and then we were startled by the sudden stutter of bats as they swooped low then twisted away again.

That night I dreamed of a café, its awning the brightest yellow against a blue frieze of sky like the postcard I used to have of Van Gogh's café at Arles. Above me is a cold glitter of stars. I sit watching people passing by. But in my dream I am on my own and when I look around me I see only young girls with flowers in their hair and frightened eyes, and then I hear her song threading itself through my dream until I become part of it, my life rising and falling with its rhythm.

I found myself with Martine again when Charlie asked us to travel out to Baran, one of the small satellite camps that ring Bakalla. Baran was about twelve miles away and he wanted us to stay overnight with some local workers and find out what they needed. I left the school in the hands of Nadra and the women she had gathered as helpers. I thought he would send Veronica with Martine but he told us she was needed in Bakalla and that Aduma would go with us. And so we set off early one morning with the wispy smoke of the camp starting its slow climb skyward. Some miles out, we passed women and children from the camp, scavenging for wood. Some waved but to others it was as if we were invisible and they looked through us, indifferent to our passing.

Martine drove too quickly over the worn paths, and Aduma and I had to hold on with both hands as the jeep bucked and bounced along. Our journey was mostly through low scrub and bush – often the path was almost indistinguishable. The noise of the engine and our bumping motion made it difficult to talk, so mostly we travelled in silence, occasionally stopping for a drink of water and to allow Martine to wipe away some of the sweat that beaded her eyes and mouth. I pulled the ends of my scarf across my mouth, trying to keep out some of the dust. As we drove through the heat of the day the sun seemed to burst inside my head and made my light-bleached senses sharp and irritable. I thought of my drive into the estate, the rain falling across the windscreen, the feeling of fear, the young woman in a white dress emerging from the greyness. I wondered where she was, what had happened to her, if she was happy. And then in my hand I saw the piece of paper with his address and the rain bleeding the ink and suddenly it changed into the scrap of paper held by a mother looking for her child and as I heard her cries again, saw Daniel's mother standing at the window, the faces slowly merged until they were one. I drank from the canister and longed for the jeep to stop, to find some shade that would bring relief.

About three or four miles from Baran we saw a cluster of mud-bricked, tin-roofed houses, and we pulled off the road. A few hens grubbed in the dirt and there was a fire collapsed in on itself but no one in sight. We looked around and sounded the horn but there was only the slight stirring of the breeze disturbing the longer grass behind the houses. I touched one of the makeshift doors and as it swung open a tiny lizard sprinted out of a crack in the wood and across my hand. Inside, my eyes struggled to focus in the dust-dappled light and then gradually I distinguished the few spindly pieces of furniture and the meagre collection of possessions. Picking up a child's colouring book from the floor I flicked the pages and saw where someone had crayoned all the pictures a single colour. On a box table were four plastic plates and cups and a coarse grey blanket hung over the back of a chair. When I went back outside the light hurt my eyes and as I turned away to shade my face I glimpsed a young boy watching us from the grass. I raised a hand in greeting but he pulled back deeper into its slow waver. I signalled to the others and told them what I had seen but although Aduma called an invitation, explained who we were, no one emerged. We went into each of the huts and left small packages of B95s. Back in the jeep, the kick of the engine seemed even louder in the silence, and I kept my eyes on the break in the grass where I had seen the child. But if he was still watching us, his eyes were masked by its shiver, and we pulled back on to the narrow road that led to Baran.

About half a mile from the camp we found the first body. It was the sudden black clatter of wings as the vultures lifted their heavy bodies skywards that caught our attention. The bunched and rucked body of a young man lay face down in the scrub, about twenty yards from the road. Across his back we found a spray of bullet wounds. It looked like he had been running away when he had been shot, his arms stretched out as if in a final effort to pull himself forward. Black flies smeared his purple flesh and as Martine touched his head it lolled sideways, almost severed by a deep rust-coloured slash across the neck. I turned away and retched and then Martine and Aduma led me back to the jeep and we sat in it and tried to breathe some cleaner air, gulping like swimmers surfacing, and Martine and I held each other's hands, trying to steady our senses.

'What should we do?' she asked. 'Go on or go back? He's probably been dead for a couple of days. What should we do?'

But we didn't know. Aduma huddled in the back of the jeep, his head between his legs, and I couldn't speak because I knew I would hear the fear in my voice and I was desperately trying to hold it in, control it. A phalanx of blue butterflies landed on the windscreen, fluttered against the warmth of the glass, then flew away again. I tasted the sickness in my throat, before drinking greedily from the canister of water and letting it splash and dribble on my face. Martine took it and also splashed some round her face, mopping the excess with the back of a hand that shook a little as she did so. Then she drove the jeep slowly forward, both hands clasping the wheel, her body tense and upright. As we moved away we caught the slow black glide of the returning vultures and the sudden break of their serrated wings as they dropped again on their prey.

A little distance on there were two more bodies – an old woman, her white headscarf soaked by the blood of a gaping wound, a young girl with her back kneaded and pulped by the puncture of bullets. Beside them the old woman's long-stemmed pipe and the girl's sandals, the yellow imprint of her toes and heels on the insteps. The brown stain of their blood joined them in the dust and both were covered by a black scree of flies. As we drove into the centre of the village we were met by the smell of decomposing flesh. At first, we stayed in the jeep and looked. There were a dozen other bodies visible, and probably the same number in the surrounding bush, those who had been pursued and executed or who had crawled away to die. We saw a mother and her baby, the child still enfolded in her arms, probably killed by the same bullets; an old man frozen on his knees like a toppled statue; two women, raped and mutilated, their clothes strewn around like rags. Martine and I walked together, unwilling and unable to let go of each other, before we turned away and were sick until nothing was left but a heaving emptiness.

Two of the huts had been burnt to the ground and a third half-destroyed. There was no one left to help, no little miracles of survival on which to cling to distract from what was all around us. There were only the bodies, swollen and bloated as if the life they once held was bursting its way out of their skin, distorting and distending their features. Only the smell. Burying them was beyond our capabilities but we couldn't leave them there, robbed of their lives and dignity, rotting like carrion. It was Aduma who decided and we nodded our heads as he took a bandage from Martine's case, tied it round his mouth and nose and began the slow job of trailing each of the bodies to the partically burnt hut. I wanted to help him but I couldn't, and when Martine tried she had to come back and sit in the jeep.

It took a long time, and when we didn't watch we could hear the heavy trail and brush of each body through the dust and Aduma's laboured breathing. At intervals he would come back to the jeep and drink some water, splash his face, and when we looked into his eyes we knew how hard it was for him to go back. It took about an hour and when it was done he stumbled towards us shaking his head and starting to cry out. We helped him into the back of the jeep and gave him a glucose drink, then bathed his face and hands. He held out his hands towards us again and again, scrubbing them desperately until he was satisfied they were clean. Then he turned his head away from us and closed his eyes. I took the metal canister of petrol and sprinkled it as best I could over the outside of the hut, the smell making me retch again. As I hesitated at the entrance Martine took the canister from me and went inside, out of sight for only a few seconds. Then she carefully made a torch from a bandage and a piece of wood, lit it and flung it on to the roof of the hut.

We waited only long enough to leave some food and basic medical supplies where they would be seen by anyone returning later to the village and then we drove off quickly, looking back only once as the hut crackled and buckled into flame. But as we followed the road back to Bakalla we carried the smell of the smoke with us, mile after mile. We could still smell it long after we had left the village behind. I wanted to drink more of the water but I knew that if I tried to drink it while we bounced over the uneven ground I would be sick and whatever my thirst I didn't want Martine to stop, to delay our return to Bakalla by even a minute. We glanced at each other constantly to see if we were all right, and once she stretched our her hand and touched my arm. The speed of the jeep was welcome now but as it careered along, the images jolted round my head like cargo loose in the hold of a ship, splitting open with every new collision. Martine's body was stiff but her arms shook with the vibration of the jeep as she sought to hold the road and avoid whatever potholes might suddenly appear. From time to time she mopped her brow with her hand and shook her head as if to clear it from sleep. Dark seams of sweat had opened on her shirt and I saw that she was crying. Making her stop, we all took turns to splash our faces with water and then she took off her shirt and quickly put on another from her bag, throwing the old one into the bush. She wanted to drive on but I got into the driver's seat and started the engine and as I drove I could hear Aduma's voice break into a kind of mumbling, the sound an old man makes when he's talking to himself. I didn't know if it was a prayer or some involuntary release of words but I wanted him to stop and then it grew slowly louder until it became a fragmented chant of lament.

I wanted Martine's voice but she huddled in the seat beside me, her knees pulled up on the seat and her head resting sideways on them so her face was turned away from me. As we approached Bakalla we passed families trudging along the side of the road, their progress slowed by the burdens they carried. When they turned their faces to us we didn't look at them, as if frightened that they might see through us to what we had seen. We felt the weight of what we would soon have to tell, and knew that words would drag into the open what everything inside us conspired to keep silent, that talking would taint us once again with the touch of those bodies rotting in the sun, push us back with sickened, faltering steps into that small clearing in the scrub.

As the first smoke of Bakalla rose in front of us I saw a young girl with a white shell in her hand, her foot trying to smoothe away the fear as she tells of a night when men came out of the darkness and killed a man. I hear her voice, see the tears about to come, and then in the silence as I drive the jeep through the shambling suburbs of the camp, I see her hand the shell to me. And all the children are staring at me, everyone staring at me, and Charlie, Rollins and Veronica are there too and at the edge of the ring my father, his eyes green and empty with the sea, and suddenly I see my own face in the broken glass of a mirror as they wait for me to speak.

Children ran alongside the jeep, their hands patting the engine as you would the flanks of a horse. In the mirror I saw Aduma lift his head and look about him as if he didn't know where he was. Beside me Martine also stirred, wiping her eyes and face with the palm of her hand, trying to smoothe away the sweat and tears. Her face was white, and although I touched her arm she didn't turn to look at me. I had become part of the reality she wanted to escape, a reminder of what she most wanted to forget. Soon she might even begin to hate me, and I knew in that moment that we would never sit together in that café watching the world pass by, that no boy would ever hold all of her in his arms. For already we were pulled deep into its undertow, carried along weightlessly, helplessly, to some place we did not wish to go. I called to her, and she turned and looked at me as if I were a stranger before she took my hand and held it tightly. She tried to light a cigarette but her hand was shaking too much and I did it for her, then had to go round and help her out of the jeep as she flicked her hair and smiled and said she was all right.

There was no one to be seen in the compound. Aduma had vanished without speaking, and Martine seemed unwilling to go any further. She sat on the steps outside the clinic smoking her cigarette. I pulled off my headscarf and felt my dry bundle of hair fall loose. There was no one in the clinic, no sound of music or sign of activity, but just as I was about to turn away I heard them. The voices came from the little back room where Charlie slept. Maybe it was Veronica's I heard first, maybe Charlie's, and as they grew louder there was the sound I recognized and turning slowly I went back out and sat on the step with Martine until they were finished.

WE have to get up very early, so early my mother has to come and sit beside me on the bed and talk me awake, and then she helps me wash and dress. My father sits in his jacket and shiny collar at the breakfast table and calls me sleepy-head, and it sounds so quiet in the kitchen because this morning there is no radio piping music and the only sounds come from the rush and bubble of water in the kettle and my father's spoon clinking the side of his dish. I am not hungry but they make me eat, telling me it is a long way and a long time before we will eat again. I have been the long way before; it means we are to travel south for my father to take the service in some other church where the minister is on holiday or there is some convention.

Outside, the world is grey and the windows look as if they should still have their curtains closed, because it feels as if the greyness pressing against the house might flow into the room. And my mother busies herself making sandwiches, arranging them in a plastic container in the way she does, using all the space without bruising or forcing anything. As I rub the sleep from my eyes my father drinks his tea and watches me over the rim of his cup and the cup looks too small for his hand, as if at any moment it might crack and the tea splash over the wooden table. Then he stands up and tells me again that it is a long way and to make sure I finish my breakfast and go to the toilet before we leave. And when he goes out to load the car I hear the click of the lock and the scrape of the bolt and when the door opens there is the soft murmur of the sea and for a second I think it will flow into the house through the open door. But then my mother comes and sits beside me and tells me that I can sleep in the back of the car, and she smoothes my hair back from my eyes.

When we leave the house everything is grey and the sky and sea seem as if they are joined, and I shiver in the coldness as my father closes the gate behind him and looks for the car keys. And he has to look in every pocket and he pats his side pockets with the palms of his hands, and then in the stillness there is a jangle and he says that which is lost is found, and he opens the driver's door and the light inside yellows the white dome of his head. My mother folds her seat forward and I climb into the back and lie down on the red tartan rug and rest my head on the cushion she has brought for me. But before we move off I sit up and look out of the back window of the car to see what the world looks like early in the morning, but all I see is the grey light pushing in on us and the only colour is the yellow dot of light out on the Point. And as always when I think of the convent out on the Point I touch my hair and try to pretend to God that I like its colour and am grateful for it. Then I wonder if there are fishing boats out in the greyness and how the fishermen see to catch their fish or find their way home, and I remember the time my father took me to Burtonport and we watched the boats unloading and I see the bright shiny eyes staring up from beds of ice and I feel the cold again and snuggle into the rug. When my mother tells me to sleep I close my eyes and pretend.

I pretend because I think they will talk as if I am not here and I will be able to listen and understand the life they alone share. But for a long time no one speaks and there is only the bump of the car over roads my father likes to complain about, and once my mother starts to hum a tune but stops and as she turns to look at me I close my eyes tighter and do my best to pretend. Always I think there must be something between my parents which is kept secret from me, which is kept only for them, like the secrets box I keep in my room. I grow tired of its secrets from time to time and take them out and they are no longer secret, but between people I think there must be big things which only they can share and which can never be thrown away. And when I am loved I will know what these things are.

When my father talks it is of money, and my mother tells him everything will be all right and that they will get by. And getting by is something I have heard her talk of before and then she talks of making do for another year and rain falls so lightly at first that the wipers scrape drily across the glass but then it gets heavier and the drops are fat splotches and the wipers flick faster. It starts to drum on the roof and I curl up tighter and the lights from the dashboard shine red and green in the gloom. Then I stop pretending and fall asleep even though the red tartan rug is itchy on my legs and smells musty. And when I wake the rain has stopped and the greyness is gone and this time it is my mother who calls me sleepy-head and my father makes a joke about Lazarus. The musty smell is in my mouth, and in the driver's mirror I see the print of the cushion on my cheek. I hang on the back of my mother's seat but my father tells me to sit down and so I flop back and watch the world.

But I see nothing new, only endless roads seamed by stone walls and beyond the walls clumped billows of yellow gorse or brown beds of heather and beyond that humped and stone-saddled mountains. We pass a reed-fringed lake and my mother points out a swan sitting on a nest, and then the road winds itself more tightly and we climb higher, leaving behind the stone-littered fields with their smattering of wind-blown sheep, and burrow deeper into the mountains through black valleys where the mist streams as if from the burnt earth. This always makes the car feel small and vulnerable and I pull my knees up quietly on the seat so my father doesn't hear me and tell me to put them down again, and when I angle my head to the window I can see mountains stretching beyond themselves into their own shadows and sometimes their sides are patched and scabbed with quarries and grey scree. When we pass the rows of peat trenches I try to count the full yellow plastic bags which lean against each other but there are too many, and sometimes at the side of the road there are crazy-angled trees with black bark and branches, hunched over the collapsed remains of stone cottages.

The car feels small as a toy, and sometimes the wind buffets it and my father asks if anyone wants to get out and walk, and then as we keep winding our way upwards we suddenly break into a shock of space and look into a distance riddled by spears of light and the scud of cloud. Then the car seems to grow bigger and my mother and father start to talk and there is a lightness in it and sometimes it includes me. My father tells me to put my feet down off the seat but I do not mind because they have been there a long time and he doesn't say how many times have I told you, it's almost as if he says it out of habit and doesn't really care. Then we drive through places where people live and he points out bungalows which are painted colours he pretends to laugh at, but sometimes I think they are only bright colours and I see no harm in them. And we pass chapels with cars parked double on the road and sometimes on the pavement, and then we have to slow right down and he complains of the time we waste.

When we have been in the car a long time he pulls into a lay-by and my mother pours out tea from a flask and offers us sandwiches from the plastic lunch box, and I never like to take the first sandwich because it breaks the pattern but if my father takes two and we take one each then sometimes the pattern becomes perfect again. The windows begin to steam up and he wipes the windscreen with the back of his hand and it makes a squeaky noise, then he puts on the heater and before long it is clear again. And when we have all finished our tea we hand him our cups and he opens the door just wide enough to reach out his arm and pour out the dregs and then my mother takes them, rubs their insides with a paper hanky and places them back inside the polythene bag which she stores at her feet. It won't be too long, my mother says, brushing crumbs off her skirt, and we set off again as the rain returns, firing across the windscreen in fine sheets, and the wipers start their slide and swish.

My father says we are in good time, but then something happens that has never happened before on the long way. We find ourselves joining a trail of cars which is hardly moving, and on the narrow roads cars are parked on both sides and so there is only room to follow the car in front. Sometimes the line of cars ahead comes to a halt, and there are other cars behind us so even if we wanted to turn round we couldn't, and my mother looks at my father but he doesn't understand. He sees no chapel and it is too early for football or hurley and he doesn't understand which makes him nervous, and he drums his fingers on the steering wheel. It is my mother who sees them first. Long lines of people on the mountain, moving through the wind and rain, some of the lines climbing upwards, others making their way down. As we get closer we see the wind blowing out the tails of coats like flags and the long hair of young girls streaming behind them like banners. And my mother says it is a pilgrimage, it is as if the whole side of the mountain is moving and then people start to flow alongside the car or in front of us and I see that many are barefoot and some of them limp and some have bleeding feet and I feel something that feels like sick. I ask my father what it means but he doesn't answer. My mother tries to explain and she tells me that it is their faith, what she calls a penance, a pain that they must suffer because they think God will be pleased. And now I feel frightened because there are so many people, some of them old, many women with their wet hair hanging lank and lifeless, and some have bleeding feet that leave prints on the road. I stare out from the back of the car as they walk in the cold of the morning and I feel frightened because they think they have pleased God and because I do not know this God.

Inside, the car grows quiet, as if we have stumbled into a

world we do not understand. As we finally reach open road I look back at the moving mountain with its top brushed by cloud and the winding lines of people hoping to please their God. And my father drives the car faster, saying we have to make up for lost time, but I think it is because he wants to get away from this place and these people, and then he starts to say things which he hopes will cheer us up. He tells us that the people who get most out of the day are the traders who lug their cans of drink to the top of the mountain at the crack of dawn and then charge everyone four times the normal price, but I don't know if he has made this up or not and my mother just stares through the side window. And nothing he says stops the feeling that we are strangers in this world, and I wonder if it is because God is angry with us because we never climb the mountain. Then my father says it's a strange religion that lets people do whatever they want and then be forgiven if they light a candle, or say some verses, or kiss a stone, but my mother still says nothing.

When we get to the church where my father will preach, it looks and smells the same as our own church but there are yew trees in front of it and a clock in the spire. Because my mother doesn't have to play we sit together in the middle of the church and there are some people around us but not many. The light shines on the dark varnish of the pews, then splashes against the gold-coloured plaques on the side walls and makes the engraved writing move. When someone coughs, the noise echoes in the vault of the ceiling and as always I wonder why God should choose such a place to live in and why he wants his house to be like this. But when my father speaks I listen because it is a sermon I've never heard before; he tells us of God's mercy and when he speaks of this mercy he calls it infinite, and he reads a story about God and Abraham and he reads it in his other voice. My mother puts her hand on my knee to stop me swinging my foot but I am listening and for a while I forget the moving lines on the mountain. The story is of how God wanted to destroy a city because the people's sin is what the Bible calls grievous, and Abraham asks God will he destroy the righteous with the wicked? And then it is like a game with numbers and it starts at fifty and comes down to ten and God tells Abraham that he will not destroy the city if it even has ten righteous people. My father calls God's mercy bountiful and infinite and says that God will not destroy the world even if there is one righteous person, and we don't have to go on a pilgrimage to be righteous because Christ had made a pilgrimage to Calvary on our behalf. When he says this I think he is looking at us but I'm not sure, and sometimes his voice drifts a little into the great spaces of the church and vanishes into the stone corners.

Then he tells us that the world we live in is full of wickedness and he gives the examples he always uses and the two women in the pew in front nod their heads in agreement, and when he has finished the world seems a bad place, so bad that it deserves to be destroyed. And he tells us that righteousness exalts a nation and says that our nation has forgotten this, and he speaks as if he is one of the righteous, one of those who saves the world from destruction. Then I don't listen any more and lean my head against my mother's arm.

When it is all over and we have had our lunch in the house of one of the parishioners we set off on our journey home, and the rain has stopped and the sun makes the roads steam a little. When we pass the mountain there is only the drift of mist and cloud. Then it starts to rain again and my mother keeps her face angled to the window and sometimes when she rubs it clean with a piece of tissue, little bits of white paper stick to the glass like snow.

DURING the next week, most of those who had survived Baran arrived at the camp. Some were wounded, all were in various states of trauma. Slowly, painfully, we were able to piece the story together. One day, in mid-afternoon, two trucks arrived bearing about two dozen men who said they were from the new army of the people and that they had come to give protection against government troops who would soon be arriving from the capital. None of the soldiers wore uniforms but all carried guns and most, said the villagers, were high on *khat*. Ordering everyone to assemble, they told them that if government troops came very bad things would happen and that everyone must flee into the bush and not return until they were told. While the leader of the men spoke to them, others went inside and took anything of value, saying it was to help the people's struggle. When the head of the village clan tried to argue with them he was brought out and made to kneel on the ground before being beaten, and as some of those watching became hysterical, the soldiers seemed to lose control and one took a pistol and shot the old man in the back of the head. Then as everyone fled towards the bush they turned their guns on them, firing bursts again and again, spraying the fleeing, screaming villagers.

Those who made it to the bush kept moving until they felt far enough away and then found hiding places and stayed there, too frightened to go back to the village or escape in any other direction. Many of their wounds were badly infected and Rollins and Wanneker worked long into the night, the yellow lights from the clinic framing it in the darkness. With Nadra and some of the others we gave out the few tents that were left, some food and water, and sat with them, listening to the shuddering rush of their words and the great silences which would suddenly shake their bodies. The children cowered in the corners of their tents, cradling themselves or clutching some object they had picked up, and when I tried to touch them they cringed and slithered away as if my hand might hurt. There was one young girl, maybe eight or nine years old, who had lost her mother and she lay where the light broke into ragged splinters, tightly curled into herself, her eyes open and unblinking. She wouldn't look at me or drink any of the milk I tried to give her. I struggled to stop my mind wondering which corpse had been her mother, remembered with shame that I hadn't been able to bring myself to touch them or help Aduma, tried also to stop that smell of burning from re-entering my senses. Her father was in the clinic with a flesh wound in his leg and although Nadra told her again and again that he would come back, I suppose she thought he too was going to leave her. I sat close to her for a long time, talking, offering her the milk. She looked at me for the first time, studying my hair under the light from the lamp and then she spoke. 'She says you have red hair,' Nadra said as the girl stretched out her hand for the milk, but I made her come for it and then she let me take her in my arms and nurse her, her wetness printing itself on my skin. Her clothes were soaked with urine and when she had finished I helped her change into clean ones and then she climbed into my arms again and I rocked her for a long time until she fell into a shallow sleep.

Wanneker called a meeting after the compound gate had been closed, and Aduma and Haneen were posted to stop anyone entering who wasn't authorized. There were blue circles of fatigue under his eyes. He sat on a table in T-shirt and jeans, the laces of his trainers trailing the ground as he spoke, swinging his legs slowly back and forward in time to his words.

'I've been on to Stanfield in the capital and told him what's happened here, and I just want to reassure you that all steps are being taken to keep the situation monitored and under control.'

In the far corner of the room Rollins sat with one leg stretched across a packing case, the other knee pulled up to act as easel for a small sketchpad. Only the very top of his pencil was visible in his hand and he didn't look up from the page or even glance at Wanneker. Martine stood in the doorway with some of the local staff.

'Stanfield has made contact with this group's spokespeople and got assurances from them that there is no danger to our work here. Supposedly Baran was the work of some rogue element and they're sending people to sort things out. But he's got a categorical assurance from the leaders of these people that they won't interfere in any way with the work of the relief agencies.'

'And has he paid them, Charlie?' Rollins asked, still focusing his attention on his drawing.

'I believe certain arrangements have been made.'

'Hope he's paid them enough, Charlie. Baran isn't very far from here.'

'I know that. And believe me, I'm as concerned as you are but I can tell you all this, if things change for the worse or the Agency has any doubts at all, then we're out of here right away. Even in the capital it's hard to get a clear picture of what's going on because there's a lot of in-fighting right now, a lot of clans trying to pay off old scores. But I can tell you something else that Stanfield told me – he believes that all the signs point to international intervention. It could be only a matter of weeks, maybe even days, away and if that happens then we'll operate under UN protection.'

'International intervention sounds good,' said Rollins, 'but it might only stir these people up. Could be upsetting a real hornets' nest. We're a long way south of the capital, could be a whole while before we see the cavalry.'

'Stanfield is already pushing the interests of the Agency in the right circles, and you can rest easy that Bakalla's name and needs will be kept to the forefront.'

'Are they going to replace the Olsons?' asked Martine.

'Unfortunately there seems no immediate prospect of replacement. I guess they're waiting to see which way the ball breaks before they decide to give us new people. So for the moment at least, it's very much a holding operation, keeping the lid on things here and waiting to see what happens. I'm sorry I can't be more specific than that. But I promise you, you're all too valuable for them to let your welfare be put at risk.'

Rollins closed his sketchbook with a snap and took his leg off the chair, and as I walked by him on the way to the door he nodded to me and said under his breath, 'Believe that, Naomi, and you still believe in Santa Claus,' then he stood up and smoothed some of the wrinkles which cracked across his clothes.

Later that night, I passed his tent, the lamp silhouetting his figure hunched over a table. I couldn't sleep, didn't want to sleep, and I walked quietly around the compound, the sand a milky colour under the thick frieze of stars. There was a drifting haze of smoke from the camp and behind the clinic the luminous, tremulous light splashed over the baobab tree, its V-shaped branches like veins against the skin of sky. From somewhere deep inside the camp came the cry of a baby, the bark of a dog, and then close by there was a voice in the darkness.

'Can't sleep, Naomi?'

He stood in the shadows outside his tent, only his glasses reflecting the light, then stepped forward a little so that I could see him. He raised a glass to me. 'Sometimes sleep don't come easy,' he said. 'Would you join me in a nightcap?' I had never been in his tent before, never known anyone who had. He always seemed private about it, as if it were a place outside the parameters of the camp, to which he retreated as soon as his work was over. It was lit by an oil lamp which hung perilously close to his head as he moved to pull another chair up to the table at which he had been working. In a glass on the table was a scented spray of bougainvillea and from the open sketchbook I could see that his painting was light and delicate, fragile as the flower itself. Pencil sketches hung around the tent, with paintings of other flowers and plants. Unlike the tent I shared, everything was neat and organized. On the upturned packing case which served as a bedside table stood a bottle of whisky, some books, a personal stereo and a box of tapes. When he handed me a glass the weight of it surprised me.

'Always drink whisky out of crystal. And always drink it neat.'

I sat at his table and sipped the drink slowly, remembering the night I sat with my mother and we tried to drink the communion wine, the red stain in the sink, but there could be no throwing this drink away – I knew how precious it was to him, and so I kept on sipping and tried not to let my face change its expression.

'You having problems sleeping?' he asked as he stirred the paint of his brush with a shake of his hand, pushing out the purple colour against the side of the glass. 'I can give you something if you like, give you a whole lot of things if you want.'

'I don't know if I want to sleep.'

'So you dream, you dream about Baran?'

'Yes, mostly about Baran. Sometimes other things get mixed through it.'

'I can't control dreams, Naomi. Wish to Hell I could, would take some of that stuff myself. Mostly this helps a little,' he said, holding the glass to the light and swirling its content, 'but there ain't no predicting it at the end of the day.'

'Sometimes you can't sleep?'

'Sure, sure, you see, I've got a whole lifetime of dreams to keep me awake – biggest collection in the world. I can take out a new one every night and dust it down, try it on for size.'

He drained his glass with a backward jerk of his head which tightened the muscles in his throat and pulled his fatigues tight across his chest. Under the light I could see the grey stubble on his face, and he suddenly looked much older.

'What did you think of what Charlie told us at the meeting?' I asked.

He poured another glass for himself, tried to give me some more then teased me about how slowly I was drinking. 'Well one thing's for sure, if Charlie thinks there's any danger to his own ass then he's out of here, and we'll be hanging on his coat-tails, so you don't need to worry about that.'

'You don't like Charlie, do you?'

'Charlie's just a rich white boy from the right side of town who's putting in some time before he picks up a nice fat cheque every month from some bigshot job. Charlie don't give a damn and he'll live off Bakalla for the rest of his life. Big-hearted Charlie, what a guy!' And he laughed until it seemed the whisky would splash out of the glass. 'Don't get me wrong, Naomi – I don't give a damn either, only difference is all my life I've been from the wrong side of the tracks and there was never any bigshot job waiting for me. And you remember what I told you – when the shit hits the fan I'm out of here just as fast as you can say Jack Daniels.'

'You wouldn't be here if you didn't give a damn. And I've seen you working – I saw you with that young girl that first morning, saw the way you talked to her, the way you treated her.'

'Just doing my job, paying my dues.'

A tiny green lizard shivered across the roof of the tent and hid itself in the rucks of a side wall. There was a moment of silence broken only by the hiss of the lamp.

'Maybe I should go now and let you get on with your painting.'

'Stay until you finish your drink. At the rate you're going it should take you half the night. And the painting's finished – it wasn't any good.'

'Looks good to me.'

'You an expert?' he asked, and the sudden edge of aggression in his voice made me blink and hold the glass to my lips. Then, standing up, he took the spray of bougainvillea and the painting and held them out to me. 'You can have one or the other, the flower or the painting. Which one would you like?' And when I took the painting he said, 'Wrong choice, Naomi, the painting don't even come close,' and he smiled and sniffed the spray. 'Maybe you made the wrong choice, too, when you came here.'

'Maybe, maybe not. Sometimes things aren't always choices.'

He nodded and placed the spray back in the glass.

'You like plants a lot, don't you?'

'Nothing as beautiful in this world.'

'Did you like them as a boy?'

'That's a long time ago. I don't remember seeing many plants, unless you count the weeds which grew along the railway line or on the waste lots behind the tenements.'

'So when did it start?'

'Longer ago than I care to remember. Those the first dead bodies you ever see?'

'The baby, a couple in the camp, nothing like that.'

'Not easy to forget – that's something else I understand. Don't suppose I was that much older when I saw my first. Saw my first before I'd had a chance to unpack my kitbag, and then they didn't stop until I caught a plane back to the world. He was a skinny eighteen-year-old, blond hair, blue eyes, looked like he should have been shooting baskets in some high school gym. He'd stood on a mine, lost most of both legs and had a hole in his chest you could put your fist in. Sonofabitch arrested three times and then I lost him. Lost him on my first day, before I'd unpacked my kitbag. Afterwards they joshed me about it. "Way to go James, way to go!" they'd say and slap my back and say I was lucky because things could only get better. Didn't get any better though, until the day I caught that plane back to the world.'

'You were in Vietnam?'

'That's right, Naomi, young, leaner, full of crazy ideas about the world and what I was going to do for it.' Above his head two small moths fluttered round the light, pinging the vaporous, hissing glass. 'By the end of the first week I knew that everything was about what the world was going to do to me, and all that mattered was looking after my own ass.' He filled his glass again, the bottle balanced perfectly in one hand. 'I guess seeing those bullet wounds brought it all back home.'

'Does it come back a lot?'

'Never really went away. Guess I just seen too much.'

I sipped more of the whisky, felt its slow burn at the back of my throat.

'I was in an evacuation hospital in the Central Highlands, but there wasn't much about it that had anything to do with a hospital. Those boys just flowed in there like a river in flood and you worked until you were done or you'd lose them, and sometimes you fell asleep in the emergency room or on your feet and then the scrub nurse had to shake you awake. All them young boys, all them boys. The ones who were conscious, I always asked them where they came from, just to get them to talk. White country boys from prairie towns I'd never heard of whose heads couldn't cope with being shut up in some hole in the ground, Hispanics from the barrios acting tough with frightened eyes, black boys who thought I might take special care of them because I knew where they were coming from, and all of them screaming for their mothers, Jesus, or cursing God, and sometimes I'd join in right along with them, curse

147

everything and everyone who had anything to do with the war. Once I had this crazy little Italian guy from the Bronx, stir-crazy with the pain, says he doesn't want any nigger doctor touching him. I leave him with a stump for an arm and two days later he apologizes, tells me I did a good job, and shakes my hand with the one he's left.

'They'd wheel them in on the gurneys, kids with sucking chest wounds, bloody stumps of limbs, multiple frag wounds, and you were supposed to work some magic and piece them together. Sometimes there wasn't anything left to piece together and we'd shoot them full of morphine, tell them everything was going to be all right. Told a lifetime of lies in Nam, enough lies to send me to Hell.'

'You won't go to Hell.'

'You think not?'

'I'm a minister's daughter. I know who goes to Hell and who doesn't. They wouldn't let you in.'

He laughed and his head fell backward where the light yellowed his glasses, then he looked at me more closely. 'You should go home, before it's too late and you've seen too many things you shouldn't.'

'It's already too late, and there is no place I think of as home.'

'Hell, Naomi, if you've got no home that makes you a refugee, so keep drinking that whisky.'

I nodded and took another sip. The hiss of the lamp seemed to have grown louder, the wings of the moths more frantic.

'When they brought in the wounded, the first thing we'd do was split them into groups, separating the no-hopers from the ones who had a chance. You'd only have a matter of seconds to decide. The men who were going to die were called expectants and you'd say something like, "You're in an American hospital and we're going to take good care of you," and then we'd ship them out to where they waited to die. Sometimes it felt that everything in that war was a lie and they'd given me a uniform and made me a part of it.'

'But you helped people too, took away a lot of pain, saved a lot of lives.'

'Sure, we did that. Some days we'd work so long we didn't know whether it was morning or evening, and when the rockets and mortars started landing we'd work on our knees in helmets and flak jackets. But the worst sound wasn't the rockets coming in over the wire but the sound of the chopper's blades and the voice shouting, "Incoming wounded!" And the worst nightmare of all was when you knew it was a Chinook, because those bastards could carry maybe fifty casualties in their belly. And there were times when twenty minutes more sleep seemed more precious than saving someone's life and if you'd been offered the choice you would've turned over and taken the sleep. Hell of a joke, spending all that time fantasizing about sleep, sleeping in some big feather duster of a bed, your woman at your side, and when it's over and it's all there right in front of you, you just can't do it. Always felt like someone, somewhere, enjoyed the joke.'

'And did you have a woman to go home to?'

'Sure did, she stayed all of six months. Went off with a pimp of a salesman who told her she could be the next Diana Ross. I don't blame her though, things weren't always easy and we weren't married or anything. One thing I knew even then – there was enough of Denise to make two Diana Rosses. Every time I see Diana on the TV she looks a skinny bag of bones, and it makes me chuckle when I remember.'

'What happened to her?'

'Last time I heard, she was married and working in a Seven–Eleven store up north. Had a couple of kids.'

'Did the army not give you help, there must have been plenty of others like you?'

'The army kicked my ass out just as fast as they could when they decided I couldn't cut it any more. Me and the army didn't part on good terms. When I came out I did nothing for a long time then had every job under the sun. Anything to pay the rent, buy the beer. Later, when I straightened things out a little, I got jobs in health programmes, mostly inner city jobs they couldn't get anyone else to take.'

'And what about the plants and the painting?'

'Always liked painting. Started to paint plants the first monsoon in Nam. It comes October to January and it doesn't stop for breath. Rain and wind and there isn't a part of you that doesn't feel wet and you can't go the length of yourself without tramping through a sea of mud. For most guys there was only drink, dope and women to help keep their heads together. I wasn't any different, but there was something blew my head more than anything. Maybe you'll think I'm crazy, but I don't have to give a shit anymore about what anyone thinks. You see I've been a city boy all my life, different cities, but all cities are the same and suddenly I'm looking at this world which is green and alive and beautiful, very beautiful. Some guys, it drove them crazy; me, I got a high out of it, seeing it, touching it and then I started to draw it. We had a guy on the base – every base had one – who could get you anything you wanted, and he gets me a kid's paintbox and I spent that first wet season in a little hole painting anything I could get my hands on. Anything that grew. Orchids is my speciality now – I grow them as well. You didn't know there were wild orchids on the Burren? The guys used to call me Vincent, ask me when I was going to slice my ear.'

He glanced at me to see what I was thinking and I looked him in the eye, drained what was left in the glass and held it out for more. And then he asked me about Baran and I told him everything. When I had finished he sat nodding his head as if he understood, but said nothing. I needed words in the silence and so I asked him how people could do that, knowing it was a pointless question, and he took off his glasses and set them on the table, then pinched his eyes with his thumb and finger. 'I've had a long time to think about that but never seemed to get any closer to an answer. Maybe there is no answer.' He flicked a hand up at the moths, momentarily disturbing the tracery of their flight, then hesitated about what he was going to say. 'Out in the field there was a big push on – they flew us in behind the troops. That's when I saw it. I flew in after a guy they called the Axe Man had done his job. Wasn't supposed to be anyone there, guess Intelligence just screwed-up or the Axe Man couldn't read a map. We dropped napalm on them – old men, women, children. There wasn't anything anyone could do when we got there. Worst fucking thing I've ever seen in my whole life. Shook up even the tough shits, and then they rushed us the hell out of there and ordered us not to talk about it. Didn't need that order. Just like it never happened. But sometimes, sometimes even now I dream that smell, dream it like they all do.'

And then I told him about my mother and that day in Derry when she put her foot on the ring. I don't know why but I wanted to tell him and as I spoke he listened, concentrating on everything I was saying and resting his head in his hands as if weary with his own weight. When I finished he tried to pour us another drink but the bottle was empty then, putting on his glasses, he used his forefinger to push them back on to the bridge of his nose.

'Naomi, you're one crazy child. If ever I thought you should go home, now I know it. Have you been listening to me, girl? This is a different world. If you think you can come here, put your foot on the ring and everything will be all right, then you're even crazier than I am. You think hard on what you saw in Baran and forget about that ring. Jeez!' He tried to pour another drink from the bottle he knew was empty. 'You remember what burning flesh smells like and get yourself in the next truck out of here. I'm going any day now, you make sure you're gone before me.'

'Why are you so frightened of your own goodness?'

'Because it's a lie, a fucking lie, and you can do whatever you like to me but don't even for a second think of painting me some sort of halo in that dreamland your head lives in.' And in his anger he swept the empty bottle to the floor. 'You know what I did best in Nam? I helped those boys to die, those lines of expectants, those kids I told we'd take good care of them. I helped them to die. Took away their screams. And at first I did it for them but after a while I did it for me, just for me, because I couldn't bear their pain any more.'

He turned his head and wouldn't look at me. I tried to speak, but he waved me away with a sweep of his hand and as I walked to the door of the tent I paused and looked back to see him staring into the shadows, his head framed by white-winged moths and paintings of plants.

EVERY hour brought new arrivals to Bakalla. Whatever was happening between the rival clans had scared people enough to make them abandon their homes and seek a safer place. There were no tents left, little we could provide for shelter, and by then everything that could have been scavenged or improvised had been picked clean, and so arriving families simply squatted in the dust and marked out a space with the thin spread of their possessions. Sometimes fights would break out over the ownership of something but they would subside almost as quickly as they started, as negotiation restored calm. Apart from the toll the journey had taken, most of those who arrived were in reasonable health and had left homes in villages where there was probably enough food to get by. In coming to Bakalla they had made themselves reliant on the Agency, but their fear of whatever was out there made it impossible for them to return home. At first we tried to keep a record of these arrivals, names, numbers, family relationships, but after a while it proved too time-consuming and eventually we abandoned it.

More children than we could cope with came to the school and Nadra enlisted help to maintain some semblance of order and purpose. But it felt as if we were being slowly over-whelmed. We needed more staff, more resources, but Charlie was pessimistic about the prospect of any early improvement and increasingly irritable and unpredictable in his manner, answering questions abruptly or simply side-stepping them with flippant replies. For a day we lost radio contact with the capital and he stalked up and down, never going out of the clinic or carrying out any medical work.

'What's happening?' Rollins asked him one evening after the compound gates had been closed.

'There's fighting in the capital, areas where it's not safe to travel. All the agencies have been trying to negotiate safe routes from the docks and warehouses but every time they pay out, someone else has joined the queue with their hand out. There isn't enough money to pay all these people any more, and a lot of the food is being commandeered and re-sold on the streets. We'll know for sure in the next forty-eight hours but there's a possibility that all relief agencies will threaten a pull-out if someone doesn't take local control and make the right guarantees. In the meantime we need to be ready to leave here at very short notice. What that means is have a personal bag packed and help get drugs and medical supplies into crates. Everything else stays. It mightn't come to it, because there's still the real possibility of international intervention, but we have to be ready – and under no circumstances should you discuss with anyone outside Agency staff what we've been talking about. Any sort of panic in a situation like this would be absolutely fatal.'

For once Rollins made no comment, seemed to accept what he had heard and made no attempt to ask further questions.

'What happens to Bakalla?' I asked.

Charlie shrugged his shoulders and at first it looked as if he wasn't going to reply, but I asked again.

'Work it out for yourself, Naomi.'

'No, Charlie. I want to hear it from you. What happens to Bakalla?'

I could see Rollins smiling and shaking his head but I didn't care.

'Please answer the question,' said Martine, coming to stand beside me.

'OK, you guys, take it easy. The best that happens is that

eventually people go back to where their villages are, try to make a go of things, or that we get intervention and relief protection and then the Agency pushes in more people and more resources.'

'But what about all those people who came here because they couldn't make a go of it and have nothing now to go back to?'

'If we pull out for any length of time, Naomi, some of those people will die. There's no two ways about it. You think I don't know that? There's still the possibility that food could be air-dropped, but that's messy and without central organization and distribution only the strong survive. But if the word comes from Stanfield we're out of here. We don't have a choice.' He shrugged his shoulders, put on his baseball cap and walked away.

Later that night I slipped through the compound gate and made my way to where Nadra lived. She sat outside her home on a strip of straw matting, trying to read a book by the light of the small fire. I sat beside her and she made me tea. I had brought something for her – a parcel of fruit and some of the daily rations that had been allocated to me. She held them in her hands and looked at them for a long time, and for a moment I thought she was going to give them back.

'You are leaving?' she asked, setting the gifts at arm's length from herself.

'I don't know yet, there is talk of it. It could be soon but no one knows for sure.' I couldn't leave a lie as her final memory of me. 'But if I go, I'll come back, I promise I'll come back.'

'Who can tell the future, Naomi? My father said he would come back.'

We watched the smoulder of the fire for a few moments and then she took a stick and pushed some fragments of wood into the flames.

'Perhaps you and the other women could go on running the school.'

'When there's no food, no one needs a school. I will have to look after my mother and sister, maybe take them to a new place. But she is old now, too old to travel far.'

'There is talk of a United Nations peace-keeping force. If it comes, then we may not have to go.'

'Many people come to our country – the British, the Italians, the Russians – and always they leave. I do not know which is worse, their coming or going. What will happen to Bakalla?'

'I don't know, Nadra. If we have to go then it's possible that aircraft will be used to drop food.'

'And how much food do you think the old and the sick, all the orphans, will get? Only the strong and the greedy will get it.'

'We don't know yet that we're going to leave.'

'But you came to say goodbye.'

'Yes, I didn't know if I'd get the chance or what exactly will happen.'

'Will you go back to Ireland?'

'No, I won't go back to Ireland. This feels more of a home to me than Ireland.'

'It is strange you find a home in a place where people have no homes.'

'Many things in life are strange.'

She nodded and stirred the embers of the fire, trying to coax some final life out of it. I had things I wanted to say to her but I couldn't say them without accepting my departure as inevitable, and so I sat in silence and stared into the fire where the final slivers of wood turned into a fine white ash. When I couldn't put it off any longer I stood up, still unsure of what to say, and she stood too and I couldn't trust my voice, didn't know anyway what to say and so I held out my hand to her and she took it and we shook hands. Then she said something in her own language and as I tried to stem my tears I promised that I would come back and more than anything I hoped that she believed me. I turned to go but felt her hand on my arm and saw her slip the thin gold bracelet off her wrist and hand it to me. I shook my head, but she slipped it on me and I hugged her before I threaded my way back to the compound, stopping once to look back at where she stood in the falling darkness.

There was music coming from the clinic as I entered the compound. The opening door threw a sudden squall of yellow across my path as Charlie stepped out on to the veranda. I knew from his speech and movements that he'd been drinking.

'Where you been, Naomi?' he asked.

'I left something at the school. I wanted to see if it was still there.'

'You've had a wasted journey then, haven't you?'

'Yes, stupid of me.'

'What was it you left?'

'Some books and things.'

'That all?'

'Yes, nothing really important.'

'They're long gone by now, buried out there somewhere, probably be used in the morning to light a fire.'

'Maybe.'

'You know you're not supposed to leave the compound at night. Anything could happen out there. I'd appreciate it if you followed that rule.'

I nodded my head and walked through the corridor of yellow, the bracelet on my wrist burnishing into light.

'Do you want to join me for a few beers? I'm listening to Madam Butterfly – most passionate piece of music there is. Always better to listen to music with company.'

'No thanks,' I said, turning the bracelet on my wrist and walking on.

'I'm a very passionate man,' he called. 'But you know that already, don't you?'

I stopped and looked back to where he stood in the doorway, holding up a bottle of beer in salute. 'You're full of shit,

Charlie,' I called and then walked on to my tent, the sound of his laughter ringing in the silence.

In the morning, word came from Stanfield that no reliable guarantees could be given on our safety. We were summoned to the clinic and told that we were to leave at dawn the next morning, transporting the medicines and portable medical equipment in the truck and jeep. Only those employed in a permanent capacity by the Agency were to be taken. Everyone and everything else was to be left. The utmost secrecy was to be preserved and no obvious packing was to take place until the final moments. Charlie was on a high, bouncing around on his trainers as if he were about to make some big play in the final stages of a game. It was supposed to be a secret but everywhere I looked, every set of eyes I looked into, it felt like they already knew and the guilt of that knowledge seeped into the smallest action. When school ended for the last time I was grateful that Nadra had gone with her mother to the clinic and wasn't there to watch as I took the little that we had and gave it out, making sure that each child got something, however small. Suddenly it seemed the most pathetic of gestures, a pitiful attempt at compensation. They smiled up at me and tugged my trousers with gratitude and each thank-you shamed me. Each smile, each pat I gave in return, became an act of betrayal, and in a short while would be the final confirmation that trust was an act of foolishness.

In our tent, Veronica was excited, glad to be getting out and closer to home. In my head I had often been hard on her, but she had survived like all of us, fighting off her homesickness, her disillusionment and the physical hardships, and I respected her for that. Martine was quiet, hardly saying anything as she threw her few possessions into her bag, not bothering to fold or pack them in any semblance of order. When she had finished she lay flat on her back and smoked a cigarette, blowing out funnels of smoke. I went over and sat at the bottom of the bed, but she didn't acknowledge my presence.

'What's the first thing you're going to do when you get to the capital?' I asked her.

'Have a shower, wash my hair, find clean clothes. Maybe find a man.'

We laughed at her, and Veronica asked her to find one for her, then went to the clinic to collect some personal possessions.

'What will you do, Naomi?'

'Wash my hair for sure, maybe swim in the sea if it's safe. I'd like to see that reef again, spend more time with the proper equipment. It was very beautiful.'

'Yes it was. I'd almost forgotten it. It seems a long time ago.' She sat up on the bed and looked around her. 'Do you think we'll ever come back here?'

'I don't know. It feels too much like we're running away, deceiving them. Do you want to come back?'

'Je ne suis plus sûre de rien. I think I want to go home but part of me says that if I go now, all I'll ever have to remember is Baran. I think I want to put something between me and it, something just as strong to carry with me. I thought I was strong . . .'

'No one should be that strong, Martine. I couldn't even touch the bodies. You were stronger than me.'

She shook her head slowly as if she couldn't accept what I said and, even though I tried, nothing would make her feel better. When she finished her cigarette she turned over on her side and closed her eyes.

After dark, Haneen drove the truck and the jeep to the front of the clinic, but nothing was loaded and they merely sat there in readiness for dawn and our departure. I stood outside our tent, wrapped in a blanket, watching Charlie, Haneen and Aduma moving about in the clinic. Once there was the sound of something being dropped and of breaking glass, but beyond the fence the camp slumbered, only the spasmodic cry of a baby bruising the stillness of the night. I thought of Daniel and the painted print of his hand on the newspaper, the pages of his book flapping open on the wet path to his house. I remembered too the musty smell when my father opened the doors of the church on Sunday mornings, the weight of the silence which seemed to surge around us as I followed his echoing footsteps down the aisle, and I knew what it was I wanted to do.

Wearing the blanket like a cloak, I moved between the fence and the truck, and quietly opened the gate, then headed for the concealing alleyways of the camp. By now I knew the place and found it with little difficulty, helped by the waxy light of the moon, and as I walked I listened for the last time to the low murmur of sleep that came from all around me. When I found them there were more children than I had seen before – maybe as many as twenty. It was hard to tell where one body started and another ended as they squirmed into trapped pockets of warmth under the polythene. I wondered how they protected it, where they hid it during the day. Its tattered ends were weighted with stones and a couple of old tyres. There they slept now like bodies frozen under ice. Ice. Daniel walking across it, it breaking under him, struggling to get out, the coldness of the water. And then I found a space, pulled the blanket tightly around me and lay down amongst them and tried to sleep.

I woke long before dawn with coldness gnawing at my legs and arms, and listened to the snuffle and whimper of the children. Sometimes someone turned restlessly, tautening the polythene and contouring each body into a new shape, or a voice would call out, speaking the language of some broken dream. As I felt the hard press of the ground beneath me I turned on my side and a child snuggled into the hollow of my back, his arm falling across my waist and tightening like a belt. Sometimes he pushed his head into my shoulders, clinging to my warmth and shelter, and I could feel the steady pulse of his breathing on the back of my neck. But soon it was nearly time to assemble and slowly, carefully, I had to ease myself out of the child's grasp, whispering and soothing his disturbance into a new fretful sleep. As I walked the length of sleeping shapes only one face turned towards me, and as I bent down I knew it was one of the blind. Walking back to the compound I felt my footsteps echoing in his head.

Thin spears of pink and yellow were lancing the darkness as I reached the compound, and the hulking shape of the truck loomed large and black, dominating the space in front of the clinic. When I got back to our tent, Veronica and Martine were just beginning to stir, slowly edging themselves into consciousness, and I lay down on my bed still wrapped in the blanket and closed my eyes. Soon I felt Veronica's hand waking me from what she thought was sleep, and as I sat up she stood back from the bed.

'You look like a nun in that blanket, Naomi. Were you cold last night?'

'Yes, I felt cold. Is it time to go now?'

She nodded her head and the three of us got ready, moving silently across each other's paths, delicately circling our consciousness of what was about to happen. Everything I had was already in a bag. I washed, then changed my clothes. It was still cold and I draped the blanket over my shoulders again, then looked about the tent, the bare table, the bed where I had slept. The only things remaining which marked my presence were the ebony mirror frame and Rollins' small painting. There was a tiny sliver of glass still trapped in one corner of the frame and I held it close, angling my reflection into it until I saw again a girl who searched another face, another place, as the grey scrawl of sea and sky seeped into the glass. And in my mouth I tasted again the bitterness of failure.

'We'll come back, Naomi,' Martine said. 'We'll come back.'

I nodded, and placed the frame and the painting in the top of my bag and pulled the draw-string. As I did so Aduma appeared at the tent and told us it was time to eat. The clinic shutters were closed and it was lit by one small lamp low in the corner. When we all sat at the long table the light distorted each face, blurring and bleaching out the features, shadowing the parts blocked from the light. On the table which had been set the night before were bread and jam, grapefruit, milk and tea. I cupped the warmth of the tea in my hands, felt the sugary sweetness flow over the dryness of my throat, but I couldn't eat anything.

'Make the most of this, it could be some time before we have another chance,' said Charlie, peeling the segments of a grapefruit and eating it like an orange. I watched Rollins cutting a slice of bread, his hunched body, the grey swathe of stubble, the knife held delicately in his hand. He looked down at me and his mouth smiled, his eyes lost in the yellow slash of light. 'You should eat something, Naomi,' he said. 'Make the journey easier for you.' I nodded and went on sipping the tea as the stuttering shadows of our hands fretted across the bare walls and ceiling. I kept the blanket wrapped around me and bunched up over my shoulders as Haneen and Aduma started to load the packed crates into the back of the truck. Sometimes Charlie looked up from the table to urge more care with the delicate contents or to ask if they saw anyone moving outside the compound, but beyond the fence everything was quiet. The only sounds were of the crates being lifted into the truck and the scrape of wood on metal as they were slid towards the cab. Through the open doorway seeped the first grainy filament of daylight. It brushed and skirmished with the yellow light of the lamp, thickening and elongating the shadows.

When the loading was finished we stood round the table waiting for our final orders. Veronica started to clear it but Charlie snapped at her to leave it and get our bags into the truck. Haneen was to drive, with Rollins travelling in the passenger seat and everyone else in the back, while Aduma was to follow in the jeep with the medical equipment that could be salvaged. Out in the compound, thin scrags of mist twisted round our legs and the wheels of the vehicles. The sky looked as if it were slowly cracking itself open, with sharpening splinters of pink and yellow breaking free from the darkness. Martine and Veronica climbed into the truck, helped up by Charlie. He held his hand out to me and I could see myself in the mirrors of his eyes.

'I'm not going, Charlie.'

He showed no reaction, as if he hadn't heard, and pushed his hand out towards me again.

'I'm not going with you.'

He pushed his glasses on to his forehead. His eyes looked small and blue, staring at me as if he still wasn't sure what I had said.

'Naomi, I don't need this shit. What do you mean you're not going? Is this supposed to be a joke?'

'No, Charlie, it's not a joke. I'm staying here in Bakalla.'

'Get in the truck! Get in the fucking truck!'

I shook my head. Martine and Veronica came forward and Martine pulled Charlie back, got down and put her arm round me.

'You must come, Naomi. You can't stay here on your own. What will happen to you? You must come.'

'I can't. What happens to me doesn't matter any more. But I can't leave.'

She hugged me, and she was crying and telling me I had to go with them and while Veronica was pleading in the background I tried to explain to her, but there wasn't time or the right words and so I said, 'You'll have to come back now, won't you?' She nodded her head and eventually I persuaded her to get back in the truck.

'Have you gone off your head?' Charlie shouted. 'I'm not leaving you here, get in the fucking truck.'

'You're going to have to, Charlie, because I'm not leaving. Put me in your report as missing property, if you like.'

'Will you stop bullshitting me and get in this truck right now!'

I shook my head again and suddenly Haneen started the engine, slowly cranking it into life until Charlie turned and swore at him, telling him to stop, and it wheezed away again into silence. He called now to Rollins who clambered awkwardly into the back of the truck, his head scraping the tarpaulin cover as he pushed his way through the crates. 'She won't get in the truck.'

'Jeez, Naomi, you're even crazier than I thought you were. Get in the truck, girl. Come home. There isn't anything here for you but a lot of pain, a lot of grief.'

'It's no use, James, I'm not going.'

He held on to one of the metal struts above his head to keep his balance, leaned towards me and whispered, 'You really think you can put your foot on that ring? You really think that?'

I didn't answer as Charlie looked at him in confusion and turned again to me. 'For the last time, Naomi, get in the fucking truck.' Then Aduma called out to him and pointed to the fence where some faces pressed against the wire. From somewhere else came the sound of voices. 'We have to go now, we have to get out of here right now. Please get in the truck before it's too late.'

'It's already too late. Go!'

'You're leaving with us if I have to put you in here myself.'

He called out to Haneen to start the engine and moved to the edge of the truck, but as he prepared to jump down I brought out the knife from below the blanket and he stopped.

'You come anywhere near me and I'll cut you open.'

He looked at the blade and then at me as the exhaust spumed out fumes into the space between us. 'You're crazy, Naomi. Crazy,' he half-laughed.

'Maybe, Charlie, but I'm not leaving.'

He hesitated, looked at the faces gathering at the fence, then dropped his glasses over his eyes and, shaking his head slowly, called out to Haneen to drive and the truck rumbled forward, its long beams of light suddenly filling the dawn with the tremble of moths.

THERE had been no plan, no preparation, and as I stood looking at the open gate of the compound I felt dazed and confused. I stared for a moment at the knife in my hand and the first threads of smoke rising from the camp, then went into the clinic and filled a pillowcase with the little of value that was left. Suddenly I heard footsteps outside and turned to see Nadra standing in the doorway. She looked at me with fear in her eyes as if she had seen some spirit, and I let the blanket fall to the floor and spoke to her until she was sure it was me.

'The truck,' she said, 'you are in the truck. I saw it leave.'

'I didn't go, Nadra. I'm going to stay until they come back.'

She shook her head as if she didn't understand, and as she came slowly closer I could see the fear was still in her eyes, so I took her hand and placed it on my hair and she felt it for a second, moving her fingers through the strands until at last she knew the assurance of her own memory.

'Why did you not go? Did everyone else go?'

'Yes, everyone has gone. I couldn't go – soon I will explain.'

She nodded her head and then she helped me gather up what was left, taking too the uncleared food from the table.

When we had finished she made me drape the blanket round myself, and then I followed her through the wakening camp to where her mother and sister still slept. I lay down on some matting in the corner and drifted into sleep, but a short while later I was jerked awake by a sound that stabbed the senses and seemed to fill each crevice of the shelter. It was one voice and many voices, voices that seemed to come from all around and swoop into each other, inciting themselves to ever higher pitches of intensity and breaking into a remorseless ululating wail.

'They know that everyone has gone. The news has spread throughout the camp.'

'It's the same sound the woman made when we told her the baby was dead.'

'It is the sound of mourning, Naomi.'

I got up and pulled my hair back from my face. 'I'll go and tell them it's only a matter of time before they come back. There's enough food in store to last everyone until that happens. Nobody needs to starve, Nadra. I'll go and tell them now.' But as I tried to leave she put out both her hands to stop me.

'You must not go. You must stay here.'

'I have to go.'

'No, you must stay here. First I will go and find out if it is safe for you.'

When finally she persuaded me to wait I lay down again on the matting, pulled the blanket round me and this time I fell into a deep sleep. When I woke, Nadra was sitting with her mother and sister, all of them watching me. As I sat up she handed me a cup of the sweet tea they liked to drink. Her mother still wore the dark mask of net over her face and I couldn't read her eyes or even guess at what she said. Nadra didn't speak but nodded her head at me in encouragement.

'I must go now and tell them,' I said, 'tell them that there is enough food to last until help comes.'

'There is no food, Naomi – it's all gone. Everything has been taken. There is nothing left. When they heard the news, people broke into the stores and took it all. There is nothing left anywhere. They take the chairs and tables, everything from the clinic. Soon they will begin to take the building itself.'

'Then I must go and talk to them. You must help me explain.'

'No, you must stay – it is too soon for you to go into the camp. Already there has been fighting. You must stay here.'

She told her sister Rula to fill a basin with water and they both came and sat beside me on the matting, then sponged my face and tried to comb my hair with a wooden comb. Sometimes it caught in tats, and when I cringed they laughed and helped each other to untangle the knots. As they worked their mother started to sing – a low song barely rising above speech that seemed to wander into the past, searching through some better store of memory.

'When will I be able to go out?'

'Soon, very soon. I have spoken for you, and many of the women also.'

'Spoken to whom?'

'To the leader of our clan. He knows you are not to blame, says you would not stay if the Agency was not coming back soon. But there are other leaders and other clans in Bakalla, and we do not know yet what they will do.'

I stayed there the rest of the day, and in the evening Nadra told me we must go to see the leader of her clan. She made me wear the blanket and a head shawl and then she gave me a netted face mask like her mother wore. I followed her through the pathways of the camp, strewn everywhere with the remnants of what had been taken from the compound. When we reached a bunched cluster of shelters she told me to wait, then walked into an area lit by a fire where a small group of men sat veiled by smoke, with women and children squatting in an outer circle. I recognized some of the women and many of the children, and as Nadra called me into the light I removed the mask and the head shawl. In the faces of the women I saw no hatred or harm. Some of the children ran towards me but were called back by the oldest man of the group. As he stood up and beckoned me forward, I saw over his shoulder, through the open doorway of one of the shelters, sacks of grain piled high.

Some hens pecked frantically where one of the ripped sacks had left a thin little line.

I stood separated from him by the fire. A small man wearing a green jacket that had come from the clinic. It was too big for him – it might have belonged to Rollins – and the sleeves were rolled into thick folds with his thin shoulders lost inside its breadth. He was older than the others, his hair a skein of white, but his body had a strength and pride and it was clear that those around the circle looked to him with respect. I bowed my head as Nadra spoke to him and he stared at me closely, as if unsure of who I was, then signalled me to sit and gestured for one of the women to bring me tea. With Nadra translating he asked many questions – why the others had left, when they would return, what news I had from the capital. I told him some truths, some lies, and always tried to be positive about the Agency's return. He listened to everything carefully, watching my face as I spoke the words slowly and with as much conviction as I could find. While I spoke I saw for the first time the young men spaced round the rear of the shelters, and the sticks they carried in their hands.

There was one last question. 'Why did you stay?' asked Nadra.

'I have no home now but Bakalla. I have no people but your people,' I said, gesturing round the seated listeners. 'Soon the Agency will return and bring more help. I want to wait here with you.'

As Nadra translated, he scratched his cheek and stared into the fire. When she had finished, there were sudden animated bursts of speech from people in the circle around us. After a few minutes he held up his hand and silenced them before calling Nadra closer and whispering to her.

'He offers you his protection and his friendship. He knows that in the past you have tried to help his people and he thanks you for that. But you must be careful. There are other clans in Bakalla, and he does not speak for them. When you hear news about the Agency or about our country you must tell him, and also tell the Agency that he has given you his protection.'

I bowed my head and thanked him. Suddenly there were cries from beyond the shelters and everyone stood up and ran to where the young men shouted and pointed into the darkness. Someone claimed to have seen members of a rival clan approaching and to have scared them off with his spear, but others shook their heads and said they had seen nothing. Whatever the truth, the incident had shifted attention from me and Nadra took my arm and led me back to her home, insisting once again that I wear the headshawl and the mask. Only when we were sitting outside by the fire that had almost died did she allow me to take it off.

'You thought I was a spirit when you saw me in the clinic, didn't you?'

She denied it, embarrassed by the question. 'I thought you were in the truck. I could not understand how you could be in the truck and in the clinic at the same time, that's all. You think I believe in spirits?'

'What's wrong with believing in spirits, Nadra?'

'You're a teacher, Naomi. You know science. Teachers must help their pupils leave superstitions behind them.'

I laughed gently at her earnestness. 'But don't you sometimes feel something else inside your head, like a spirit or a ghost from the past?'

She looked to see if I was teasing or testing her in some way, then asked, 'Do people in your country believe in spirits, ghosts from the past?'

'Yes, I think some people believe there are things beyond themselves. They call them by different names.'

'In my country, many people believe in spirits. My mother, she believes, but she is old. Many believe in the gelid – this is when a helpless person sends his spirit to trouble the person who has done him harm.'

'Do you believe it can happen, Nadra?'

She shrugged her shoulders and didn't answer. Somewhere in the camp, voices called out to each other.

'Why did you not go in the truck?'

I didn't know how to explain. The voices volleyed back and forward across the night with increased urgency. 'Maybe I have a spirit sent to trouble me. Maybe I thought that staying in Bakalla would get rid of it, make everything right.'

'You think that someone has put a curse on you, someone you have done bad to? But you have not harmed anyone.'

'No, perhaps only a little by my foolishness, the times when I believed stupid things.'

'Then why should their spirits trouble you?'

'I don't know. Maybe it's only in my imagination but sometimes I think of all the people who have . . .' My struggle for an answer was stopped by the sound of someone running through the narrow alleyway, the pound of bare feet in the dust, the heavy draw of breathing, and as the figure passed us close enough to touch we could see the tight press of fear on his face. Then from somewhere behind came the sound of his three pursuers. Even in the thickening darkness we could see the knives in their hands and as their sandals slapped against the soles of their slathering feet we pulled ourselves into the shadow of the shelter. The dwindling smoke from the fire puffed into our faces and I heard the clatter of other feet on a pavement, the slither and scrape as they kicked the crouching figure in the doorway, knew again that there was something which threads and links through time, as real as the bruised prints in the dust. I felt it then as I felt it on a Belfast street, and I was afraid. And as the pounding feet and the knotted, ragged breathing vanished into the heart of the camp we turned our faces away and went inside for shelter, kicking our own dust over the final stirrings of the fire.

Great fault lines slowly began to open in the camp. Ancient feuds that had lain dormant long enough for some to believe they had been forgotten, started to move and shift. A fight at one of the wells, some stolen cattle, a dispute over a sack of grain, the body of a young man found on the river bed with his throat cut. Accusations and counter-claims, funerals and calls for vengeance, the re-formation into tribal enclaves. I watched from behind the mask, moving silently with Nadra's guidance through the areas which were safe for me, and knew that the longer Bakalla went without food and aid, the closer we would slip to disaster.

Sometimes they brought the sick to me and asked for help. Nadra did her best to explain that I wasn't a doctor but they didn't understand, wanting desperately to believe that I had the knowledge that would cure their children, and I touched their heads, a blessing of ignorance, and then they were taken away to live or die. The days passed; the food controlled and distributed by the clan leaders grew more meagre and I watched the children consume it more ravenously. The little I had, I tried to share with the orphans who wandered through the camp begging for scraps and scrambling for cast-offs, but there was never enough. Sometimes they pulled at my pockets, urgency flowing through their thin reeds of arms. Often I turned them away empty-handed and then they would slink off to find shelter from the sun and flies. Most of the people I met were friendly, often offering to share the little they had, but sometimes I met others who cursed me and once as I walked with Nadra from the well, two small children threw stones at me at their mother's prompting until they fled in the face of Nadra's fury.

For a couple of days we tried to organize some place for the children, but we had no equipment or materials and nothing to give them and so the numbers dwindled as they found more immediate attraction in the sense of danger and loosening control that rippled through the camp. Most of their time was spent searching for wood at steadily increasing distances, and the long trudge drained them of their energy and concentration. When they filtered through the camp they were constantly on the look-out for anything that might be useful, and then they fought fiercely with other gangs for possessions of such objects. At the sound of an aircraft they would drop whatever they were doing and flood out onto the plain beyond the boundary of the camp, hoping to see food falling from the sky. But nothing came, and as the days passed I too waited and listened.

Sometimes we would go to the wells with the other women and draw water to wash our clothes. Then for a short while at least I would hear laughter, the ripple and gush of gossip and snatches of song. The heads of children bobbed on the women's backs like seals as they kneaded and pumped the dust out of the clothes, twisting them to tight knots and splashing them against stones. They would ask me questions through Nadra and she would apologize for the ones she considered too personal. Was my father rich? What did he own? What age was I and why was I not married? Was it true that in the West women could take many lovers? I answered everything, sometimes enjoying shocking Nadra and making her give replies that made the women squeal with girlish laughter and clap their hands. Most days when the work was over they would sit in a group and one of the older women would start some story she remembered from the old way of life, often decorating it with sprigs of song, and her listeners would follow intently, constantly nodding their heads in affirmation. At first Nadra tried to translate for me but then I stopped her and tried to listen for the meaning myself, remembering my mother singing in Gaelic as my father listened secretly behind a paper or book. Later Nadra would tell me that the stories were of great wedding feasts, beautiful brides and long journeys across the plains in search of water and grazing; of children born on the way and great warriors of the clan who fought off thieves and bandits and saved the herd. When one teller grew tired another would take up the tale, passing the telling round the circle like drink or sweetmeats, polishing and elaborating on what was already familiar to all. Even then, even in Bakalla, they would sing, and gradually I came to know fragments of the songs, began to grasp some of the complex rhythms, and they would clap their approval as I joined my voice with theirs.

After almost a week had passed I was summoned again by Osiba, the head of the clan. As before, he sat with a group round the fire. When we approached he stood up and gestured to where we should sit. Then from inside the folds of his green jacket he produced a Bible, a small black Bible, and he held it up to me and flicked the pages carefully before speaking.

'He wants to know if this is your holy book,' Nadra said.

I nodded my head, and he asked me to swear on it that I would answer all his questions with the truth. He held it out towards me and I placed my hand on it and swore. When he was satisfied he sat down again but I remained standing, watching him through the smoke.

'Why do your people not come?' he asked.

'I don't know. I think it must be because there is fighting in the capital and they think it's not safe to travel here.'

'What do you know of this fighting?'

'There are many clans who make war with each other. Many people have been killed. They ask the Agency for much money to allow them to bring food into the country.'

'Will the Agency pay this money?'

'If it can. But if there are too many people asking for money, there might not be enough to go round.'

'Why do planes not come as you promised?'

I said I didn't know but I thought they would come soon. After my answers he discussed some things with those sitting closest to him but it was difficult to gauge what was being said, and then he asked me if I was important to the Agency.

'Yes I am, very important,' I lied.

'They would not leave you here if they did not mean to come back?'

'That's right. They will come back for me. They will come back to Bakalla.'

He broke off his questions to discuss my answers and as the exchange became more heated, with voices splintering into each other, Nadra whispered that some of the men thought they should make their way back to their old territories while others argued that it was too dangerous to move outside the camp and they should wait for the return of the Agency. As evidence Osiba held up the Bible on which I had sworn and waved it round the group. Finally there was an uneasy agreement. They would stay and wait, but a couple of the younger men would make the journey and report back on what they found. When the discussion was over, Osiba called for tea and we sat drinking while other business was sorted out. A widow came to ask for his approval of an offer of marriage for one of her daughters, two men sought arbitration over disputed ownership of some goats, and an old man presented an account of a dream he'd had for many nights which he claimed a holy man had interpreted as a portent of coming disaster.

As fireflies bled into the darkness and cicadas locked into their steady scream it seemed that all the business had been completed. But when I gestured to Nadra that we might leave she told me there was something else, and as I felt her hand touch mine I looked up to see a group of young men pushing and pummelling two stumbling figures into the firelight. One of the group carried a machete, another a cane. As they came closer, I saw that their two prisoners were Ahmed and Iman, and I could see also the cord that tied their hands in front of them and linked their ankles. It seemed to pull Iman's legs into even more of a concave bow as he scurried forward, each faltering step or hesitation punished by flat-handed blows to his head. Their guards pulled them into place before Osiba, keeping a tight hold of their arms, and in the light from the fire I could see the bruises on their faces. I went to stand up but Nadra pulled me down as Osiba started to pass his sentence.

They stood with bowed heads as Osiba shouted and pointed at them, his finger jabbing through the smoke of the fire. When I asked Nadra what he was saying she told me that he was telling them of all the punishments that might rightly be given to them, and as words burst about their heads the two boys leaned into each other, fear trembling through their bodies. Before Nadra could stop me I stood up, ignoring her whispered warning and the tug of her hand on my skirt. But I said nothing until Osiba had stopped and turned his focus on me.

'Tell him I wish to speak for them.'

She shook her head and tugged again at my skirt, but I shouted at her to tell him and she did what I wanted. The two boys turned their heads and saw me for the first time before slaps drove their gaze to Osiba again. He beckoned me forward and silenced the shouts of dissent which came from some of those seated closest to him.

'What is it you wish to say? They have admitted their guilt. It is right for them to be punished.' As Nadra finished his words she shook her head at me.

I tried to ask that he would show mercy to them because of their age, because they had no families. I told him how they had helped with the school and looked after the younger children, that I would take responsibility for their future good conduct. As Nadra translated, he shook his head slowly and turned his eyes from me to stare into the fire. I grew more desperate, started to promise things I couldn't deliver, talking as if the Agency would return at any moment, listing the special privileges he would receive. Finally I ran out of words and Osiba silenced me with a dismissive sweep of his hand. Some of those around him were shouting at me, plucking little handfuls of dust and throwing them into the space between us, while impatience bristled in the bodies of those guarding the boys.

The young man with the machete turned it in the air, cutting the drifting smoke of the fire, and again Nadra pulled at the hem of my skirt but I remained standing.

There was more discussion, more argument, and sometimes shouting broke out between opposing factions. Ahmed tried to look at me again but received another blow to the side of his head and then I saw that Iman was crying, lifting his bound hands to wipe away his shame. Some kind of decision was reached and agreement ricocheted round the nodded heads, with those who were opposed either shrugging their shoulders in resignation or spitting on the ground in open disgust. I was called in front of the fire again. As Osiba stood, one of the sleeves of his jacket rolled down over his hand and he struggled for a second to fix it. The two boys were known thieves and had stolen food from the mouths of those who needed it, he said. Justice demanded that they be punished for their sins and that others know that they had received punishment as a warning and an example. I felt Nadra's hand touch my back as she told me that he had heard my words and that this time, but only this time, their crime would be punished by a caning. But there was a condition to this lesser punishment. I turned and looked at Nadra's face to confirm in her eyes what I had heard. 'Do it or it will be worse for them,' she whispered. 'Do it, Naomi, you must do it.'

In the corner of my eye, I saw the firelight edging the machete, saw the resolution in the tier of faces, and knew there was no other way. So I stretched out my shaking hand and took the offered cane as the boys were made to kneel in the dirt and darkness, their ragged shirts ripped from their backs.

'You must do it with all your strength until you are told to stop. Do it, Naomi, or it will be much worse for them.' And so I cut the cane across their backs, cut it again and again until their screams mingled with the shouts of exhortation and my breathless, sobbing cries.

THERE was a raised tracery of red weals fanning across their backs, and they winced and squirmed face-down as we tried to salve them with cream salvaged from the clinic. On Ahmed's back one of the ridges had slit open where several strokes had fallen across the same line, blood oozing out as I tried to clean it. His whole body stiffened under my touch and all the time I kept saying, 'I'm sorry, I'm sorry,' trying to make my touch light and expressive of what I felt. Iman turned his head away as Nadra worked but I could see the shiny slither on his cheek where his tears slid into the dust. Their wrists and ankles were rubbed raw, making it look as if they wore manacles. I kept willing a face to turn to me, a face like Daniel's in the doorway, which would draw me in and smile up at me and tell me that everything was all right. But there was no absolution, only the constant flinch and tightening of broken flesh. And behind her mask, Nadra's mother sat rocking, cocooning her spirit in some incantation of the past, the low drone of her voice unrelenting and unforgiving.

In the morning I went with Nadra to one of the wells and stood in the long line which had already formed, hoping to miss the heat of the day. I wore her clothes, the head covering and mask, and for the first time I was glad because it served to hide me from the world. Sometimes young children chased each other through the queue and were shouted away as they threatened to topple the containers, but we held tightly to our silence, shuffling forward slowly over the threadbare earth.

It was when we were close to the well that we heard the

sound of approaching trucks. At first in my confusion I thought it was the return of the Agency, but then we heard the shots fired and as Nadra pointed, I saw three vehicles moving slowly through the camp towards the compound. The first one was what they call a technical – a small truck with a machine-gun mounted on the roof of the cab, the sunlight bouncing off the brown and gold belt of bullets which trailed like teeth from the gun's mouth. Behind the cab huddled four men, their arms draped across each other's shoulders. They wore a mixture of army uniforms and T-shirts, with either black berets or baseball caps on their heads. Behind was a larger truck, crowded with more men, all hanging on to whatever support they could find as it bounced over the potholes and rutted pathways. Among them we saw the two young men who had been sent to scout their former homeland. Some of the soldiers fired Kalashnikovs into the air and there was laughter on their faces as children scrimaged to retrieve the spent shells. Last came an open jeep with another tight hive of men hanging on to each other for balance. When they pulled into the compound they jumped down and while some guarded their position, pushing the barrels of their guns through the holes in the fence, others pressed forward into the clinic, buildings and tents. Slowly, and with a mixture of caution and curiosity, the people of Bakalla walked towards the fence, led by the excitement of the children. The shooting had stopped and the faces of the soldiers seemed to invite the people forward. Some of them called for water and as it was poured through the fence they drank it greedily and splashed it over their faces or doused their heads, shaking off the excess with sharp flicks of their necks.

They were young mostly, a couple still probably in their teens, and the black sheen of their weapons contrasted with the ragged variety of their clothing. I watched with Nadra from the back of the growing crowd as an older man in a tailed beret came out of the clinic and climbed on to the back of a truck to address the camp-people, shouting through cupped hands to make himself heard. They brought no harm to anyone, they were friends of the people. They had come to give protection from those who had done things like at Baran. They would hunt them down and punish them like the dogs they were. He talked of the future, the need to build a strong country free from foreign influence and control, told them that the Agency had deserted them, that they must rely on themselves from now on. That the foreigners sought only to make them weak and divided.

When he had finished the people stood motionless, staring impassively, as if they were still straining to hear his words. He turned for a moment to speak to those who had carried out the searches, and his frustration was obvious when it became clear that the compound held nothing but empty buildings. Then, calling for the leaders of the camp to come forward and meet with him in the clinic, he warned the people that they must be on their guard against the renegades who had attacked Baran, that an attack could come at any moment and they needed to be alert and report anything suspicious that they saw or heard. When he climbed down he was replaced by one of the younger soldiers who sprayed a burst of automatic fire into the air then held the weapon in one hand and punched it into the sky. Some of the crowd cheered, but others shrank into themselves before drifting away.

When the leaders of the clans reported back it was to tell the camp-people that a tithe of food was required, and was to be brought to the compound that evening. There was a list of other things that were required in the way of equipment. That night the compound was lit by a large fire over which a goat was roasted, and as the flames and smoke scuttled skyward they revealed the silhouettes of guards perched on the roof of the clinic, their arms and chins resting on the guns they cradled in their laps. Later, as the fire started to subside, some of them came into the camp looking for women, content at first to persuade with promises of food and money, but when this failed there was the sound of screams and shouting as women were taken by force. Once a clatter of gunfire ripped the night, a final angry assertion of will, and when later all fell silent the camp drifted into a sleep haunted by dreams and memories of Baran.

In the morning, smoke still curled from the ashes of the fire and on the roof of the clinic a solitary figure hunched in sleep, his body skewered by the line of his gun. From the frayed edges of the camp began the first slow run of families, their possessions strapped to their backs or balanced on their heads. Small children carrying their own weight struggled to balance themselves. At times, something would slip, opening a gap in the line as the straggler sought to redistribute his burden and scurried forward to make up ground. Others stood in motionless groups, watching the departures, their thoughts lost in the frieze of faces. More families appeared from various parts of the camp, heading in different directions but all distinguished by the same sequence and rhythm, their slow progress tainted by resignation and uncertainty. Sometimes the lines and directions intersected, weaving a pattern across the open plain that spoke momentarily of purpose and order, but then the lines would circle or suddenly collapse in a huddle on the ground.

As we watched, the jeep and technical drove out of the compound at speed, their wheels slewing up showers of dust, brakes squealing, as they pushed a horn-pumping path through the alleyways of the camp, threatening to collide with the fragile shelters. Breaking free, they bounced and bucked over the uneven ground, weaving through aisles of thorn trees and groves of spiky aloes. In the back the soldiers clung to each other in a tight scrum, one arm around their neighbour for balance, the other pointing out the snail-trails of departing families. They swept round in front of the largest groups, blocking their path and shouting at them to return to the camp. Shots were fired into the air and possessions were shed or dropped as the families fled back towards Bakalla, the single file fanning out in panic, small children being carried by parents or left behind to cry out in terror. Again and again the vehicles circled round departing families, and each time the effect was the same until the plain was filled with the return of running, stumbling people, desperate to re-enter the shelter and anonymity of the camp. We watched too, as one small group was made to kneel in the dust and a soldier urinated on them from the back of the jeep.

An hour later everyone was summoned to the compound fence to hear the commander tell them that no one was to leave without his permission. They were under his protection and he could not guarantee their safety outside the camp. They must stay in Bakalla until he told them they could leave. There were many dangerous and armed bands in the surrounding area who would kill them and steal everything they had. If they waited in Bakalla he would arrange for food to be brought from the capital, from the warehouses and docks his people now controlled. Those who did not obey his orders would be punished. His speech ended with the firing of more guns into the air, and their stuttering recoil as they fell back like lovers into the young men's arms.

Families still left, but at night. The camp was too big to police the boundaries effectively, even though they tried. Families vanished into the darkness, their departure marked only by the soft scuffle of feet, the clink of pots, a nervous guiding whisper, and in the morning their empty shelters were dismantled or claimed by others until there was nothing left to show that they had ever existed. Nadra's clan met to discuss whether they too should go, but they had many old people in Bakalla and it was decided that for the moment they should stay.

During the day I stayed mostly in the shelter, at Nadra's insistence, until the sweltering heat turned it into an airless crucible. Then she would reconnoitre and, if it was safe, walk with me or lead me to where the other women met. And always I wore the mask and the cover of her clothes. At unpredictable times the soldiers would patrol the camp, their eyes exploring people and possessions and storing whatever knowledge was useful to them. The children would imitate their swaggering walk with fearful admiration, and sometimes they would be allowed to touch the guns. I remembered the boy in the airport who had pointed his wire gun at me, and soon the children of Bakalla too began to fashion their own weapons, firing them in simulation of their sound and movement. Many of these children had come to the school.

Perhaps it was one of the children who told; perhaps it was someone from a rival clan. Everyone was summoned to the compound by the firing of shots, and the leader of the soldiers spoke from the truck, his words spreading out across the serried rows of listeners who passed them back to those too far away to hear for themselves. They knew that a European was hiding in Bakalla, a worker from the Agency, no harm would come to her if she came forward, they wanted to talk with her, send her back to her own people. She must be brought to the compound right away. All those standing around me knew who I was but no heads turned to look at me and no one spoke as the crowd started to disperse.

We sat in the shelter that had become my home. Nadra's mother was sleeping while Rula fanned the flies away from her face. 'You must not go,' Nadra said. 'You must not go to them. It is not safe for you to go to them,' her fingers plucking out her insistence on the ground.

'Sooner or later they will find me. Someone will show them where to look.'

'You have been given the protection of our clan. No one in it will betray you.'

'But there are others outside the clan who also know I am here. They have no reason to protect me. Maybe I should leave during the night, slip away with some of the others.'

'No one will take you, Naomi. No one will take another mouth to feed or risk the anger of the soldiers. You must stay here and hide with us. Perhaps they will leave soon, there is nothing in Bakalla for them. Soon they will grow tired and then they will leave. Maybe the Agency will come back and we will be teachers again.'

I nodded, but as the days passed I began to doubt the Agency's return.

At first, the searching seemed completely random, with groups of soldiers selecting a shelter and ordering everyone outside before ransacking and looting everything of value. Where they met with protest or any semblance of opposition they lashed out with their feet or the butts of their weapons, and sometimes when they had finished searching they smashed and toppled the flimsy structure into the dust. As it went on they grew more angry at their failure, more ready to inflict punishment on those they believed to be helping their prey evade capture. At midday, when the sun was at its most fiery, we were summoned to the compound. It was safer to mix with the flow of the people than risk staying in the shelter and being discovered by the following sweep of searchers, so I stood in one of the tight huddles of women with my head bowed and face and hands covered.

The anger in his voice and body made Nadra's translation unnecessary. I had to be given up immediately and those who were hiding me were enemies of the people whose souls had been bought with foreign money. Too much time had been wasted in searching and if I was not given up, all those who helped me would be punished as traitors. When I heard this I tried to speak to Nadra, but she silenced me with the clutch of her hand on my arm and I felt the other women press closer to me, screening and strengthening me. Then, when he had finished, three soldiers climbed into the truck and sprayed round after round over the people's heads. There was panic as people turned to run or flung themselves to the ground, and the air was filled with the sound of children crying. Again I told Nadra that I must give myself up, but the women bundled me away, brushing aside my words with their own.

Afterwards the searching became more systematic, with small areas of the camp sealed off and no one allowed to enter or leave, and each search ended with the cries of women and children. Always they demanded *khat*, and when there was none to give they vented their anger on the shacks, laughing when they collapsed. It seemed only a matter of time before they found me, and I decided I must risk leaving the camp by night rather than bring punishment to more people. I knew Nadra would try to stop me but there seemed no other way.

As I sat planning how I should deceive her, two young women burst into the shelter. The soldiers were coming; they were sealing off a large area and we would be caught inside that ring. Nadra's mother broke into a rising wail, her hands lifting and falling in lament, and Nadra was angry with her, telling Rula and the two young women to take her to another shelter. They led her stumbling and protesting through the doorway, and in that moment I looked at Nadra in the half-light and told her that I must go to the soldiers before they found me. But she was angry, telling me that perhaps it would be possible to slip through the circle and out into the sheltering scrub of the plain. Then other women came to the doorway to report and there was an argument and rising anger in the exchange before it suddenly subsided and they all turned to look at me.

I took off all my clothes as I was told and sat naked while they stared at my skinny white body, then Nadra told me what was going to happen. When I told them I wanted to go to the soldiers they silenced my words and shook their fingers at me as if I were the most foolish of their children, and I bowed my head and accepted the reassurance offered by the touch and pat of their hands. I lay down on the woven bed of matting where Nadra's mother slept each day and looked up at their faces bending over me. Their eyes were the last thing I saw as they rolled and wrapped me in the fibrous webbing, then tied the top and bottom with rags and girded the middle with a knotted rope. I felt their hands lifting me but my eyes distinguished only a flecked and grainy patina of light. My arms were pinned tightly to the sides of my body and my head could only move a couple of inches to either side. When they carried me through the doorway of the hut I felt that I might suffocate, but knew too that if I panicked I would scream and those screams would bring punishment for all who had helped me.

I thought desperately of other things, tried to focus my mind on anything that would distract me for even a few moments. I felt the cool rush of the sea as it engulfed my body and washed me clean and whole. Diving below the shimmer and swell of its surface, drifting once again through those arching corridors of coral. I closed my eyes, shut out the grainy press of matted light and tried to see again its colours, touch the verdant bushes and the gold tracery fine as filigree. Someone stumbled, and I heard a breath of voice at my ear, felt the firm press of a hand. I wanted to cry out and kick my body free but I couldn't and so I flicked my feet in the water, pushed my body through the caverns of coral. Breathing, breathing gently, slowly gliding in the slipstream of water, feeling its coolness on my face. I chanted a mantra of silent words to myself – O'Grady says do this, O'Grady says do that, O'Grady says do this. Then I heard the women's song twist itself through my head and I tried to follow its slow lamentation. I remembered lying in my bed with the shuffling sea outside and the voices filtering up from the radio in the kitchen. The slow process of my father between hedgerows flecked with white. My mother brushing my hair, her voice singing of some other world. Then suddenly the song of mourning collapsed into a ululating wail as I was lowered into the place of the dead.

Wrapped in my shroud I could see it only in memory. At first it had lain beyond the camp but as Bakalla grew, the distance between them had disappeared until it squatted on the very rim of the living. A place of open graves which could not be shovelled shut until they contained their fill of bodies, where a marked plot or a coffin were things unknown. They brought the bundles wrapped in their sleeping mats, tied and trussed, and there they lay until bloated and ready to burst, waiting for the grave to be filled. I lay on my back on the hard earth and felt the heat of the sun worm its way through the matting and saw the flies moving across my face like writing across paper.

Separated and shrouded from the living, I tried desperately to catch sounds from the outer world, but the voices of the women had gone, Nadra's promise that they would return as soon as it was safe the last words I had heard. I tried to focus on my breathing, to force myself into a steady calming rhythm, and hoped that they would come back soon. I wanted to touch the gold bracelet I wore on my wrist, but couldn't move my arms.

For a long time I lay in the place of the dead, and then I was not alone any more for beside me were the two soldiers whose bodies were left on waste ground, the baby we buried in the dirt, the old woman and the young girl of Baran. My father too, his eyes full of the sea, his head crowned with weed and shells. We lay together in the place of the dead as the black fly-writing scribbled across my face and I breathed the woven fibrous membrane which separated me from the world. I heard their voices calling to me, speaking my name, but the words were lost in the swirl and cadences of the women's song of grief and I struggled again and again to hear what they were saying but always it faded into the rush of my breathing and the rising beat of my heart. And then above me, standing around the grave, I saw the hunched figure of McCarroll; the young boy who spat in my face and called me 'a Fenian bitch'; the ring of men in Derry, their broken shapes reflected in the black skin of the cars. And their voices join in my obituary – 'short and sweet, good enough for her' – and they drop soil on my corpse and curse me with their laughter.

I started to struggle, trying to free my arms and rip the covering from my body, but then I thought of Nadra and gradually forced myself into a broken calm, my body into stillness. And so I lay for a long time, trying only to resist the rising pressure of heat which streaked my body with sweat and left me dehydrated and dizzy, desperate for water. Then, as I started to grow faint and think that I would suffocate, I suddenly felt hands opening the shroud and heard voices talking to me. They helped me sit up and washed and dressed me but let me drink only a little at a time. A damp cloth was pressed against the back of my neck and hands helped rub the circulation back into my arms and legs. I tried to stand up but my legs buckled under me and then as they continued to minister to me I looked round the women's faces. I felt dizzy again and splashed water into my eyes and attempted to focus once more on the faces. I listened to the voices murmuring all around me and tried to pick hers out but couldn't, and then I asked for her by name but there was no reply and when I called out more loudly, the women fussed round me trying to distract me with their kindness and the hush of their voices.

They had taken her to the compound. Someone had told them that she spoke English and had worked with me in the school. Too frightened to protest directly, they could only watch as she was led away. Now there was no choice. When I was able to stand, I told them that I must go to her, get them to free her. They didn't try to stop me but as I looked at their faces I saw only sadness in their eyes and an unspoken acknowledgement that the decision was mine alone. Silently they stepped back, opening up my path, and I walked through them and down the narrow alleyways which had hidden me. I passed houses which had been broken and toppled during the search, and the families rebuilding them stopped and watched me in silence. Once, two small children came running to greet me, but a father's voice summoned them back. An old man, a stretched frailty of peeling papery skin, lifted his lolling head from his chest to utter some blessing or curse.

The soldier on the roof of the clinic saw me first, and as I walked into the clearing in front of the compound he stood up and shouted to those below. At the open gate they swarmed out, holding their guns in readiness but no one came close or tried to place me under his control. I kept on walking; past their staring faces, and then one of them made a joke and they laughed and someone shouted and there was more laughter.

He was waiting for me on the veranda outside the clinic, flanked by two of his men. When I reached him, I bowed my head and told him my name, then gave my nationality as Irish. At first he didn't understand, asking again and again if I was American or English. It felt safer to be Irish, less important, and finally he understood what I was saying but there was suspicion in his eyes.

'Where have you been hiding?' he asked.

'Outside the camp. In the bush.'

'Who has helped you hide?'

'No one. No one has helped me.'

He smiled his disbelief and said something in his own language to the soldier beside him and they looked me slowly up and down, feeling no need to disguise the intensity of their examination.

'Why did you come here?'

'Because I heard you were looking for me and that you would do me no harm.'

'Who told you this?'

'Some children. I do not know their names.'

'Why do you wear the clothes of my people?'

'I have no other clothes. I wish to be as one of your people.'

He shook his head as if denying the possibility of such a thing, and then broke into conversation with the two soldiers, emphasizing his points to them with slashes of his hand through the air. For the first time I was able to look openly at him, and saw that he was tall, with a sinewy body that didn't fill his uniform, and just below his high-pointed cheek bones his skin was marked by dark ridges that looked like tribal incisions. As he grew more animated his right hand moved rapidly, like a tongue, its speech full of urgency. Once he looked briefly at me and pointed, his finger insisting on something to the other men. I shifted slightly and silently, trying to see past their bodies and into the shadows of the clinic, but as the argument ran on they moved constantly, readjusting and realigning themselves with their differing points of view. Finally it was finished and as they turned again to me, whatever divergencies had existed had vanished, replaced by a cohesion that showed itself in the way they angled themselves to each other.

'There are many questions. You must answer everything with truth.'

I nodded, following when he motioned me into the clinic. As I stepped into the cooler, shadowy air, at first I saw only the two soldiers slouching on the chairs, their guns resting on the floor and held loosely between their knees. I tried to hide my desire to rake the room with my eyes, knowing that my indifference would serve her better than my concern, but as they gestured me to a seat, my eyes found her where she stood with her back against the wall, half in shadow and half in the light of the open doorway, and in the seconds before I turned my glance away I saw the cut and bruise of her face. She didn't look at me but stared at the floor, holding herself motionless and silent as if part of the wall itself.

He stood a few feet in front of me looking down, and I tried to hide my fear and look openly at him without bowing to the weight of his gaze or trying to evade it. Other soldiers came and stood in the spaces of the room, and the scent of their sweat mingled with the cold oiled smell of their guns. One of them sat jangling a bunch of keys he had found in a drawer.

'Why did the Agency leave?'

'After what happened in Baran they were frightened. They were given orders to leave because it wasn't safe.'

'Where is your passport and your belongings?'

'They were all taken on the truck.'

'Why did you not go also?'

'I don't know. I wanted to stay and help the people of Bakalla.'

'Are you a doctor?'

'No, I am a teacher.'

'Have you food?'

'No, I have no food.'

'Then how can you help Bakalla?'

'I don't know. I was confused. I just wanted to stay.'

The bunch of keys jangled more loudly. Over his shoulder I could see only the part of Nadra's face that was in shade. He came closer, blocking her out.

'Perhaps you are a spy left to report to the enemies of our country.'

'I am not a spy.'

'Where is your radio?'

'I have no radio. I am not a spy, I am a teacher.'

He took another step towards me, and when he spoke I felt the angry warmth of his breath. 'Tell me the truth. Why did you stay in Bakalla?'

'I stayed because I was ashamed to leave, because I wanted to help.'

He shouted an order, and one of the soldiers grabbed Nadra and pummelled her forward, almost making her fall to the ground. Then they pushed her to her knees in front of me and pulled back her hair so that her beaten face was raised towards me, but still her eyes refused to meet mine. I turned my gaze away from her and back to him.

'She taught in the school. She is your friend.'

I shook my head, saying she meant nothing to me, that she was of no importance and they should let her go. Above us, a soldier was walking on the tin roof, each step rattling in the snatch of silence. The leader stretched out his hand and lightly touched a strand of my hair, then quickly pulled away again. Suddenly he was shouting at me in his own language, and at his order they pulled Nadra off her knees and lifted her on to the trolley that served as an examination bed in the clinic. I told them again that she was of no importance, that she had done nothing wrong, but the rising panic in my voice betrayed the truth, and as they pinned her arms to her sides he turned again to me.

'You are a spy.'

'No, I'm not a spy. I am a teacher.'

And then they pulled away her lower clothing, and at first she didn't struggle or make any sound but suddenly she started to squirm and tried to free her limbs from their grasp, but they held her more tightly and as he took his gun from its holster and placed it between her open legs, she fell back motionless, only her broken, frightened breathing pleading for release.

'Tell me the truth.'

He pushed the gun against her and then, looking at me, started slowly to enter her, turning the butt from side to side, until over the top of her rising cries I screamed for him to stop and as they turned their excited faces towards me I shouted, 'I am a spy, I am a spy!'

THEY shut us in one of the buildings that had been used as a store for food. It was empty now; only some ripped hessian sacks making a mosaic of the earthen floor, and the sprinkled flecks of grain like dried-up confetti, indicated its former use. The walls were bare, unplastered blocks of concrete, and where they met the tin roof there were regular ventilation gaps which let milky-white light filter into the darkness. Nadra sat slumped against the back wall with her face pushed into her raised knees. She hadn't spoken or looked at me since we had been locked inside, the laughter of the soldiers and the clang of the metal bucket they had thrown after us our final contact with the world outside. When I knelt down beside her she didn't move or turn her head, but slowly I felt her body lean into mine and I put my arm round her and cradled her. Sometimes the silence was broken by voices shouting in the compound, and once there was the sound of an engine starting and driving away. But when they faded there was only Nadra's broken breathing and the fistle and scurry of a rat down in one of the far corners of the shed as it sought out the remnants of the grain. Sometimes it seemed she was asleep, but then she would move her hands or nestle her face more tightly in the cushion of her knees. A long time passed until, able to stand it no longer, I knelt in front of her, my face close to her bowed head.

'I'm sorry, Nadra, I'm sorry.' But the words seemed only to freeze her even stiller, pull her body into a tighter knot. I was close enough to see the rucked and mottled bruising on her cheek, the swollen cut in the corner of her mouth, and I stretched out my hand and touched her chin, slowly raising her face until it was level with mine. But her eyes still wouldn't meet mine, staring instead into the layered pools of shadows at the base of the wall. 'I'm sorry. I'm really sorry.' And then it broke inside her and she started to cry, but silently, until everything inside her was subsumed into the shudder of her body and her hand clamped itself to her eyes trying to staunch the tears that washed the bruise of her skin. I whispered it again and again and then I took her hand away from her eyes and held it to my lips and she looked at me for the first time and when I held out my arms she came into my embrace. I held her gently, until her sobs broke free, her cries beating like startled birds into the hollow spaces of the shed and echoing back from the corrugated roof. As I rocked her I talked, told her that everything would be all right, tried to ease the shudder out of her body with the only salve I had, until gradually it seeped away and she slipped into a steady rhythm of breathing. Using the hem of my skirt I cleaned the smear of tears, careful to avoid the pummelled, livid bruise of her cheek. As the pearly light squirmed into the shed, opening the shadowy corners and lightening the dark bevel where floor and wall met, we sat with our backs against the wall, and then I gathered the hessian sacks and made a bed for her, covered her with them as she lay with her head in my lap.

She dozed a little, sometimes speaking in her sleep, her body twitching then searching out a new position as she sought respite from her dreams. Once a rat came close, snuffling and sniffing for grain, and I threw a stone at it, sending it scuttling away into a dark corner. Then finally she curled into herself in a deeper sleep.

Their questions had gone on a long time, the same ones over and over, things about which I knew nothing but for which I invented answers, guessing at what they wanted. At first they assumed I had some close knowledge of the changing political situation and the West's response. It seemed foolish to know either too much or too little, so I tried to strike a middle course, but as the night wore on their aggression drained away and I think they knew I had told them the truth when I said I was a teacher. They asked questions about the West and the way people lived, the things a man might own, the position of women. Sometimes there would be discussions about what I had said and, when the leader's questions dried up, others would clamour to ask theirs, using the translation of my replies as proof of their own knowledge, to score points off their comrades. Then they concentrated on establishing exactly which agency I worked for and where it had its base in the capital. Eventually, I understood that they would hold me until they could extort as much money as possible. I tried to ask the leader for Nadra's release, promising that I would co-operate with them, but he dismissed my pleas and I knew that they valued her ability to speak English and the leverage with me she gave them. As the questions went on I watched two of the soldiers share out half a dozen stems of *khat* which they carefully unwrapped from a banana leaf, peel off the leaves and bite into the stems. Soon their jaws were working it into a green paste and spitting out the excess from time to time on the clinic floor. One of them came over to me and offered a stem, his lips flecked with green, and the others laughed until the leader's angry shouts silenced them again.

I looked round their faces, the faces of young men. When I stared at them, they were embarrassed by my gaze and turned their eyes away, preferring to study me from the safety of the group, but I saw too the excitement that their sense of power over me gave them. A couple were no older than Iman and Ahmed, carrying themselves and their weapons with self-conscious nonchalance, proud of their election to manhood but betraying themselves with expressions and movements which belonged to childhood. I wondered with what zeal they had sought to impress the older men, what it had cost them to win their spurs, and saw, when they became bored, how their attention turned to their guns, the soft caress of their hands as they balanced them in their gentle grasp. Others rummaged in the cupboards and drawers of the clinic, inspecting the little that was left with curiosity and stashing objects in their pockets.

When the interrogation was over and the leader had walked out to the compound, one of them came over and sat on the chair opposite me. He wore a green T-shirt and a red cotton macawis and his gun rested across his lap. He said nothing for a few moments, then asked me the name of my country.

'Ireland, I come from Ireland.'

'Where is your country?'

'Ireland is an island close to England. It is a small country.'

I don't think he understood but he nodded his head as if I were telling him something he already knew. I asked him where he had learned to speak English, and eventually I grasped that he had worked in the docks. Before the fighting he had been given a job in the customs office. When the fighting was over, he would go back to it.

'Why did you come to our country?'

'I came to help your people, people who have no homes or food.'

He shook his head. 'You want to buy our people with your food, you want to make them your slaves, to have power over us. Now we take our country back,' he said, patting the gun on his lap.

'How will you help the people of Bakalla? These are your people, how will you help them with that?'

'Bakalla?' he said, and spat on the floor. 'They have made themselves weak. They deserve nothing. They bring shame on us.'

I saw the anger in his eyes and said nothing, turning my head away to watch one of the soldiers squirt water from a syringe at where Nadra slumped on the floor. From the compound came the sound of voices and beyond the fence the low murmur of the camp itself. Above our heads, the sentry walked across the roof.

'You are a spy. We can shoot spies,' he said, searching my face.

'I'm not a spy. You know I'm not a spy.'

He shrugged his shoulders as the man with the syringe came over and stood by my side and squirted water on my cheek. I wiped it off and turned to look at him. His eyes were fixed on the gold bracelet on my arm. The soldier opposite smiled a little and leaned forward on his chair.

'You are frightened? He has killed many people.'

I said nothing and tried to keep looking at his face, but the soldier with the syringe grabbed my wrist and I pulled my arm away. He tried to grab my wrist again, pulling me towards him by the hair, but stopped suddenly as the soldier in the red macawis jumped from the chair and knocked his arm away. They shouted at each other, standing almost toe to toe, then pulled apart, and as their hands tightened on their guns the other soldiers jumped up in readiness, their voices joining in the argument. But just as it seemed that a sudden movement might start them shooting, the leader burst into the middle of them, screaming and pushing them apart, ordering everyone into the compound, shoving those whose exit wasn't quick or submissive enough. Then he too went outside and there was the sound of more shouting, until eventually a kind of calm settled, broken only by the short snap of his final orders and the rush of feet.

When he returned his face was glazed with sweat and he stared angrily at me as if I had provoked the soldiers. He said nothing as he turned his back and leaned against the door frame. A thin dark gully of damp ran down his shirt, and his shoulderblades pushed at the thin stretch of cloth as he scanned the world beyond the fence, and when he moved his face the light caught the black flanges on his cheek. He seemed to have slipped into his own thoughts for a few moments, oblivious to anything else. When he turned to look at us his gaze passed over me and lingered on Nadra, who sat still and silent on the clinic floor. He spoke to her in their own language, but she didn't lift her head to look at him and when he stretched out his hand, almost gently, to touch her, her body squirmed away and he pulled back again. As he walked towards the door he glanced at me and I felt his hatred, his blame for what he had done. He hurried into the compound and then there was the angry shout of his voice and a few minutes later two soldiers bundled us out and locked us in the shed.

The shed where Nadra slept under hessian sacks with her head in my lap, and where I sat with the coldness of the wall seeping slowly into my back. Flowing about me was the malleable light. I felt I could stretch out my hand and scoop a cold handful of it, let it trickle through my fingers. To let yourself be carried by a current, to stop struggling against it and let yourself be carried further and further out, must be a beautiful thing. No need to think or struggle any more, the coldness numbing and anaesthetizing. There would be no flash of past life or memory, only the letting go, the sweet joy of letting go, the first time in life when you could give yourself entirely. But they had found him in the end, tangling him in the trawl of their nets, pulling him back into the world. White blossom on the hedgerows brushing the black coats of the procession. In the house, the sudden empty spaces where the present re-formed and settled in a new pattern, old lineaments blurring and realigning. Our laughter fountaining above our heads before falling back silent as snow. And into the shed flowed the silver light, a swirl of sea, and I wanted to give myself to it, to stop struggling and drift beyond even the reach of the nets, beyond the taint and tug of fear. But in my lap she moved her head and I looked down at the stain of her cheek and knew it couldn't be.

Towards dawn she woke, looked up at me and for a second

strained to remember where she was, but her hand brushed her face, she remembered and shivered. I smoothed her hair and pulled the sacking on to her shoulder and she closed her eyes again, as if she was in a dream and wanted to wake to a different world. I had to move and stretch my legs, but when I stood up they almost buckled under me and I reached out to the wall to hold my balance. She stood up too and draped one of the sacks across my shoulders like a cape, and together we walked the circulation back into our limbs, moving round and round the shed, until gradually we pushed some warmth into our bodies with our breath puffing in front of us like thistledown.

'What will happen now?' she asked.

'They will contact the Agency and ask them to pay money to get me back.'

'So they will not harm you?'

'They need me alive to get the money, but nothing is certain with them, nothing except that they want to hurt us.'

'I don't work for the Agency, Naomi. No one will pay money for me.'

We walked on, pulling the split sacks round us like cloaks, the smell of the hessian and must spuming into our faces. 'We must find a way to get out of here and away from Bakalla. Sooner or later they will hurt us both. We have to try and get away.' She nodded and we went on walking, determination quickening our pace and joining us in a sense of purpose. With the slow return of body warmth we crouched against the wall and talked about what had happened. She told me everything. I had already seen the worst. And when silence flowed into the wake of our words we stared through the ivory light at the shed which enclosed us.

We tried the door first, but it was locked with a chain that rattled loudly when we pushed against it. Through the narrow gap between the metal doors we could see the truck in the deserted compound, and a square of yellow light in a window of the clinic. There was a gap of a few inches between the bottom of the doors and the floor, but when we tried to scrape away the earth we met the concrete blocks of the foundations and could go no further. The ventilation holes proved no better, for although we could support each other long enough to reach them, we couldn't sustain it long enough to widen the hole, and even if we had succeeded, only one of us could have clambered out, leaving the other stranded. By now the grey wash of light had risen and thickened, leavening the darkness and revealing most of the shed. We walked around it again, feeling along the walls with our hands.

It was Nadra who found it, down low in the corner farthest away from us. At first it looked just like another shadow, a dark patch of shade and indeterminate shape, but as more light filtered through the gap in the doors and ventilation holes, we saw that in a space occupying the size of a concrete block, mud bricks had been used. A shortage, a miscalculation, maybe a change of mind about ventilation – it hardly mattered.

We started to scratch at the mortar with our fingers but made little impression; the bricks were baked hard and impervious as stone. But we kept on, taking it in turns to scratch, until our nails broke and the tips of our fingers were red and raw. We needed a knife, some sort of blade, but the best we could find was a hair clasp belonging to Nadra which had a metal fastening, and so we gouged away with that until slowly and painfully we succeeded in digging out the granules of mortar. We knew dawn was coming quickly and it spurred us on to greater effort, one working in a short burst of intensity, then resting and trying to stem the soft papery blisters, while the other worked on. We scraped away enough to know that we could probably kick out the bricks and squeeze through the narrow space into the compound, and then we stopped and looked at each other. Suddenly the shed felt safer than what waited outside. There was still the compound fence, still a soldier on the roof of the clinic. Neither of us spoke, but as we looked at each other we recognized each other's thoughts. We sat with our backs pressed against the wall on either side of the opening. I glanced over at her and saw her finger the side of her face, and knew that we had to go.

I draped one of the sacks over my feet to muffle the noise, lay on my back and kicked out. On the second kick the bricks pushed out almost noiselessly, and with my head sideways to the earth I wriggled my shoulders and body through the narrow slit and helped her to follow. We stood under the sky that was beginning to redden, its greyness burnishing into a coppery band. The back of the shed was about thirty metres from the compound fence, and if we picked the right angle it shielded us from the clinic and the gaze of the guard stationed on its roof. The earth at the fence was sandy and we burrowed and scooped it away until we were able to slip under it then ran, crouched low, across open ground and into the shelter of the huts which straddled the rim of the compound, hearing in our heads at every step the warning shout and the crack of gunfire that never came.

We knew we could not seek shelter in the camp itself, but had to make our way into the bush beyond and put as much distance as we could between ourselves and Bakalla. Our breath streamed ahead of us as slivers of yellow sky began to cut open the strands of red, and gradually as our run petered into a walk the cold clutched at our bodies and made us shiver and the whisper of our voices was fretted and tremulous. I wanted the warmth of the sun, but knew that with it would come the light and the discovery of our absence. All around us the shelters looked frozen in sleep, laced with the mist and grey seepage of light, silent except for the occasional baby's cry. We passed through the tight narrow alleys, separated from the life within, until we worked our way through the rings of shelters which led to the open plain. But as we reached the open stretch of scrub we saw the bouncing, blinking lights of a jeep slowly circling this outer area. They were still too far away to see us and we pulled back and crouched in a space between two huts. Then I followed Nadra as she wove her way towards the south of the camp and the river bed. Without her saying anything, I understood that it was probably our best hope of escape. But as we headed towards it, the lights of the jeep suddenly changed direction and cut across the open plain at a sharp angle, forcing us to seek shelter. We were already beyond the last straggle of dwellings with only a few minutes to avoid being caught in the open, and so as Nadra pointed we scurried into the field of sunflowers.

Even after the stripping of everything left by the Agency, the crops of sorghum and sunflowers had remained untouched. The serried rows of flowers stood tall and heavy-headed, the splurge of yellow drained away by the grey light. We moved slowly, deeper into the thickening screen, conscious even then of the smell of greenness and flower, until we reached what must have been the centre and lay down, letting the white tails of mist snake around us. Too frightened even to whisper, we listened to the sound of the jeep's engine become louder, hoping and hoping that it wouldn't fall into silence. The headlights fanned through the rows of plants, throwing their light over our heads and then away again as the jeep moved back to the surrounding band of scrub.

We lay facing each other in separate drills, a double line of plants between us, and I saw her face gilded and framed by the ovate leaves, her hair braided with tendril and leaf. We lay there in silence a long time as the light tightened and stretched itself into a blue thinness, stirring new scent from the plants and stiffening the yellow faces of flower as they lifted their heads to the morning light.

'We must stay here until it is dark,' she whispered, 'then follow the river bed.'

'Can we not go now?' I asked.

'It is too dangerous. They will search for us. They will find us by daylight if we are in the open.'

I nodded and stretched my hand to her through the stems of the plants, and she took it for a second, and then we curled back into ourselves again and tried to find some comfort on the thin bed of earth. Slowly, bit by bit, the rising heat of the day crept over our bodies, loosening the tight knot of our limbs and stirring a restlessness for which there was no respite, but we stayed where we were, afraid that movement or noise would betray our presence. We suffered ant bites, and constantly had to brush away the insects which flitted through the terrain in which we were trespassers. Once, a couple of drills away, a snake slithered languidly through the base of some plants and we threw small stones to scare it away, and with the rising heat came the first powerful pangs of thirst but there was nothing with which to satisfy them; we could only push deeper into the dappled shade and try to distract our minds with other thoughts and focus on how we would make our escape.

By then we knew they had discovered our disappearance; there was the frequent angry rev of engines and bursts of voices from many different directions, but only the excited voices of children drifted close by, the high tremble of their laughter lingering after them like the notes of a wind chime. I imagined their faces, for a second almost wanted to call out to them because then everything would be a game, a game that children played. As the day wore on and the heat pressed tightly against us I longed for water and tried to force myself into sleep but it eluded me, throwing me back into other worlds. Some of the swelling had gone out of Nadra's face and the badge of bruising had softened and lightened in colour, like a smear of childish make-up. Once she pulled some leaves from a plant and held them tightly to her cheek while above us the heads of the sunflowers stared blankly like children's paintings of yellow suns, their faces ringed and whorled by a black penumbra of seed. Sometimes small birds swooped through the narrow drills or hopped between the rows, their wings bright snaps of iridescence.

Hiding as a child in the dunes, darting through the tussocky tunnels to spy on strollers on the beach, watching their solitary skirting of the tide, their ritual stooping to finger some shell or stone. An old couple throwing sticks to a dog, the surf foaming and splashing white around its paws. Lovers arm in arm, their tight enclosure shutting out any eyes that might follow their synchronized steps. Their deliberate printing of the moment in the sand. Sometimes, after they have gone I walk in the woman's steps, imagine the consoling, protective arm of her lover around me. Sometimes I sit and wait for the encroaching tide to swirl away the traces. When the sharp-edged grass cuts like the slice of paper, it's so fine it doesn't bleed.

We lay there all day trapped in our silence, starting at every sound that came close, our movements brushed by leaf and stem, and I wondered what memories she sifted through. Sometimes her face was turned towards me, so close I could have stretched out a hand and touched it, and then suddenly, despite everything I knew about her, despite the time we had spent together, I realized there were great areas of her past and present that I knew nothing of. She lay so close, and yet I didn't know what world her mind wandered through or what future she constructed for herself. I looked at her eyes, ebony, beautiful, and the olive sheen of her skin and wondered in what place or time our lives could touch. Because by then I wanted our lives to touch. I had known this for a long time but had tried to keep it hidden, preserved in the memory of a cloud of grain falling softly across her face and the touch of her hand on my hair. When they had brought me back from the place of the dead, hers was the only face I wanted to see, her voice the one I wanted to hear. Her absence had freed the truth. Every day we were together I added another image of her to my secret store, preserved in memory and studied like the photographs we had taken of the children in the camp. Sometimes words came to my lips, words that came from somewhere I didn't know, but I stifled them and pushed them back into a nervous silence. For there was another voice, a voice like the one my father used when he spoke for God, and it warned and mocked what it insisted was an unutterable foolishness, perhaps even the greatest and most dangerous of all. I heard its insistent thud, like a hammer hitting an anvil, and sometimes it vanquished all other words. But sometimes too, that grip would slip and I fastened only on the blink of her eyes, the white whorled skin on the tips of her fingers, the electric rustle of her hair, and I would feel the life that coursed through all my being.

I stared at her through the drill of sunflowers, the silhouette of her face framed by the ornate decoration of leaf, and I was frightened that what I felt might only serve to hurt her. He had said that we wanted to buy his people with our food and make them our slaves, to have power over them. How could I love her – for by that time I had allowed the word to remain in my consciousness – and not let that love seek to take away her freedom or subsume her into a world that was mine but could never be hers? She stirred in the gully between the drills, propping her head on the pillow of one hand and fanning away flies with the other, and when she smiled I felt a shard of shame for the thoughts my returning smile disguised. It seemed like a deception, another example of self-assumed superiority patronizing with half-truths and lies. What would she do or say if she knew? I touched her gold bracelet on my wrist but when I searched amidst the shared moments which had brought us to that place there was only the slow shift of uncertainty.

As the day lengthened and seemed to stretch into its own eternity I wanted to speak to her, to let our voices pass through the barred stems of the plants. I started to whisper but the long silence and the heat had dried my voice, and when I went to speak the words croaked out too loudly and suddenly she silenced me with a finger across her lips. I read her eyes and the turn of her head and knew she had heard something and as I listened I heard it too – at first no more than the gentle brush and rustle of plants disturbed by the wind, but the air was heavy and still. Then slightly louder, somewhere in the far corner of the planting. We lifted and turned our heads, straining to catch the slightest disturbance, but for a few moments the stillness settled again. Just an animal perhaps, even our imagination, but as we relaxed we heard it once more. Footsteps, slow footsteps, the rustle and brush of plant. Coming further into the crop. She stretched her hand to me and I gripped it, trying to stem the fear, but as we held each other the sounds faded once more and suddenly I was conscious only of my breathing. A small bird, its breast and plumage an electric shock of blue, shot over our heads, making our eyes lift skyward to the blue swathe of sky, and then into the silence slipped the sound of music, a tumble of notes on a flute which seemed to snake and lilt between the plants until it circled and held us tightly in its grasp. I turned from Nadra and scurried along the drill, propelling myself forward with kicking movements then easing through the rows, following the music. I saw them through the curtain of plants, standing at the edge of the flowers, Ahmed's flute rising and falling in rhythm with the music. When they saw my face the music stopped, but only for a second, and from inside the tattered rags of his clothes Iman passed me a plastic canister of water and a little parcel of dried meat. Then without words being spoken they turned and walked away, my final memory of them obscured behind a screen of leaf and flower.

THE closer the past comes to the present, the less certain it becomes. Things blur a little, sometimes blend with dreams and take on new forms so I have to struggle to order their shape, try to pare away what belongs to the distortion of memory. Maybe it is the drugs they give me to ease the pain which cloud and layer those days and mix the memories with some other world outside time. But to remember, to remember clearly, is one of the things that is important, and I remember the rising hysteria of the cicadas, the sky above our heads slowly branding itself with a fiery filament of light, the dark buzz of mosquitoes looking for a feast and across the drill of plants her eyes like amber, the patina of her skin dulled by the softening of the light. Soon it would be time – and we waited, rubbed our legs and stretched them into life, sipped a little of the tepid water, using our tongues to push it round the dryness of our mouths. Already the night birds had started their guttural cawing and from time to time voices ricocheted across to us from the camp. The falling of darkness seemed to stir a stronger scent from the sunflowers, and shadows drifted into the gullies where a faint breeze stirred the rows. Stirred them like a whisper, rippling through the field like little tongues of sound, and suddenly there was a security in the shelter of where we lay. Beyond that security extended an uncertain journey, and into that uncertainty flowed the fear-driven imaginings that made me want to delay our departure. The hundred or so metres' stretch of open ground to the river bed magnified itself in those final moments, assuming the proportions of an epic journey which would surely thrust us into the spotlight of searching eyes.

But there was no other way, and I tried to counter my fears with the knowledge that each step would take us further from our pursuers. Through the filter of leaf, the moon seemed sunk deep in the sky, its scarred surface brushed lightly by yellow, vaporous mist, and about it a scattered spray of bone-white stars. The air was still warm and thick, but drained of humidity and weight, it pressed down on us making the movements of our bodies seem slow and heavy. A stronger breeze riddled the leaning rows. We started to scuttle along the gullies towards the edge of the crop. When we reached it we paused and peered through the final wisps of plant at the open stretch of scrub which separated us from the river bed. There was nothing to be seen except the lazy flitter of moths and the fine clouding of insects around some bushes but we both hesitated, waiting for the other to make the first move, and in the night sky the stars hung frozen and trapped in their remote silence. I touched her arm and nodded that I would go first, and as I rose to a crouch the journey flashed in front of me – a nightmare of flailing limbs, a slow-motion run, the opening of the clouds like curtains in a theatre pulled back to reveal a light-drenched stage, the bitter mocking laughter of the audience. I saw again the faces of the soldiers as they sat staring at me in the clinic and suddenly I hated them for filling me with that fear, that sickening loosening of the stomach, the unravelling reel of images projected across the stretched screen of my senses. I hated them with an intensity that fired energy and strength into my body and I set off, pounding my anger into the dust, indifferent to the rough, uneven ground below my feet, holding my face up to the sky and drinking in the sudden sense of space. Sometimes I almost tripped over stones, and thorns brushed my legs, but I knew nothing would make me fall or stop even for a second, and a few moments later I was sliding down the shaly sides of the river bank, tumbling and rolling in an ecstasy of relief.

For a few seconds I lay there staring at the night sky, and then I clambered up the slope with my feet dislodging little avalanches of earth and stone, to crouch where bank and plain met. I waved my arm at the oscillating shadows that were the field of sunflowers and waited for her to emerge. I waved again, my arm working stiffly like a metronome, calling her forward, but there was no parting of the shadows, no one emerging from the slow tremor of plant. Rising to my knees I waved more frantically, listening all the time for some sign of her approach. I wanted to call out and knew I couldn't but just when I thought of going back I saw her soft shape slewing a path through the moonlight, and I willed her on, starting forward each time she stumbled but making myself hold back, watching as her features slowly formed in the darkness. As she ran I listened desperately for the sound of an engine or a warning shot, but none came, and then she was dropping on to the soft bed of the bank, gasping for breath. We lay on our backs and stared into the sky until she was able to speak.

'I almost fell,' she said. 'I tripped over something, I thought I would fall.'

For some reason I laughed, and after first pretending to be angry she did too, until the laughter screwed up our eyes. And then the words came tumbling out, flooding the long silence we had endured and which had held us separate. Only the moon-washed river bed coiling below us reminded of a time beyond the present.

'We have to travel by night, hide during the day, until we are far from here,' she said.

'They will search for us, won't they?'

'Yes, they will search. You are worth much money to them. They will try to find us.'

'They're probably out there right now.' And as I spoke I knew that they would punish me through her. Standing up, I helped her to her feet and we slithered down the steep slope to the dried-up bed below. In the gauzy, flint-coloured light we started to follow its sinuous course. Sometimes we stumbled over clusters of stones or the tattered brambles of some thorn which had taken root. As we walked, the black buzz of mosquitoes hunted our steps. The ground below our feet was yielding, as if we were walking on a cushion of sand, but this only increased the feeling of uncertainty that each step brought. Gradually, too, the steep slopes on either side disappeared, to be replaced by broad borders of scrub, and so our progress was more exposed but we kept on walking, encouraging each other with looks and gestures.

After about an hour we passed through a section which was littered with limestone rocks and large stones, and then our feet would slip and slither over the loose scree, banging and bruising our ankles and draining our strength. We sat on a dome-shaped rock and rested, pressing our hands to the knobs of our ankles and trying not to scratch where the mosquitoes had bitten. By then all the water and dried meat had gone, and the rest brought the first pangs of thirst, but to think about it made it worse and after a short while we pushed on, knowing that we needed to cover many more miles before dawn. Once we came across a solitary waterbuck sniffing the cold memory of water before it took off into the bush, its sudden speed through the silvery light like the tremble of mercury. And on the plain, acacia trees were framed and frozen by the monochrome light, while on either side of us the distance stretched like a bleached moonscape.

We walked on, taking rests only when we had to, the warmth of our bodies dropping with the falling temperature. It felt like a dream, a dream world, in which I had slipped from my bed which faced the sea and walked through the door my father had secured and bolted, then passed through the funnel of coarse-spiked dunes until I walked along the shore. Spectral, my body diffused only by the grit and grain of light, blown by every breeze and current, unshaped or formed by any consciousness other than the sift of dream, I walked in a trance, the journey passing through me, gnawing at only the edges of my senses. I remembered the walks on the beach when I followed my father's footsteps, his shoes sunk deep in the crust of sand, the wide stretch of my legs as I tried to follow in his stride, the whine of wind splashing my face and slapping back my hair. Trying to narrow the gap between us to shelter in his broad wake as he strode through it, his head unbowed or distracted from its forward gaze as he headed for the black ligaments of rocks which marked the end of the beach and his turning point. Sometimes I wished I could be younger still, small enough for him to lift and carry inside the folds of his coat.

But now as he walks I move about him, made of nothing but silver particles of light, and I speak to him in a voice that breaks inside his head like the heave and fall of the sea, and I ask him about love and show him the photograph of my mother, the wedding dress flowing round her feet like surf. And we stand together on a pavement and watch her move shoes in a window, move them gently while the light glistens on the bright leather and buckles. We come close to the glass and stare through our own reflections into the world which stands behind her – the rows of green and white boxes on wooden shelves which reach to the ceiling, the steps with their long upright arm, the little sloping footstools with green leather centres – and suddenly she looks up and sees us both and smiles. It is a smile of love and it falls back on us equally, and we're standing so close to the glass that our breath clouds the glass and I have to rub it clear to see her perfectly again.

I move about him silently, invisible, made of nothing but light and the wind that whips the sand into little fists, and I ask him how love feels. And I see their bed that first time and feel their fear, the strangeness of solitary lives meeting in a moment that can never be rehearsed, and I ask did he put his love in words. And I look through the window again where my prints have smeared the glass and I see her climbing to the top step, scanning the rows of boxes, then stretching for the right one. I see the care with which she handles the box and holds it in the palm of her hand like an offering and when she opens the lid there is a sprinkling of coloured tissue. And then she kneels and lifts the lid away and offers the shoes and I ask again did he ever put his love in words. And when he looks through me with his eyes full of the grey swell of the sea, I ask him why that love was not enough to heal him.

My hand flicked mechanically at the insects which shivered about my face, and a dull pain throbbed in my head. Sometimes it seemed the moon was dropping steeply towards me, its owl face hunting out some new orbit and swallowing all conception of time. He tries to stride away from me with his face clasped to the black ridge of rocks but I won't let go and I flow about him and ask him about his God and if when he sat in his study each night his God came to him and brought him comfort, but when he opens his mouth to speak the only sound is the rush of the sea, and then he walks through me and into the ocean. I call out to him but I too have no voice and I hear only the clack and suck of the waves shuffling back over a bed of pebbles. He strides away, straight-backed, bare-headed, and I try to follow him but am bound to the shore and he is swimming out deeper with his head buried between each trough and then he is gone, gone from view, drifting into depths where even I can't follow.

Something flurried across the moon – a bird, a cloud, I didn't know. Nadra had stopped walking, I almost stumbled into her back. She held up a hand to silence any speech and we stared into the pearly light which flowed down the river and saw where a beam of yellow light stretched from bank to bank. And then it was gone but its image petrified in the imagination. We moved slowly to the nearest bank, conscious of every tiny noise our feet made, the rustle of our clothes, and I had to fight the impulse to run. As we walked it seemed our movements left our shapes behind in the light and I wanted to brush them into nothingness with the swirl of my hand. But I followed Nadra closely as she made her way up the gently sloping banks and into the frayed tatters of bush. Her head was turned towards where we had seen the light, but there were no engine noises or voices and that intensified our uncertainty.

She tugged my sleeve and I kept close to her. We walked back along the path which beaded the river bed and then she pointed to a thick clump of tall bushes and trees squatting in a bed of ragged grass. As we walked towards them dampness feathered our ankles and sometimes our feet caught in roots. We pushed our way between the bushes, scratched by the springing whips of branch and torn, but tunnelled into the deepest part and climbed into the branches which hung close to the river's edge. The cold wash of moonlight seeped through the veil of foliage and below us the road of river vanished into the smoulder of shadows. We hugged the rough-barked branches, and peered out through the flecked screen.

We heard him before we saw him – a faint scratch of stones pushed together underfoot, the rustle of clothes, and then he came. Ghostly, moon-bleached, he walked slowly down the middle of the bed, the gun across his chest. Picking his steps carefully over the uneven ground, his gaze divided between the ground and the terrain above him, and when his eyes flickered up to where we stood watching, even though his face was washed clean of features, I knew he was the one who had tried to take my bracelet. He stared through us then turned a slow circle, scanning the banks and scrub before kneeling down and touching the ground with his hand. I felt again that something of our presence lingered there on the bed, tangible, shaped by the scent of our bodies and the intensity of our fear. He looked up again then cupped a hand to his mouth and called like a bird, the sound looping through the night. Even though I knew he couldn't see me I pressed my face to the coldness of the bark and felt its raddled blotches on my skin. When I looked up again a second soldier had emerged, walking through the wall of shadow where the river curved into the night. I knew from the way he walked and the way he held his head that it was the leader. When they met, their voices joined in whisper and then they split up, each broad-stepping up a bank then walking in parallel along the smooth ribbon of riverbed.

Sometimes they glanced over at each other and paused to search the straddle of scrub. Suddenly there was the turn and kick of an engine, and its headlights shot beams of light and a few seconds later we saw the jeep slowly bumping along the bed. On the far bank the leader waved it on with his hand, then motioned it to stop, and the engine died and the lights vanished into themselves again. Two more men got out and walked on either side of the jeep, their slow movements bringing them into gradual focus like prints developing through a filmy fluid. I clung more tightly to the tree as my urine stained through my clothes. Every part of me seemed drawn into the beat of my heart. The soldier we had seen first was now no more than thirty metres away from where we hid, and his stealthy movements made me a prey to each of his steps. He held his head up towards the sky and for a second I thought the night currents would carry the scent of our presence, but I forced myself to look at him and saw his etiolated face, the blurred nebulous void of his eyes, and then I stared at the Kalashnikov he held across his chest and saw for the first time that it was beautiful, and I longed to have it in my arms, to turn its power on those below in a sudden burst of anger and payment for what they had done, for what they still would do. And not from that miserable hiding-hole, but striding into the open in the clear light of day so they could see their justice coming and would know too the churn and shudder of fear. There was no other way – no words could carry such strength, such finality of judgement. I wanted to stretch out my arm, take its righteous incorruptibility and turn its force on them. Short and sweet, good enough for them. But down below he held the gun tightly in his grasp and so I clung more tightly to my hiding place, stilling and tightening my body, feeling only the shame of my fear.

He came closer, his movements a silvery blur in the moonlight, his face glazed by the wash of light, and as he passed along the path below us I heard the faint draw of his breathing and his light slow steps on the dust of the path. Then as he moved on and out of sight the jeep's engine started up again and the yellow light shot past us, moths and insects dancing in the beams. It moved slowly past us, the beams lifting and falling over uneven ground, until gradually the sound faded and into its wake flooded all the other sounds of the night that fear had shut out. But we stayed motionless, not even turning our faces to each other, and tried to construct what we couldn't see from the sounds. The call of a bird sent us scurrying deep into ourselves and once something rustled through the scrag of grass behind our den. Then there was nothing, nothing that could be distinguished or separated from the pattern of the night, and we allowed ourselves the luxury of movement, the silent shift of weight, but we both knew that many more hours would have to pass before we could risk leaving the protection of our hiding-place.

Places to hide. Always places to hide. Secret chambers of the heart. For some reason I thought of the school where I had started to teach, the place where I had once believed my future lay. I saw it in my mind, imagined it squatting in the silence of the same scrub of moonlight, the spokes of narrow streets around it held fast by the closed embrace of sleep. I walk through its narrow corridors, brush my hand along the green walls and hear the echo of voices tumbling from the distant corners of empty rooms. The ring of a phone, the slamming of a door somewhere, the hollow bump of a ball against an outside wall. I open my classroom door and stand in the tremble and shock of moonlight and their faces lift momentarily and stare right through me. I speak to them but the words drift aimlessly like motes of dust. I try again but no head lifts and in desperation I walk to the back of the room, to the boards covered in their work – the poster of a desert island with palm trees and yellow sands – and the faces stare down at my approach. Shadowy faces, the African tribe performing a dance, the statues of Easter Island, a dark figure wearing a combat jacket and a balaclava. They stare at me with their indifferent eyes but I reach out and take the shell in both hands and then, as one, the children's heads turn to me and their eyes look at my red-blotched skin, the dried-up gauze of my hair, my strange dust-smattered clothes, and I try to tell them about being afraid, about the baby we buried in the dirt, about everything, but my words start out only to vanish into the smear of moonlight. Then they turn their heads away again and as the shell cracks and crumbles into dust only one face is open to me. It is Sinead's. I see her tears swimming from her eyes like tiny silver fish. I reach out my hand to her but it passes through her and the silver fish of her tears are nothing more than the quiver of dust in the shiver of light.

But Daniel, where is Daniel? I sit at my desk in an empty classroom during a lunchtime when the rain fills the corridors with children and streams and sprays against the windows. In the playground younger children splash and dance in a puddle. I sit and wait at my desk, listening for his running feet and the sound of his laughter, but he doesn't come and there are only excited squeals and the smack of feet on the black sheen of the playground. I drop my head and try to concentrate on my work but the rain raps more loudly on the glass and when I look up his mother's face is at the window, her hair plastered flat to her head, her tears mirrored in the frame of glass.

Now everything fades in and out of dream. Sometimes as we walk along the river bed I am enveloped by the closing light, and as I follow Nadra I struggle to keep pace with her until I look up and she has vanished round a distant curve. When I cry out my voice is dry and brittle and breaks into fragments of dust and so I stumble on alone, my feet bruised and blistered by the long trek through the night. Then her face looms up ahead of me and she helps me when I want to stop. I walk somnambulant, oblivious to the landscape melting silently on either side of the bed. Hour after hour we trudge on, until the light begins to thin and fret itself into a new pattern. I slip on a scree of shale and suddenly the sky forks and cracks with blue shots of lightning and my head fills with the roar of thunder. And the rain comes, gentle at first, and I hold up my face and feel it kiss my skin, then heavier and unrelenting as it beats angrily against my body. And I imagine the vault of sky splitting open and the roar of some great flash flood bursting into the dried-up course of river bed and a roll of water swirling through its empty veins and though we try to run there is no place to hide and it breaks over us, carrying us with it, helpless and inseparable from the vagaries of its will.

JUST before dawn we climbed up from the river bed and headed further into the bush in search of some hiding-place for the daylight hours. We stayed roughly parallel with the river, ensuring that we held to our easterly course which we hoped would lead us to the coast. Once an antelope kicked up its heels at us and skimmed the silvery light before vanishing into taller grass. Groves of giant cacti with smouldering rosettes of pink flowers and around us the plain was badged with sandy patches, like the coat of a mangy dog. Sometimes small birds shot up from the grass and the clap of their wings echoed the startled beat of our hearts. It had grown misty and cold but I knew it wouldn't be long before the sun scattered these last vestiges of the night and the prospect of a full day spent trying to shelter from its heat, without food and water, seemed to slow and weight our walk until eventually we ground to a halt and hunkered in a blotch of sandy soil.

'We won't be able to walk much further unless we find food and water.'

'You're hungry already?'

'And thirsty.'

'Talking about it will only make it worse. Think of other things.'

I inspected the bites and cuts on my legs then tried to soothe away some of the pain from my feet, but there were blisters on my heels and under my toes.

'How far do you think we've gone?' I asked.

'Not far enough. A jeep might come,' she said, coming close

and looking at my feet. 'But you are right, we need to find water.'

I looked around us. 'Are there things here in the bush we can eat?'

'What things, Naomi?'

'I don't know – things like berries and leaves.'

She smiled. 'You think I know lots of secrets about the bush, that I will be able to do magic, find food and water from leaves and plants?'

I smiled too and shrugged my shoulders, feeling foolish. 'Well, do you?'

She laughed and widened her eyes. 'No, Naomi, I have no magic, but maybe we can dig a big trap and catch some wild animals and have them for our tea. Maybe find an elephant and ride on its back to the coast or shoot it like George Orwell did.' I kicked up a little dust at her. She pulled the trailing tails of her head-covering tightly round her neck like a scarf. The side of her face was bruised and the corner of her mouth was seamed with a thin black line.

'What do you dream of, Nadra, when you dream?'

She slithered her foot over the sand, pushing it into a little ridge then flattening it again. 'I dream the same dreams as you.'

'But what do you dream?'

'Of happiness, of something better in the future.'

'And what will be better in your dreams, Nadra?'

'Different things. Greenness, greenness spreading out over the desert like water; a school in every village; books. A home under trees. Things like that.'

'And do you ever dream of love?'

She laughed and chased away an insect with a quiver of her hand. 'No, I do not dream of love.'

'Why not?'

'To dream of love would be a disappointment. I must wait for what is given.'

'Who will give it to you?'

'A man who God will give. Is it different in your country?'

'In my country a woman can look for her own love.'

'And do they find it?'

'Sometimes, sometimes not.'

'And have you found yours?'

'No, I haven't found it.'

'Then you must be patient.'

I felt the first slow stirrings of warmth as the light quickened on the landscape, painting in the details that before had been insubstantial and unformed.

'Why do you ask these questions, Naomi?'

'I don't know . . . maybe it's because I don't know what you're thinking. Like when we hid in the field of sunflowers, or last night.'

'And that is why you ask about my dreams?'

I nodded my head and watched her hold her face up to the sun.

'Dreams are the worlds where spirits live,' she said, closing her eyes and tilting her face upwards. 'Dreams are where spirits talk to us, where they come to visit us.'

'You said once that spirits were superstition.'

'Yes, superstition, only in dreams can they live and move.'

I went to say something else, but she stood up and beat some of the dust from her clothes, slapping out little puffs into the air. 'We should go now,' she said. 'Will you be able to walk?'

'I'm fine. Will we keep following the river?'

'For a little longer. There is smoke in the distance. Maybe someone there will help us with food and water, but we must be careful.'

And so we set off again, hugging the edge of thicker scrub and pausing for a few seconds before we ventured across open ground, trying all the time to subdue the desire for water. Keeping my eyes fixed on the slow drift of smoke, I found comfort in the hope of what might be found there. I walked a few steps behind her, listening to the quiet ripple of her song, trying to keep pace with her steady stride. Eventually we broke out from the bush and across an open grassy plain, walking through a shock of green grass which fanned around our legs and felt cool to the senses. Little eddies of breeze vibrated across it, and butterflies like painted brooches lingered on the tips of grass or lazed into tremulous flight. Beyond the plain we found a path leading through thick corridors of thorn and we followed it, getting closer all the time to the smoke. Nadra wanted us to get a look at the place before we made ourselves known, but as we moved along the path we heard the startled voices of children and their flight through the undergrowth as they raced ahead of us to warn of our arrival, and so there was nothing we could do but walk on and take our chances.

It looked as if the whole village had turned out to witness the strangers' arrival. A dog barked round our feet as we approached the straddle of shelters, all of which were built with mud bricks and grass, some strengthened with bits of wood or coped with sections of tin. In a makeshift corral some goats and a few thin cattle were grazing. As we came closer to the group of people it was obvious which was headman, and I followed Nadra as she bowed and spoke to him. His face was grained and ridged with age and his eyes were full of suspicion. As he listened, the women and children fanned round me, unable to restrain their curiosity. Some of the children touched me then pulled away again, as if frightened to let their hands linger too long. I smiled at those staring at me but their faces registered only caution. I didn't know what story Nadra was telling but it felt like she was struggling for a response and once she held up her empty hands in a gesture of poverty, showing that we had nothing to give them for the help we sought. When she had finished the headman turned his back on us, and there was an animated discussion with those closest to him.

'What did you tell him?' I asked.

'That you work for the UN and they will get a big reward if they help us.'

'And does he believe you?'

'I don't know. They are frightened of trouble. He wanted to know why we were walking in the bush, why we were on our own.'

'And what did you say?'

'That our jeep broke down, that we got separated from the others. I have told him that many people will look for us, and if they help us they will be given American dollars and food.'

But it was clear there were other considerations to be taken into account, things about which we could only guess, and the length and animation of the discussion made it clear that there were conflicting ideas about what their response should be.

When at last the headman turned to us it was to say that we could have food and water, but then must leave the village again. We were grateful even for that, and we sat in one of the shelters where they gave us bowls of something that looked like porridge, and ate it ravenously. A group of women looked after us, bringing a basin of water for us to splash our faces in, and milk to drink. They fussed about us, shy but curious, keen to show us kindness. When some of the younger girls giggled behind the screens of their hands one of the older women silenced them sharply. I wanted to repay them, but there was nothing I had to give them except my thanks through Nadra. They bowed their heads solemnly in response and then for the first time seemed to relax and chatter openly amongst themselves. Nadra told them about my feet and one of the women inspected them, clicked her tongue against her teeth, and ordered fresh water to be brought. With it came glossy funnel-shaped leaves, and she broke and squeezed their sap into the water then gently eased my feet into it, rubbing and kneading my skin with the tips of her fingers. She made me sit for a while and I saw her looking at my white legs and ankles with their red tracery of scratches, and when her eyes moved to my face I smiled at her but she looked away, happier like the others to study surreptitiously. Then she lifted my feet from the water, knelt in front of me and patted them dry with a piece of red cloth the size of a handkerchief. One of the other women took a wooden box from a corner of the shelter and, opening it carefully, took out a glass phial, opened the top and poured out a small drop of scent on my feet, then rubbed it into my skin. As she rubbed, the sweetness of the scent spread through the whole shelter, and again I felt the urge to give something in return, but could only sit and receive.

A little girl slipped her way through the adults to stand and stare. Her mother called her back, but I held out my hand and after a second's hesitation she took it and I reeled her closer. Through Nadra, I told the mother that the child was very beautiful and asked her name. When I tried to pronounce it they laughed and the little girl repeated it again like a teacher, nodding when I eventually got it right. They made me drink more milk, but just when they started to ask questions about the country I came from, two men came into the hut and told us that we must leave. None of the women spoke. They looked down at the earthen floor as we walked out into the brightness of the morning, and then they joined the other villagers to watch our departure.

We were given a guide who would lead us to where a road ran in the direction of the coast. He was a young man and he looked at us impassively, shrugging his shoulders when Nadra tried to speak to him, as if he didn't understand her. When we set off he walked ahead, never looking back at us or checking that we were keeping pace with him. Before we had gone very far there was the sound of running feet and we looked round to see the little girl pursuing us. The light caught something in her hand as she ran, and when she reached us I saw it was the little phial of scent, which she handed to me. I waved back to the group of women, but no one raised a hand, and we turned again to follow our guide. He wore a green shirt and a

223

patterned macawis, and his body was held stiff and straight as he led us along narrow paths and into the bush. We passed a couple of boys herding goats and they raised their sticks in the air, but he gave them only a cursory glance then fixed his gaze on the way ahead.

Gradually we left all traces of the village behind and turned in a direction which took us towards higher ground, through a series of rises and ridges, and beyond it stretched the blue, glowering shape of mountains. Soon we had left the grasslands behind and begun a slow climb, winding our way upwards along a single track which led through a series of gullies, the steep sides flecked by grey swathes of stone and groves of aromatic shrubs. And as the climb became steadily steeper we struggled for breath, but there was no slowing in the pace of our guide, and only the dark stain of sweat shadowing his spine revealed his exertion. Once Nadra called out to him, but he ignored her and so we walked on until finally she took me by the arm and we plumped down on some rocks. She shouted angrily and he finally stopped and turned to stare at us. For a second I thought he was going to shrug his shoulders and leave us, his face a mask of disdain, but after a few minutes he came towards us and sat a short distance away.

'Ask him his name.'

But she shook her head. 'We must ask nothing of him. As soon as we know which direction to go we must get away, travel on our own.'

'You think he means us harm?'

'Maybe. I do not know, but we should not trust him. Soon we must send him back to the village.'

He crouched in the shade of an overhanging rock and watched us, making no attempt to disguise his gaze.

'Ask him how much longer the journey will take.'

Reluctantly she turned and asked him the question, and the answer came back that we must walk the same distance again. Then he asked her what we would give him for acting as our guide. When she told him that we had nothing he shook his head in disbelief, pointing to me. He said the way ahead was very dangerous, that he was the only one who could lead us, and for that he must be paid. It seemed wiser to have that argument when he had taken us to where we needed to go, so I nodded my head to appease him. Then, as I loosened the laces of my shoes, he suddenly came to where we were sitting and stood over us, looking down but saying nothing. I looked up at him with what I hoped passed for indifference, but then he turned his eyes on Nadra and uttered something that came out as a low rush of air. And immediately Nadra hissed a reply.

As he walked back up the path I asked her what he had said. She hesitated at first, but I made her answer.

'He says that the foreigners make our women into servants and then into whores.'

'What did you say?'

'I told him it was he who wanted the foreigners' money, not Nadra.'

We scrambled off the rock and hurried up the path, following him as he started a new climb. He walked ten metres ahead, never looking back to check if we were with him or making any allowances for the increasingly difficult terrain. After about an hour we started to drop into a long stretch of ravine, shaded from the sun by gnarled and twisted trees leaning out from the stony sides and terraces. Great swathes of thorn bushes and yellow-barked acacias meshed through each other and looked as if at any moment they might tumble and slip over the top of us. On either side of the narrow path we were brushed by tall, tawny-coloured grass, and as we pushed deeper into the ravine most of the trees appeared dead, their rotting branches jutting out at crazy angles and dripping with moss. The path was no more than a step wide and curved round the outcrops of rock and vegetation before straightening out again. We walked one behind the other, our approach startling birds and starting up little flurries in the undergrowth. Above us the sky was squeezed into a sliver of blue. I wanted to talk to Nadra but there was a stronger surge of silence flowing about us, broken only by the rustle of the grass or the sudden beat of wings.

We entered a series of tight little curves and then, as we broke into a straighter stretch of path, we saw that there was no one in front of us. Where he had been was now empty path and on either side of it the lazy fanning of tall grass. We stopped and stared along the way ahead, listening for footsteps that no longer existed, searching the emptiness for the little puffs of dust made by the slap of his sandals, but there was only the tremble of grass.

There was nothing we could do but walk on. Going back was not an option: our only chance seemed to be to follow the path and hope that it would lead us out of the ravine. We could only guess at the length of it, trying to remember what we had seen as we dropped towards it from higher ground. There could have been a mile still to travel, maybe more. We tried to tell each other that he had grown tired of his burden and, rather than lose face in front of us, had simply doubled behind and was making his way back to the village. Perhaps he accepted that we really had nothing, and to journey any further with no prospect of reward struck him as an act of foolishness.

We walked close together through the shoulder-high grass and thorn, and past clearings where stumps of trees stuck up out of briars. At first we tried to speak as we walked, but our voices seemed too loud and intrusive and so we fell back into silence, scanning the dense curtain of growth on either side of the path. We had only gone a short distance when we both knew that he had not returned to his village. We knew he was there. I felt his presence close and real, and I knew she felt it too. I saw it in the sudden stiffness of her body, the hesitancy in her step, the way she flicked her head towards every new sound. He was close and he was watching us, watching from the shelter of the grass. A bird took off suddenly towards the narrow slice of sky and we hesitated for a second then kept on walking, but each step we took only seemed to lead us further into his power. It felt at first like a power game, but I knew that soon it would not be enough for him. We walked on, forcing out each step, trying to hold our heads straight, and all the time watching for what was going to happen. Perhaps he wouldn't have the courage, perhaps we could shame him with an outward display of strength that would send him scuttling back to his village, where he would hurt us only in his dreams or in the shared laughter of young men sitting round a night fire.

We walked on, beginning the climb again up the far side of the ravine, sometimes passing under arches of thorn or the dead branches of trees which were smothered with wiry grey moss. As I looked up I felt suddenly dizzy, made faint by heat and thirst, but I walked on, too frightened of being separated from Nadra to pause or slacken my pace. And suddenly in a blur of movement he was there ahead of us, dropping on to the path from some rocks, stumbling a little as he searched for his balance, and as he straightened we saw the knife he was holding, its bronze-coloured blade angled across his chest. For a few seconds we did nothing but stare at each other and wait, then Nadra spoke to him and her voice sounded as if she were pleading with him, promising him whatever it was he wanted.

He came towards us and grabbed her by the arm and bundled her into the undergrowth by the side of the path. And then we were both screaming, and suddenly she was shouting at me to run but I followed them as they slid down the little bank that sloped away from the path and levelled out in a narrow terrace before it fell away again down steeper scrub into a gully strewn with rocks. He had pushed her to the ground and was kneeling astride her, holding the knife close to her face, but his head was turned towards me and he was shouting, while all the time she was telling me to run, to run as fast as I could. And then he held the knife blade up under her chin and she fell silent and he was talking to her, telling her something. I stood motionless at the base of the slope, but when I started to speak he screamed at me and pushed the knife closer to her and I fell silent.

'He wants you, Naomi,' she whispered.

He turned his face towards me as she spoke, and I nodded my head again and again. 'Tell him yes, Nadra. Tell him yes, tell him to let you go.'

He listened to her words, turning his eyes away from me to look at her, and the hand holding the knife relaxed to his side. And in that second I had grabbed a stump of wood off the slope and as he turned back towards me I already had it high in the air and though he tried to squirm aside I brought it down on him, striking the side of his head with a blow that almost shuddered it out of my hand. He tried to stand but Nadra pushed him back with her feet and I clubbed him again, and as it hit him the wood splintered into a spray of fragments and he stumbled backwards, staggered forward a few steps with skittering eyes, then lost his footing on the loose scree and slid down into the gully below, rolling and tumbling down the slope until he lay face down on the rocks below. We stared down at him, saw him move slightly then fall still again. Nadra picked up the knife he had dropped and we stood looking at it and then back down into the gully. She sidled closer to the edge but I put out my hand and stopped her, and then without speaking or looking again we turned and clambered back to the path.

AFTER about an hour we finally climbed out of the ravine, only gradually losing the urge to look over our shoulders. Nadra still had the knife, but she kept it hidden under her clothing and we hurried on, stopping for only the shortest of rests. Down below us, we saw a band of scrub crossed by broad shallow watercourses that were now dry beds of sand, and beyond this a stretch of plain that looked as if a fire had burnt it black. But there was no sign of road or village, and we were faced with no alternative but to continue following the narrow path and hope that soon it would lead us to somewhere we could find help. It meandered across the scrub until it brought us to a landscape that stopped us in our tracks, as if it belonged to another world, a dream, and I stared at the earth as I felt the last fringes of grass disappearing under my feet, to be replaced by the hardness of stone. Nadra looked confused, and I knew from her face that I didn't dream it. All around us stretched a black lava bed, strewn with igneous rocks, many of them sculpted into conical spires and pinnacles like children's sandcastles shredded by the wind. A ridged and cratered world, suffocated by a compression of thick black ash, where nothing grew – no crevices or pockets of plants – and where all sound seemed to have been distilled into the whine of wind that shaped and eroded the rock. There was no path, and only the blue-domed mountains beyond the blackness beckoned us on.

Sometimes the wind whipped the dust into our faces, and we covered them so only our eyes were bare. In places the rock was sharp underfoot, pressing into skin already blistered; in others we sank into troughs of thick, granular ash which made walking difficult and pulled at the muscles on our legs. We passed through narrow corridors of black rock with riddled, pockmarked surfaces and which stretched upwards into fluted and grooved configurations. Across wave-shaped ridges where the spray was frozen into pitted curves of stone, and the sun that beat down seemed powerless to stir anything into life or unlock the deadness. The ash left a bitter taste in the mouth and I tried to spit it out but couldn't, and we trudged on, accompanied by the strange, high whine of the wind rushing through the pipes and channels it had fashioned over centuries.

I tried to think of other worlds, of the sea, of the coolness of the blue mountains, but nothing seemed strong enough to resist the black press on the senses. Past and future were absorbed into the slow trek across the lava bed until I no longer knew if the world around me belonged to some blistered past beyond time, or the time that was called the future. All around, the contorted, broken rock seemed to channel us into a world from which there could be no human escape, and then I thought of God. And of a mountain that moved. The top of the mountain brushed by cloud, the women's hair hanging wet and lank over their weary faces. Watching through the car window as long lines of people moved up and down the mountain, climbing the stony paths with their bloodied, frozen feet. People hoping to please God through their act of penance, wanting to make themselves righteous through their pain. We had listened while my father ridiculed their superstition. Maybe I had stumbled into God's punishment, His penance imposed for my foolishness, for a man's body lying in a gully, for my sin. But I walked on, crossing the black bed of ash as the wind piped and squirmed through the fissures in the rock and dust flurried round our faces.

Where our hands touched the rock, or our clothes brushed against it, dark smudges were left and, as the strengthening wind stung our eyes, we walked with bowed heads, barely looking beyond the next few steps. We passed rocks covered with lizards, their languid bodies slowly inflating and their long tails curled like question marks. We took turns to walk in front, allowing the other to find some shelter, and then after what seemed like many hours I looked up to see the shapes of trees, and through their branches a waving flag of greenness. We pushed on with new determination, and in another short while the rock formations petered out and the blue mountains seemed within reach. The lava bed came to a jagged end, with long black fingers of ash stretching into the softness of the plain, and when we had left even these behind we slumped down to rest. But darkness was only a short time away. We had to find food and water while we still had strength left, and so after a little while we trudged on, walking mostly in silence.

They saw us before we shook ourselves free of our stupor and noticed their existence. Standing motionless like part of the landscape, momentarily forgetting their grazing sheep, their thin white whips thrown back over their shoulders. Two boys, maybe twelve or thirteen years old, standing as if frozen to the spot, watching as we walked towards them. We didn't shout or even raise our hands, frightened that any sudden gesture or sound might send them fleeing into the bush. But they held their ground, with their heads angled in animated conversation, perhaps unwilling or unable to leave their sheep. Then Nadra led us closer until we could see their faces, but she stopped, leaving a short distance between us. As she spoke, they looked at each other and past her at me. When she had finished, one of them took his skin-covered water carrier and held it out to us, and we took it and sluiced the tepid water round our mouths and splashed our faces. Then we followed them towards the base of the mountain, and in the falling darkness we found a straggle of makeshift shelters, and rearing up behind them a cliff pitted with caves. In the entrances burned scores of fires so the whole rock flickered with flame. As we came into the light people seemed to pour out of every crevice and flood around us. A hundred voices spoke at once. Nadra answered them and I knew she was telling the same story she had used in the last village. But when she said that we had come across the lava bed they rustled with surprise and some heads shook in wonder and disbelief.

An elderly woman with a shock of white hair came forward and, taking us by the hand, led us to a fire at the base of the cliff, then gestured us to sit and had food and drink brought to us. We drank thick warm milk from green plastic cups and ate tough strips of meat. Women we thought were her daughters brought water in a zinc bucket, and when we had finished eating we used it to wash. Slowly and painfully we eased off our shoes, and when they saw our bloodied feet they brought more water and cloths to bandage them. There were few males to be seen, apart from the young and the very old, and the woman told us that there had been much fighting round the villages where they had lived, and to escape the warring factions they had fled to the caves. The men had stayed behind to protect their homes or to join the struggle, but nothing had been heard from them for many months. Too frightened to make the journey back, they had chosen to stay until they were sure it was safe. There was a natural spring from which they could draw water, and good grazing for the sheep, goats and few camels they had brought with them, and so they lived there in the rickety shelters or in the colander of caves. They seemed to accept us as displaced people like themselves and the help they gave us seemed genuine, umprompted by other motives. Even their curiosity about us was restrained and discreet, and soon other families came to offer tokens of help – blankets, a wooden comb, a cooking pot, soap, a plastic canister for water.

Some of the women led us up a path and showed us to a shallow pocket of cave as if to an empty room in a lodging house. Their children carried little bundles of wood and soon they had a fire lit, and it felt as if we were ensconced in unspeakable luxury, hidden somewhere between the earth and sky. The fire flickered into the cave, smoke drifting lazily upwards, a fine gauze which shielded us from the gaze of the world. When we spoke, our words echoed slightly then lingered in the stillness until other words came to replace them, and as we sat on the blankets it felt as if our physical exhaustion had taken us beyond sleep, to a place where only words could expel what we carried inside, and so we talked into the night and sometimes there was laughter. I watched her add new fuel to the fire from the supply they had left us, and as she did so there was a dark shift of air as hundreds of bats wheeled across the face of the cliff, for a second eclipsing the moonlight. When she sat down again she was silent.

'Are you worried about your mother and Rula?'

'Yes, I wonder what is happening in Bakalla.'

'Maybe the Agency will have returned. Maybe they'll use planes to drop food. There's nothing there now for the soldiers, soon they will grow tired and look for somewhere else. You said that yourself.'

She nodded her head and stirred air into the fire with a stick. 'Who looks after your mother, Naomi?'

'She looks after herself. She lives with her parents now. They're old and she takes care of them. They have a shoe shop and she works in that.'

'Do you miss her?'

'I never feel she's separate from me. Even though I don't see her, I always feel she's with me and that I am with her. Does that make sense?'

She nodded and stared out through the smoke. 'Do you want to go back to your country now? You must think this is a very bad country with bad people.'

'I don't think that. I never think that. And I don't want to go back to Ireland, not for a long time.'

'But you must think that we are very backward people, very

superstitious, very cruel.' And she turned her face to me to catch my hesitation or evasion.

'All countries have their superstitions, their cruel people. My country as much as yours. You shouldn't feel like that.'

She shook her head in disbelief. 'The West calls us the Third World because you think we are backward, because we are poor.'

'My country has more money than yours, but that's all. I come from people who worship stone statues they think can move or cry tears, people who believe it pleases God for them to climb mountains in their bare feet. And in the north of my country people kill each other because they belong to a different tribe.'

'But you have books and education, schools and universities.'

'Some things are stronger than education.'

'Like magic?'

'Like magic, and dreams, Nadra. Like history and the past. The hate men have in their hearts.'

She shook her head again. 'Nothing is stronger than education, Naomi. You're a teacher, you should know that.'

I let her scold me, knowing it was pointless to argue, perhaps even cruel to damage the hope she held so tightly to, and so I listened in silence as she talked about how only science could make the desert green and only education could change the future. From somewhere on the cliff face came the slow dance of a woman's voice and the sound of children singing the chorus. We lay on the blankets, listening as the music floated in to echo in the chamber of the cave, and it made our own voices sound loud and hard and so for a little while we fell silent. And I remembered the young girls with white flowers in their hair as they sat in the gloom of the bar, heard the whirr of the fan and the song that drifted up to me through the clink of glasses and slap of hands on tables. His cry as he came in me.

'What is the song about, Nadra?'

'It's a song for children about catching birds. The words are foolish.'

'Would you like to have children?'

'Yes, I would like children, but I think maybe I am too old.'

'Too old? How are you too old?' I laughed.

'Most girls my age have been married for ten years. My family is poor and there is no dowry to give. I think no one of any worth will want me.'

'But among the young, the educated, many will want you for yourself.'

'It doesn't matter if they are educated, their families will still expect them to marry someone from a good family, or else they will not give their approval. I have no father to give a dowry or to act for me now.' She paused and then lifted the wooden comb, turning it over in her hand to look at it. 'Maybe I have to find my own love, like the women in your country.' She started to comb her hair, smoothing it first with her hand then slowly lifting and working it with the comb.

'Perhaps your father will come back.'

'No, he won't come back, Naomi.'

'How can you be so sure?'

'Because he has told me he will never come back.'

'Told you?'

'When I spoke to you of my father, I didn't tell the whole truth. I didn't want you to know of our shame and so I didn't tell everything. I must tell you now. When my father left my family, my mother sent for me. He had been gone many months and the letters did not come any more.' She stopped combing her hair and set the comb down on the blanket. 'It was decided that I should go to the capital and try to find what happened to him. When I got there, I stayed with the family of a girl I knew at university, who works for the government. But I did not tell them why I had come. I said I was looking for a new teaching job, a better position.' She hesitated.

'You don't have to tell me this if you don't want to. There's no need.'

'I want to tell you, Naomi. We should only tell each other the truth now. You told me about your father, I must tell you about mine. There was an address on his letters and I went there. It was a place where people stay who travel to the city to look for jobs. Men come and go all the time but it was the only address I had so I went there each day, very early in the morning, and stood and watched as men went to work, but he was not there. I didn't know other places to look – the city is very big and has many people – but I didn't want to go back with no answer for my family and so I went on looking. I told the family I was staying with that I was taking a class in the University, so they did not suspect.'

Something in the heart of the fire sparked and crackled into a fleeting blue flame. The song had stopped, and outside the night seemed to have settled into a drowsy stillness.

'One morning I was there very early, standing on the pavement, when a man spoke to me. Someone told him who I was looking for and he said he knew someone who had seen my father and I was to come back that evening and speak to him. All that day I sat in the bus station pretending I was waiting for relatives to arrive from the country. When I went back to the place the two men were there but at first they made jokes, did not tell me anything, and then I got angry and they told me he worked in a workshop that made radios, and the man told me an address where I could find my father. But it was getting late and it was difficult to find in a place which was strange to me. As I walked the women cursed me and men called after me so I couldn't ask for help. And then I found the place – an old man sitting in a doorway pointed it out. There was a courtyard and children playing and many open doors with steps up to them, and suddenly I was frightened. I almost ran away. But I spoke to the children and they showed me which door. Before I reached the top of the steps my father came out and saw me. He greeted me but in his eyes I saw something else. And as I sat in his home I heard someone in the other room, the room where he slept, but at first he said there was no one there but then he called out. It was a girl, maybe the same age as me, and he told me she was his wife and that she was going to have his child. When I asked him, will he come back, he said that his past life was dead to him, now he must have a new life. He had to leave the old world behind because it was no good and his future belonged in the new world. He said I could understand because I was part of the new world and that I could live with them, that I could be like a sister to his wife. He told me how much money he earned and the things he could buy with the money, and he showed me some of the things he had bought. But when I asked again about his family he said the past must be dead to him and that it was the will of Allah. Then I left and he called to me to stay but I kept walking and got lost in the dark streets, but I just kept walking and I never saw him again.'

She lifted the comb again and ran the tip of her finger along the teeth.

'Did you tell your family?'

She shook her head. 'When I went back I told them that I hadn't been able to find him. Maybe it was better to tell them that he was dead and then they would no longer wait for him, but I didn't tell them the truth.'

'Am I the only person who knows?'

'Yes, you are the only one I have told the truth to.'

I took the comb and knelt behind her, then carefully worked it through her hair in the rhythm I had watched her follow many times, using my fingers to tease out where it was turned and twisted, and soon it felt oiled and fluent, quickened into life. I let my hand touch my own hair and felt only a brittle dryness, a sun-baked lacquer of dust, dead as the lava bed we had just crossed.

'If you wanted, you could go and see him again. If that's what you wanted.'

'He doesn't want us any more. He has his own life now. We are not part of it. I think I would only remind him of the world which is dead to him.'

I lifted a thick bunch of her hair and gently pulled it back from her head, cupping it like water in the palms of my hands then letting it spill again over her shoulders. 'I didn't tell you all the truth about my father either, Nadra.' She turned her head sideways and I smoothed some hair behind her ear, but it sprang free again and fell across her cheek. 'I've never spoken all the truth to anyone, not even my mother.' I hesitated, but she turned round to face me. 'My father was an unhappy man for longer than I knew or understood, and I think he came to feel that there was no other life than the one that had been given to him. And slowly he felt frightened by that life, like it was crushing him, and he grew tired of struggling with it. My father was a good swimmer. . . . I think he just stopped struggling, let himself be carried out to sea. It was what he wanted and he knew it would look like an accident. I think my mother knows too. But she won't say it because she loved him and it would hurt too many people.' I heard my voice shake, the little echoes that trembled into the corners of the cave. 'I think he loved us but in the end that love wasn't enough.'

'But your father was a holy man. A holy man would not take his own life.'

'He was a holy man, but somewhere, somehow, he must have lost his closeness to God and couldn't find it again. Maybe it just slipped away year by year, I don't know.'

'And you are angry with him for what he did?'

'Once I was, but not now, not any more. I just feel sorry that it had to be like that, that he couldn't tell anyone. I think he must have been very lonely for a long time, but because he spoke for God he felt he had to hide it, even from those he loved.' I looked at her and didn't try to stop the words. 'Once I too thought it would be good to let go, to stop struggling and just let go . . .'

'What stopped you?' Her voice was a whisper, as if she was suddenly frightened by what she heard.

Too late for lies. 'Love. The bruising on your cheek where they beat you. The sound of your breathing, the touch of your hair.'

She sat still and silent and I turned my eyes away from her gaze to where a current of air fanned smoke from the fire. Then she was kneeling beside me and I felt her hand on my hair and the slow movement of the comb as it broke open the dryness and separated the strands. There was no sound but the crackle and rustle of my hair and the little clucks she made when the comb caught. She lifted and straightened, moving the comb the full length of each strand, and when the wooden teeth touched my scalp it made me shiver. When she had finished she went to the canister of water and, using a little cloth, she washed my hair and face and then she opened my robe and when it fell free she washed my shoulders, the hollow of my back, and the water felt cool and clean against my skin. After it was done I did the same for her and her body was beautiful, and as I touched it my hand shook a little and she smiled and guided it with her own hand. But my touch felt clumsy and heavy, as if it might break the moment into pieces. When she stood up I thought I had destroyed it but she came back with the phial of scent the child had given us and pressed it to the tip of her finger and smoothed it on my eyelids, the nape of my neck, between my breasts, and I closed my eyes as the cold sweetness of its scent filled my senses. Then in this place that felt balanced between the earth and the sky we lay down together on the blanket and watched the fire's slow slide into darkness.

WE stayed with the people of the caves for three days. To have stayed longer would have made too many demands on their generosity. They had been good to us, sharing the little they had without expectation of payment, without question. If they felt relief when we told them that we were going to try to reach the coast, none showed it. Instead, some of the children tugged at our clothes and tried to persuade us to stay. The older woman told us that two of the older boys would lead us through the mountains and show us where there was a road which led to the next town, and before we set off they filled our canister with water and gave us a little package of dried meat and rice. We left just after dawn, before the fires had been lit, when the caves were still silent pockets of darkness and dreams.

They led us through a mountain pass which burrowed into steep-sided rocks. Sometimes we were watched by gazelles perched on narrow ledges or precarious vantage points, their thin, bony legs propelling them to new ground. The journey was shorter than we expected, and after two or three hours we had worked our way out of the mountains and were in sight of a brown dirt road which curled into the distance. We passed other people walking and sometimes greetings were exchanged. At other times people glided across our path like ghosts, never turning their eyes towards us or showing any consciousness of our existence. One of them was an old man, naked apart from a ripped pair of trousers, his brown papery skin creased and wrinkled like a tied-up parcel. In his hand he carried a branch broken from a bush, and he shook it in front of him as if he were sprinkling incense. There was a family – father, mother, grandparents, five children – all weighted with an equal share of possessions and walking in single file, disappearing one after the other into a screen of bush.

When we reached the road the two boys left us and headed back towards the mountains, and we started along the road in the direction of the town. It was a long time before we heard the sound of an engine. We stood on either side of the road watching as it churned up a fan-tail of dust in the distance, the waver of heat making it difficult to see what it was. For a second I was frightened that it might be the soldiers, but as it came closer I saw that it was a car – a black saloon-type car that looked as if it belonged in an old film. We stepped into the road and tried to wave it down, but our frantic gestures were met only by a burst of horn and a spray of dust as it sped past us and into the distance. We walked on. As the day got hotter we were passed by few other vehicles – a couple of trucks, one other car, a man on a motorbike wearing a yoke of bamboo cages filled with hens. No one showed any sign of stopping. We had rationed the water with scrupulous meanness, but already half of it was gone and we had no idea of the distance to the next town. We left the road to find shade and ate some of the dried meat, pulling and gnawing at its stringy toughness, listening all the time for the sound of an engine. But all we saw was a man herding a couple of camels, his long cane pushed in syncopated rhythm against the creatures' necks as he steered them.

We walked on again, exposed to the constant pulse of the sun and the spumes of dust kicked up by our feet. Gradually the credit our bodies had accrued from three days' rest began to drain away, and our pace slackened. I don't think Nadra heard it at first because she walked on, locked in her own thoughts, and as I stopped to stare back down the road I had to call out to her. It was another truck, slowly forming out of the melting tremble of distance. It came closer. A blue-fronted truck with slatted wooden sides and a green canopy billowing up like a sail, bouncing over the bumps and ruts of the road. It wasn't going to stop. No one was going to stop for two women walking along a road when every road was filled with walkers, whole families of them crossing the country, their destinations and motives often uncertain. The truck was about a hundred metres away, filling the whole width of the road, its windscreen a jagged frazzle of light, blanking out the driver's face and making any kind of personal contact impossible. We stood facing it with our arms extended as if we were signalling a bus to pull in but I knew it wasn't going to stop, and then about fifty metres from us it slowed a little to cross a patchwork of potholes and with Nadra's screams in my ears I stepped into the middle of the road and let my head covering fall to my shoulders. I held up both hands in the air. There was a fierce stamp of brakes and the truck shuddered and skidded to the side of the road as its locked wheels gouged through the dirt. Spitting stones and dirt it slithered to a halt, half on the road and half off it, and then for a few seconds there was nothing but the sizzle of heat from its engine and the slow fall of dust.

He got out of the cab with a heavy spanner in his hand. A small man, smaller still as he stood against the side of the truck, wearing a ragged red shirt and a cotton macawis but it was clear from his eyes and the way he held on to the driver's door that the weapon was for defence rather than attack. Nadra called to him and gradually the tension drained out of his body and a little swirl of relief washed over him. He threw the spanner into the cab, his eyes and mouth creased into a smile, and surrendering with a shrug of his shoulders, he gestured us to climb into the cab. He had a crop of bananas to take to the capital. He could take us there too. He didn't speak or respond much to what Nadra said to him as he drove, but glanced constantly at me, the mirror angled slightly so he could see me. But when our eyes met I saw only curiosity. Holding the wheel with one hand he stretched behind and handed us some bananas which we ate greedily, our feet resting on what looked like a box of engine parts. Sometimes he would reach for a leather swat on the dashboard and use it to squash insects that fluttered against the glass. He would lean across to our side, holding the wheel with one skinny arm, and then the truck would veer to the side of the road, straightening out again only after the smack of leather on glass.

At regular intervals we passed lines of people and little camps hugging the side of the road, where families seemed to have collapsed around tiny heaps of possessions. Some of them held their hands out to us but we sped past them as if they were invisible. Once we passed two bodies rolled in cloth and tied with string, as if left out for collection, and later there was a group of half a dozen young children wandering along the road, some of them without clothes and with no adult to be seen. The younger ones held hands and all of them had a dazed, bewildered look. One of them trailed a red blanket as he walked, its tails slithering through the dust. It was their only visible possession. As we passed them they bunched together and closed their eyes as we showered them with dust. The child holding the blanket tugged it back, as if frightened that it might be pulled under our wheels. I watched them in the truck's side mirror as they set off again down the road, until the red blanket vanished into the distance.

My throat was sore and sometimes I felt dizzy. I knew my temperature was rising, but when I tried to sleep the noise and bump of the truck made it impossible. Hot air streamed into the cab and my clothes stuck seamlessly to the back of the seat. We might have been better off sitting in the back among the bananas. Then I remembered what it was like for those walking the road and tried to feel grateful. I said nothing to Nadra about how I was, frightened that if we were to stop and get out, the truck would carry on without us. By then I knew I couldn't have walked more than a short distance. I think she realized that I was suffering, because she spoke to the driver then told me that in another hour we would reach a small town and that he planned to stop there for a short rest and to refill his tank. She pushed my head on to her shoulder and as I tried to doze my eyes fixed on the dashboard, where there was a magazine picture stuck on with black tape. It was a picture of a young woman with blonde hair in a white T-shirt and shorts, drinking from a bottle of Coca Cola. As she tilted back her head the T-shirt tightened over the shape of her breasts. Behind her on a white sweep of beach was a group of teenagers enjoying a barbecue. Two of them were dancing, and behind them a girl was throwing a beach ball in the air.

The closer we got to the town the better the road became, and I slipped into sleep. When I woke I was conscious only of silence. The truck had stopped outside a green-walled building with a flat roof. There was a wooden stool beside its open door, and on the wall above, the green paint was flaking off in great blisters, revealing the brown surface underneath. In front of the building stood two thin petrol pumps, streaked and spotted with dust. The driver disappeared inside and we climbed out of the cab. I stood on the little stool and tried to fan some coolness against my face. The town seemed little more than a main street with a few narrower streets off it, there was little on the fronts of buildings to indicate if they were shops or dwellings, and in the strangeness of the silence there was no one to be seen. Halfway down the street a bicycle lay on the ground, light reflecting off its spokes in a way that made it look as if the wheels were turning, and further away a scatter of cardboard boxes rested on their sides, empty apart from scrunched newspaper.

When the driver came back he was holding two bottles of lemonade, and handed one to us. He drank his in two quick gulps, tilting the bottle steeply to drain the last drops. The pumps were empty but the truck carried its own emergency canister of petrol and he poured it into the tank, careful not to spill any. While he was doing this some movement, some glint of light on the opposite side of the street, caught my eye. In a gap between two houses was a white-walled building with double wooden doors. Above the doors a black cross was embedded in the plaster. As I looked, both of the doors opened slightly, forming a narrow seam of black, then through the widening gap stepped a child, but when she saw us she turned and vanished inside again and the doors pulled tightly closed. I got up and walked across the road, with Nadra following a few steps behind and urging caution. As I paused before the doors I heard the jangle of a key. The sudden surge of silence; the musty air which clings to my face like web; the clack of his heels as we walk down the stone-floored aisle; the echoes swallowed by the great vaulted mouth of the roof. In church the light is always strange – dust-flecked, grained and coloured by the high windows, always moving. And I never look up, because I think I will look into the face of God and something terrible will happen.

My hands rested on the hot iron rings of the doors for a moment, and then I pushed them open. There was a silence, broken by the faint rustle of women's clothing. I breathed the fetid air, searched the gloom, saw the women who sat singly on the wooden chairs or in little groups of two or three. The children sat on the floor at their feet or knelt with their heads on their mothers' laps but no one spoke and nothing stirred the moment into life. One woman lay curled on the floor, her face turned to the wall; another crouched at the side of the altar. Above them was an alabaster statue of a white Christ blessing a kneeling black man. Both faces were pocked and blotched with white where they had been disfigured. Scattered about the floor were ripped vestments and empty beer bottles. As I walked among the women I tried to speak to some of them but they clung to their own silence, their eyes glassy and focused on nothing but the tight circle of their own space. When I touched one she shook my hand away and her children buried their heads in the folds of her clothes. Nadra knelt beside a young woman who nursed a baby, and suddenly the silence was broken by a whisper of words and a low whimper. At first I thought the sounds came from the baby but they grew louder, more insistent, and I realized that they came from the woman herself. She sat bent over her child and her bare feet slithered back and forward over the floor. One foot had a cut caked with dried blood. Slowly the noise seemed to penetrate the pockets of silence the women had pulled about themselves, and their faces turned to where we stood and gradually the cry was taken up by others, and it spread round the church until it broke against the walls and sought to break into some space beyond the one confining it.

I knew before Nadra told me. They had been raped. They had been raped and some of their husbands and sons herded into cattle trucks and driven away. Anyone who resisted was shot. They had come to the church to hide, but the soldiers had found them. The priest who had tried to protect them had been one of the first to be killed, and afterwards the attackers had dragged his body through the town tied to the back of a jeep. Their men had been taken away for questioning. Almost a day had passed and still there was no sign of them. Now they were too frightened to leave the church and go back to their own homes. There was nothing we could do for them, nothing we could give them, and I looked at Nadra but she shook her head, and when we went to the woman curled to the wall and tried to comfort her, her body was stiff and indifferent to our touch. Their cries had fused and grown in strength and I wanted there to be anger in them, to be able to join my voice with theirs, but there was only the steady, rising sound of despair, of suffering beyond endurance, and we were excluded from even that. As I stood there under the broken, blasted face of Christ, the wailing voices burrowed deeper and deeper inside me until it felt as if what little strength I had left would collapse into nothingness. There were children's voices too, rising high like some descant, and then Nadra was tugging my sleeve and I heard the truck's horn warning that it was leaving and we turned away, closing the doors of the church behind us.

As the truck drove quickly along the main street, faces peered out at us from hiding places, and once a door slammed shut. A solitary dog ground itself into the dust and growled as we passed, then ran barking after us but wearied after a few seconds. At the end of the main street there was a body lying face down, the head framed by a dark pillow of blood. Leaving the town we passed a row of advertising hoardings, some of them plucked and ripped with bullet holes. Do I dream it? Have I confused it with something else? The last one hangs loose, broken off from its supports and daubed with paint. On it are two black hands, one male, one female, with bright red fingernails and a clustered diamond ring, and they are holding two glasses of Guinness. Underneath it says in English 'The Power of Love'.

As we drove out, we tried to fill the silence with talk, and spoke only of what we should do when we reached the capital. We had no real plan other than contacting the Agency for news of Bakalla and returning there as soon as it was possible. Nadra said we should stay with her father until we were able to go back. I knew she didn't want to go to him, but there were no other options open to us and we knew nothing of what was happening in the capital. Our driver could tell us little, other than that there had been much fighting and that different clans fought for control of different areas. It was clear that he grew more nervous the closer we got to the city. When we started to pass the first scattered outcrops of housing he steered the truck off the road and told Nadra that it might be dangerous for us if I were seen by the wrong people. He asked us to travel in the back and to keep my face covered until he was able to drop us off. And so we climbed in among the piled heaps of bananas, sitting with our backs to the cab.

The road was full of traffic now, and where other roads joined the main one vehicles and bicycles flowed into it without stopping, and the air was filled with the angry blare of horns. Young men riding scooters or motorbikes weaved in and out of the slower traffic, their shirts billowing out. High-sided carts pulled by donkeys plodded dispiritedly along, indifferent to the noise and rush around them. The city streamed out behind us, spinning out through widening tree-lined avenues bordered by white-walled buildings and the sudden climb of minarets from blue-domed mosques. Sometimes too, there were burnt-out cars, their blackened shells pushed to the side of the road, children playing in them, climbing through the windscreen or bouncing on the roof. As we drove on, we saw the first badly damaged buildings, their crumbling brickwork punctured with holes, sections sliding into collapse or lurching precariously over the street. Once there was the screech of brakes and a technical raced past in the opposite direction, the long thin barrel of a machine-gun bisecting the space between the driver and front-seat passenger. On either side of it sat three men, weapons resting across their laps, and behind the gun, looking down its sights, was a young man in a white shirt. As the technical swerved, he clutched the struts to stop himself falling. There was another sound, one that I recognized, and I looked up through the slats to see a white helicopter hanging high in the sky, then dropping lower. For a few seconds it disappeared as we passed under a great archway, some other culture's monument in stone to its moment of triumph. Then, with the sound of the helicopter still lingering in the air, we sped on until the traffic and crowds slowed us to a crawl. Lying flat on the floor of the truck, I peered out through the wooden struts at the people we passed and felt the hot stream of faces and noise wash over me.

Then we were turning off the broad avenues and into narrow streets where the house-fronts were draped with drying washing like unfurled flags, or rows of bamboo birdcages with tiny coloured birds. In the narrower alleyways the houses tilted so close together that it seemed their tops must touch, and from the open windows people leaned out, studying the world below. Past waste ground with makeshift shelters and market traders and penned livestock, until eventually the truck came to a halt outside what looked like a row of warehouses. There the driver called out to us, and after a brief offering of thanks we left him and set out into the night streets. We paused in the doorway of a derelict building for Nadra to arrange my headcovering so that it covered most of my face, and smear dust from the road onto the skin that was still visible. Then I followed her, my head bowed, through the tight mesh of streets. Many of them were lit by what looked like kerosene lamps and front rooms open to the street were like little grottoes, each revealing a different scene. In one of them an old man sat cutting leather to make shoes; in another a woman wove a cane basket, the cut rods beside her soaking in a bucket of water. But we hugged the shadows, skirting groups of people, avoiding eye-contact with those who passed us and hurrying on without ever breaking into a run which would draw attention to us. Sometimes Nadra hesitated, confused about which direction to take, and once she made me wait a short way ahead while she went back to speak to some women.

Eventually we found it, and it was just as she had described it in the cave. There were children playing in the courtyard, throwing small stones and hopping to pick them up, so absorbed in their game that at first none noticed our arrival. As we climbed the stone steps we heard the sound of a baby crying, and for a second Nadra hesitated. When she called out to her father her voice was strange to me.

He was younger than I expected, not so tall as his daughter but with some of the fineness of her features. He seemed confused at first, and his greeting was a mixture of formality and affection. As she started to explain who I was, he hurried us indoors, dropping the beaded curtain quickly behind us. In the doorway of an inner room a young woman stood, trying to nurse the crying out of her baby, its head resting on her shoulder, but as Nadra's father brushed clean a wooden chair for me, she vanished from view and only the intermittent cries of the child revealed that they were still there.

While Nadra and her father talked I looked round the room, taking in the few pieces of furniture, the radio-cassette player, a pink-coloured glass tray with tiny glasses, a hand-driven sewing machine beside what looked like a pile of pillowcases. I had taken off my head covering, tried to clean my face. He glanced at me, nodding his head at what Nadra was saying.

'I have told him that you work for the Agency and that you have become separated from them, that tomorrow we will try to go to where they have their offices. He says we must be careful, that foreign soldiers have come ashore from their ships and there has been fighting. In some places foreigners have been attacked. While we are here we must not go out or draw attention to ourselves.'

I nodded that I understood. The woman brought us thick black coffee, and when she served Nadra their eyes never met and no words were spoken. He was curious about the West and for a while asked many questions, but sometimes Nadra answered them herself without translating and gradually her voice became flecked with irritation. Soon after the questions stopped he went out for a while, and when he returned he told us that in the morning someone from his workshop would drive us across the city to the area where the Western agencies had their bases. That night we lay on the stone floor, hearing the staccato rattle of gunfire and the hollow rumble of explosions. Once when we got up and looked into the night sky we saw what looked like the red scream of tracer bullets. When we turned round the woman was standing there with the baby in her arms. He was awake but not crying. I think she had just fed him. We stood looking at each other for a few seconds, embarrassed by the silence but not knowing what to say, and then she came towards us and offered the baby to Nadra, holding him with outstretched arms into the space between us. Nadra hesitated, glanced at me, then took the child in her arms and held him close.

In the morning a small three-wheeled van arrived outside the courtyard. We sat in the back, squeezed between spare tyres and wooden boxes of tools, and the smell of exhaust fumes seemed to seep back inside the van. I hoped the journey would be short, but the roads were already clogged with traffic and when we hadn't come to a complete stop the van swerved in and out of other vehicles and we had to use our feet as brakes to stop ourselves sliding across the floor. Once we were caught in a jam at crossroads, and then the faces of cyclists peered in at the back windows but as I tried to hide my face the van moved off again, jolting and rasping through changes of gear.

After about half an hour, we turned onto a broad boulevard, lined on either side by high white walls. Almost immediately the driver shot his foot on the brakes and the van slewed out of control, finishing side on to the road. As we spun, we caught sight of the burning cars ahead, heard the angry bursts of gunfire and the screams of running people. Suddenly the smell of smoke filled the van, and as our driver jumped out we kicked open the back doors and scrambled out. People were running in every direction, knocking into each other, stumbling, sometimes falling in the frantic search for escape. Gunfire sprayed over our heads and the air was raw and riven by the smell of burning and new explosions. As we hesitated in the confusion, a technical veered towards us from a side street, its machine-gun pointing at the sky, and suddenly there was a deafening rush of air as a helicopter swept low over our heads. The swivelling gun of the technical spurted shuddering volleys into the sky. In a moment's pause in the firing we ran across the street, heading for the partially open gate of a courtyard, but before we reached it there was the sweeping slash of sky and another helicopter swooped over the tops of the buildings. It hung so low that I could see the occupants' faces, and then there was only a molten flare of light and the sear of pain and I stumbled into the courtyard, hearing nothing but my own screams as hands tried to scrape away the burning rags of my clothing. And then somewhere in the darkness, the darkness that isn't night, Nadra's voice is screaming that I am a European and a voice says Jeez, Jeez, and then it tells me that he is an American soldier and he will take good care of me and I remember and think that I am an expectant and that they will ship me somewhere to die. And I do not want to die. As I scream his hands move over my body and he's talking to me and sometimes he forgets himself and says Jeez again under his breath, and then I realize that the soldier is a woman. And she's shouting, shouting for a stretcher, and then there is the clatter of feet and nothing but a deep well of blackness.

'WHY did I come to Africa? It's always better not to ask that, Basif. It only encourages lies.'

'What about telling me the truth?'

'Why do you want to know? What difference will it make?'

'I'd like to know, to help me understand. That's all.'

'So you can decide if I'm crazy or not.'

He laughs a little and I hear him strike a match, draw his cigar into new life. 'I don't think you're crazy. No crazier than anyone else. Anyway the Irish are all a little crazy, I think. I met this guy once in Paris – his name was Marty Sullivan, do you know him? He was a very crazy man.'

The children have started to sing. I try to follow the melody and slowly recognize it as one of the songs Nadra taught the children in Bakalla. I shake my head at his question and try to listen to the song, but his voice pushes in over the top of it.

'Do you think you're crazy, Naomi?'

'Like you say, no crazier than anyone else. I think Stanfield might say something different. But you've talked to him about me, haven't you?'

'Yes, I've spoken a little to Stanfield. Not much. Just a little.'

He has the advantage over me. I have to listen for his evasions, his half-truths, can't see them in his face. 'And Stanfield thinks I'm crazy?'

'He thinks you're young, that you've seen many bad things. He thinks maybe some of these things have affected you.'

'And what do you think?'

'I don't know, Naomi. Some people come here and have big

253

problems with what they find. They've seen it on their TV and then they come here and it's not like TV and they aren't strong enough to deal with it.'

'What happens to them?'

'They go home again and try to get it out of their heads.'

'And you think I should go home?'

'I don't know. Maybe. But I know you're strong. When they brought you here your injuries were very bad, very painful. You were brave, and now your body heals well. Soon you will get back your sight. Maybe even by the time the Swiss doctor arrives.'

'You shouldn't promise things you can't deliver, Basif. Do you make promises to all your women?'

'Of course, Naomi. Apart from marriage. And I always deliver. It's my trademark.'

He laughs at his own joke. The children are singing a new song, one I don't recognize, and I can hear Nadra's voice mingling with theirs. Above my head the branches move slightly and a little slip of light brushes my face. I think he has given up, will soon get bored with me and leave, but I am wrong.

'So, are you going to tell me why you came here?'

His persistence arouses my curiosity. It is a quality I don't associate with him. I could lie to him, of course, concoct some tale that he might believe, but the effort it would involve seems wearisome, unnecessary, and there is no need for lies any more – the lies you tell because you're frightened that your own truth isn't good enough. I turn my face to where I hear him shift in his seat and I start to tell him.

'I came partly because of a boy.'

'Ah,' he says, as if that one sentence makes everything clear to him. 'It was – what do you call it? – an affair of the heart. That's it, isn't it?'

'Yes. It was an affair of the heart. But not in the way you think. He was a young boy I taught in Ireland.' I hesitate, but there is only the wispy swirl of smoke from his cigar and the silence of his attention. And I tell him about Daniel, tell it in a way he will understand, and as I speak the words, my voice sounds strange to me and the story I tell travels to me from a different world, a world which I can only reach through memory. When I have finished, told the part he will understand, there is silence, and for a second I think I have been talking to myself, but then there is a knock of his feet against the chair and the rustle of his clothing.

'And did you ever see this boy again?'

Did I ever see Daniel again? Yes I saw him. Only once. And only for a short time. It begins with a letter I almost throw away because it is mixed in among all the pieces of useless paper which fill my pigeonhole in the staffroom. A small white envelope addressed to me in thin blue writing, and I think it is a note from some parent to excuse an absence or request permission for a pupil to attend an appointment, and so I leave it lying until break. But it is from Mrs McCarroll and it says that Daniel is in a young offenders' centre. There is a visiting permit in the envelope. Beside his name is an inmate's reference number, and in writing which I recognize is my name and the address of the school. There is nothing else, and it answers none of the questions which run through my head. When the bell rings for class I fold the paper carefully and place it in my pocket.

The afternoon of the visit I am nervous, more nervous than I can remember being about anything. Nervous about what to wear, what to take, but mostly about what I will say. In the end I take only the book his brother Sean had given him and make the short drive to the edge of the city; turn into a winding tree-lined drive which too quickly leads to the high wire-topped walls of a prison. In a few minutes I am standing at a metal gate, studied by two officers inside who tell me to push when I hear a click. Inside they look at my pass, write my name and address in a ledger, and inspect the book I have brought. They flick the pages, turn it upside down and shake it, then check it against a list of banned books. The older officer calls me 'Love' and points me to a waiting area, where I sit beside a fish tank with a poster of a tropical island above it. The rose-coloured carpet is blackspotted with cigarette burns. I am the only person there and I wait until another locked and barred door is finally opened.

There is a perfunctory search of my bag, and then I enter the visiting area. On the walls, large circular, convex mirrors throw back my reflection. At a raised platform a prison officer inspects my pass, tells me the number of my table, and then he too flicks the pages of the book. When they bring him in I almost don't recognize him. He is taller, broader, and his hair is cropped so short that it's almost drained of its colour. He comes to me with a casual, loping walk and I look into his face, search it for his smile, but it isn't there, only a slight creasing of his eyes and mouth. For a second I think of offering my hand, but as he reaches me he looks away and pretends to concentrate on taking his seat at the other side of the table.

'Hi, Daniel,' I say, without meaning to, already slipping into my teacher's voice. He looks at me properly for the first time, as if he is struggling to remember who I am.

'Hi,' he says, nodding his head several times after he's said it.

'What happened to your hair?'

'I got it cut like this a while back. It helps me look like a hard man.'

'Does it fool anybody?'

'Yeah, I think so. Sends out the right messages. Maybe you should try it.'

'I don't hate my hair that much. I brought you a book,' I say, as I hand him it in its polythene bag.

'A book? Bad for my image.' And pretending elaborately to check if anyone's watching, he removes the book from the bag delicately with his finger and thumb, as if it's something dangerous. When he sees what it is, he's surprised and flicks to the flyleaf to check for the inscription. 'Where did you get it?' he asks.

'It was one of the books your father threw at me as I was leaving your house. He thought it was one of the ones you'd borrowed from school.' He holds the book for a few seconds, staring at the flyleaf, then sets it at the side of the table as if it doesn't belong to him.

'Me da said you'd come, but he never mentioned the books.'

At the table across the way a young woman with a boy of three or four is talking to an inmate. The boy kneels on a chair and drives his car across the table's formica top.

'So you met me da, then. That must've been a treat for you.'

I shrug my shoulders and smile. Across the way the child has climbed on to the table.

'We had a row about three weeks ago, he hasn't been back since. Me da'd fight with his own shadow. So, how's school, then?'

'Same as always. Trying to keep my head above the waves, not make a fool of myself too often.'

'So you've stopped looking for that boy Axl Rose then?'

'You're never going to let me forget that,' I say, but I'm smiling. At the other table, the girl smacks the leg of the child and pulls him back down on to the chair. 'A lot of your class passed their English. I don't know who was more surprised, them or me.' He doesn't say anything and in the sudden silence I look at our reflection in one of the circular mirrors. We listen to the voices beginning to rise at the next table, and then he drops his own.

'He has two other kids by two different girls. Some day they're all going to arrive here at the same time and then there'll really be a row. Do you want a cup of tea?' I nod my head. 'You'll have to go to the vending machine for it – I'm not allowed to move my arse from the chair.' When I return with two cups he says, 'Don't be making a mess now, because I have

257

to clean up after you've gone.' We sit sipping the tea, which tastes like something else, and there is silence again and it feels as if the first safe rush of conversation has gone. The young boy comes and stands at the end of our table with his eyes level with its top, and he raps it with the car before his mother calls him back.

'So what's it like in here?' I ask.

He shrugs his shoulders. 'No problem.' The child's mother is saying 'What do you know?' louder and more angrily, over and over, her only response to what the youth on the other side of the table is saying. We both glance over, and when I turn back to Daniel he says 'No problem' again and his face is closed and proud. An officer walks between the tables, lingers a little, then walks on with his head still turned towards the argument.

'How do they treat you?'

'I've been treated worse. They don't come round every day and beat you with rubber truncheons, if that's what you mean.'

'I didn't mean that.' Then I don't know what to say. At the other table the girl has stood up, and is grabbing the child as she hurries to leave. The youth looks embarrassed and folds his arms, then brushes the table with the edge of his hand. The child's car is still on our table, the child is pointing at it, but his mother ignores him as she rushes to the desk with her pass. The child is slipping into panic. As we stare at the car an officer comes and lifts it then gives it to the child, who grabs it tightly, and then the same officer comes and takes the prisoner away. Daniel exchanges the slightest of nods as he passes.

'Do you ever go back to Donegal, then?'

'Sometimes during the holidays. Not as often as I should.'

'You still think the sky and sea are suffocating you?' he asks, and he's almost smiling.

'When you don't have to live somewhere, going back isn't too bad.' He half-smiles again, as if I've said something funny. 'Are you taking any classes, going on with your education?' I ask.

'I'm learning hairdressing. It was a toss-up between hair-dressing and bricklaying. At least if you become a hairdresser you get to work inside and don't have to stick your hands in cement all day long.'

'Would you like to be a hairdresser? What about your exams?'

'What's the point? There was never any point.'

'You're not going to be here for ever.' I sound like a school teacher. He's playing with me, making me say the predictable, and I can't help it. 'You talked about going to America.'

'America?' he says, as if I've just made it up. 'I'm not going to America. I'm not going anywhere. There's people here who'll look after me now.'

'Do you believe that, Daniel?' He looks away, stares into one of the mirrors, then drinks from his cup.

'Do you know what I really hate about this place? It's the wee things. Like the drawers. You have three drawers for your clothes and things and you have to keep everything in the same order, like your socks have to be down the middle of the second drawer. And they inspect it every morning.' He screws up his face as if he can't believe his own words, then half-smiles again.

'How long will they keep you here?'

'With good behaviour and remission, about another year.'

I want to say something but don't know how, and he sees it and so he says, 'Are you still playing those games with the shell?'

'Not so often. People find it hard. It's always easier to side-step it, to bottle it as you said.' He nods and stares at me and I feel sick inside, wonder what my voice sounds like. 'Are we going to talk about it?' He looks away again. I follow his eyes to where the officer sitting at the raised desk watches us without interest.

'You always want to talk about things,' he says. 'Why do you always want to talk about things? You think it changes anything, makes things go away?'

'I don't know why. Maybe it helps. Makes you feel differently about things.'

'And that's why you want to talk? You want to hear me say I feel differently about what happened? I suppose it would make you feel better, go home happier.'

I shake my head but know it's the truth. He leans across the table and I smell prison off him.

'This isn't school, it's not a place where you play games with shells. This is the real world. Do you know anything about the real world?'

His words spit into my face like hail, and each one hurts, and I have to say something to try to stop the sting. 'I know what happened to those men was terrible. As terrible as all the other things that happen in this country. And I know you couldn't have been a part of it.'

'Everything's simple to you. You want everything simple like it's those two gangs of kids on that island, and one's led by Ralph and one by Jack and you want to be in Ralph's gang and everybody you don't like is in Jack's.'

'Maybe it is simple, Daniel.' As soon as I've said it, it sounds stupid, pathetic, but it's too late.

He shakes his head in a way I've seen him do before, as if I'm a child who will never understand, and for a second it looks like he's going to walk away but then he remembers he can't. We sit in silence for a while and everything in the room seems drawn into the mirrors, trapped in their repeated reflections. Words start into my head but they seem feeble and incapable of conveying what I want to say, so I say nothing.

'What about Sean? What about what they did to him? What about the people that Stone killed?'

I have no answer for him, and just for an instant in the tight hunch of his shoulders and the bite of his voice I see and hear his father, but I try to push the thought away, hold on to something else. Everything floods in – his mother's face against the glass, the girl in the wedding dress, her train caught by the wind – but then it collapses into nothingness and I hear only the voice of some young man, a young man without a face, and suddenly I look at Daniel and feel the sickness welling up inside. And I say it in a whisper but loud enough for him to hear, ' "Short and sweet, good enough for him." Is that what you said, Daniel?'

He looks at me and his eyes blink, and for a second I think he's going to say something but the words vanish in his throat. And then he's standing up, raising his arm to the prison officer in the corner, and without looking at me he lifts the book and turns away. But the officer calls him back and points to the two cups on the table and he stands staring for a moment into the officer's eyes. I say his name but he doesn't look at me or speak, just bends to clean the table and drop the cups and book into the bin. I watch him walk away shadowed by the officer, and then there is the rattle of keys and the clunk of the metal gate opening and closing. I never see him again.

I tell Basif enough for him to understand, but he doesn't speak at first and only the smell of the cigar tells me he's still there. I imagine the smoke drifting slowly into the branches of the tree and curling towards the light. I move my head, tilt it slowly upwards, and wait for him to speak.

'I saw it on TV – the car, the soldiers at the funeral,' he says, but his voice is slower than I know it, opaque, difficult to gauge.

'I suppose they showed it round the world.'

'I had forgotten it, but as you told it I started to remember.'

From the room used as a school comes the sound of Nadra's voice, a child breaking into a hollow cough, the clap of hands.

'Will that do you, Basif?' I ask, turning my face once again to where he's sitting. 'Will that do for a reason? Part of a reason?'

'Yes, that'll do. Maybe we have to be old before we can understand all the things that happen to us.'

'So, Basif,' I say, 'will you tell me why you're here?' But I expect only lightness, a good story that will amuse and change from telling to telling, for I think I know this man I have never seen, and so I tease him with my curiosity. He shifts in his chair and I wait for him to talk of himself.

'There are many reasons why people come to Africa.' His voice is strangely clouded, moving in some unfamiliar orbit. 'To help people, of course, and maybe to help themselves too. Sometimes to punish someone else or even themselves. Or to pay the price of something. You understand?' I nod my head, but he pauses a little before he continues. 'My family live in Beirut. We are Christians, Maronites. Before the fighting Beirut was a very beautiful city, as beautiful as Paris, I think. We had a good life there. My family was rich, we had many businesses, and my father wanted me to run these with my brother, but when I decided to be a doctor he was happy too. I trained in Paris. But I love Lebanon and know I will always go back there.

'When I was a boy my favourite place was the racecourse. My father had racehorses and sometimes he took me to see them training. I would sit high up on the wall and watch the horses and jockeys. Afterwards he would take me to a restaurant owned by my uncle in the Place des Martyrs, and there were crowds and shops and no one cared who was a Christian or a Muslim. When the war came everything changed, everything was destroyed and the city was divided in two, with Christians in the east and Muslims in the west. Many bad things happened, very bad things, too many to tell. My family supported Bashir Gemayel and the Phalangists, my brothers joined the militia, so when I went to work for the Red Cross things became difficult. Often I worked in the refugee camps with the Palestinians. They couldn't understand this. They have a saying: "One Palestinian in the sea, pollution. All Palestinians in the sea, solution." We argued, my mother cried, then we didn't see each other very often and it became too dangerous to travel across the city. For a while I worked at a hospital in West Beirut, but then the Israelis invaded in '82 and it was the end of everything. Arafat and the PLO were surrounded, it was hopeless – they had no choice. The Americans helped negotiate what you call a safe passage, and in August they sailed out of Beirut.' He stops, I hear him exhale in a slow stream. 'Do you want me to go on? This would be a good place to stop.' There is something in his voice I have never heard before – a nervousness that slows and dulls his voice, makes him cautious about the words he chooses – but I ask him to go on because for the first time I don't know where his words will lead.

'There were two large refugee camps called Sabra and Shatila. I had worked in both. Very poor places, very primitive – block houses, open sewers and rubbish piled high. Open sewers flowing everywhere you looked. After Arafat left, these camps were left with no protection. There is an old Lebanese proverb which says, "If you are a sheep among wolves you will be eaten." The Israelis surrounded the camps but didn't enter, then the Phalangist militia came in trucks from where they were waiting at the airport. The Israelis gave them the job of what they called "searching and mopping up". They were in the camp for three days and they massacred all the men, women and children they could find. I heard from another doctor of the strange rumours that were going round but I didn't believe them. But we went to Shatila, got there just as the first journalists were arriving.

'We saw the first dead in the entrance. It looked like a family who had tried to escape, the children still held in their parents' arms. We were doctors, we had to go on, but we never found a single life that could be saved. We were too late. Now I wish I'd never gone, never seen.' He stops, and I hear his feet shuffle in the dust, the rustle of his clothing.

'Go on. Tell me what you found.'

'Why do you want to know? There are only bad things to tell. What good will it do?'

'Do you believe in spirits, Basif?'

'Spirits? I don't know.'

'Unless you tell it, the spirits of those people will curse you.' I do not care what the words sound like or if he thinks I'm crazy. 'Please, go on.'

There is only silence for a few seconds, and the sound of his breathing. 'We found the bodies everywhere; on open ground, in the houses, the narrow alleyways. Piled on top of each other, twisted and stiffened into terrible shapes – for some had been dead for a couple of days. Some of the bodies were swollen and black and the smell was almost more than we could stand, and we couldn't speak because of the clouds of flies that gathered about our faces. I think they had grown so used to feasting on the dead that they didn't realize we were still alive. There were twenty, thirty bodies of young men with their hands and legs tied, lying at the base of a wall. Bodies of women and children covered by thin soil. Many had been shot but many had been killed by knives. At the start they used knives to stop the panic spreading too quickly, so as not to warn others. Babies, many babies and children, with their throats cut. Old women with single bullet wounds in their foreheads, shot at close range. They even killed the animals – we saw horses with their stomachs ripped open by bullets. The people who survived sat in the dust and held out their hands to us, but what could we give them? An old woman followed us, wailing, holding up a photograph of her family as if we might find them for her. Then more people arrived and the cameras came to show the world. Did you see it, Naomi?'

'I saw some of the pictures. Before they showed it they said, "Some viewers might find these pictures disturbing," and they showed a little. I only watched some of it, because I was frightened of what I would see.'

There is a sound that starts like a laugh but collapses into something else. 'Maybe it's good not to see, Naomi.'

'I don't think so, Basif. Not any more. The Israelis said they didn't see what was happening.'

'The Israelis heard it, Naomi, and watched it. There was a radio message to the Phalangists which they picked up. It said, "Do the will of God." '

'How many were killed?'

'So many we stopped counting. Later they said about a thousand. There were probably more, and ones who were never found. I knew many of them, recognized their faces. I had treated them in the clinic, especially the children.' His voice falters, breaks a little. 'There was a young girl called Salah, ten years old. I had treated her a week before, put a dressing on her arm and told her that soon it would be better, that she would live to be a very old woman. I found her lying in a space between two houses. I think she had tried to hide. She was lying on her back and her eyes were open, looking up at me.' I hear him cry, a low broken sob followed by ragged breathing as if something is choking him. 'I think as she looks at me that she's telling me I lied to her and I have to look away, try to hide the truth from her, that my brothers did this thing. And because of that, her blood, all their blood is on my hands.'

Then there are no more words but only the choking, ragged breathing, and I reach out my hand towards it but touch only space, and as I call his name I hear his steps rushing away. Then there is nothing but the stretch and creak of the branches above my head and the spiralling echoes of his words.

NADRA says the rains will end soon. I know she is right but I have grown used to their sound, find reassurance in the familiarity of their rhythms. Already the thunder seems far off, slipping like a lizard into some distant sky, and the anger of the rain – its beat and clatter on the tin roofs, its sluice through the gullies – seems almost spent. Something in me wants to hold on to its sounds, finds comfort in its fury, but I feel it fading into the loosening strictures of the air and know it is the start of the fierce heat of summer. Parts of my skin feel tight and stretched across my body, like the skin of a drum, and without warning or pattern pain can strike. The worst time is when they change the dressings, and then I have to send Nadra away, or she will argue with the nurses and criticize their clumsiness. But I know too that my body is healing, growing stronger, and now they let me sit in the courtyard, sheltered by the tree, for longer periods each day. It is a good place to sit because it feels as if the life of the hospital filters through it, and I am close to where Nadra teaches the children and so can hear her voice and the voices of the children. From the open corridors comes the chatter of the nurses and patients, the squeak and rattle of wheels, the smells of food and medicine. Some days I hear another sound, one which I have come to recognize – that of American AC-130 gunships and Cobra helicopters. I know they bring wounded from the capital, sometimes their own soldiers, and I listen to the blades thresh and slice the air, can even distinguish the particular sounds of their engines.

The arrival of the Swiss specialist to examine my eyes has been delayed, because there is fighting round the airport and some planes have come under fire. But they tell me he will come soon and that they think the signs are good. I think my eyes will heal, heal like the rest of my body, but I must be patient and not seek to rush things. Perhaps Stanfield was right after all and I have been lucky. I think he would like to hear that.

Now everything is seen through thought, screened by the process of memory, and the darkness forces me to shape what I have seen, to fashion it into some permanence before it drifts away and is lost. So I sit and try to call it into life, sift and store it where I know it will be safe, where no one can take it from me. Sometimes I touch the bracelet on my wrist with my gloved hand, make it rub against my skin and it doesn't matter that some, like Stanfield, will think I have been a fool, for none of that matters any more, and I feel the lightness of that indifference. The only thing I don't try to shape is the future. I resist that temptation because it is one foolishness I won't be guilty of. I have no wish to taste the bitterness of disappointment.

It is the faces which start to give me trouble. Just when I think I have them fixed and locked away, they blur and slip out of focus. Sometimes they run and smudge like ink. I hold them in my mind like I held the piece of paper with Daniel's address, and then a squall of rain slants down and the ink bleeds across the page. Sometimes I lose my father's face and as I bring him something in his study there are only his hands, flat and crusted like starfish on his desk, and beyond, the seamless band of sky and sea. Sometimes I even lose Daniel's, and then I think of that first morning and a boy crouching in a doorway and wait for his face to turn to me with a sudden seep of smile, but sometimes it is the face of someone I do not recognize. When the faces do come back I try to freeze them in my head, but as I turn them over and over like the Polaroids of the children in

Bakalla, they slowly drain of feature, dissolve into amorphous ghosts which drift between past and present worlds.

Now, in the darkness, I lose my own face, find it mirrored only in the memory of someone or something else, and then I see myself in Wanneker's eyes as he looks down at me from the back of the truck, but the face I see is the one he imagines and as the truck drives away it slowly vanishes into the greyness of the dawn. Frightened, I grasp for my face in the sliver of glass left in the frame Nadra gave me, but as I try to turn it to the light its surface clouds and I see only the little scrap of paper and the word Bakalla, and then something falls on the writing and it runs into nothing. I go desperately to the one place which always holds my reflection, see the mottled glass with its rusting clips, but there is no one there and even the trapped sky seems uncertain, as if it is only a vague memory of itself. For a moment I forget and lift a gloved hand to my hair, then drop it again. But then I force myself to laugh at my fear, smile when I remember Basif's promise to me, that he would make me beautiful. I shall remind him of it, threaten him with legal action if he fails, no matter how difficult the task proves. He will like that and tell me again that all women are beautiful, talk about Loren, tell me that my eyes will be as beautiful as hers.

He came to see me yesterday for the first time since we talked. I had heard his footsteps a couple of times before but they only came so close, then turned away again. When I asked him how he was he made a joke, talked like Basif, and so I said nothing, played the audience to his performer, listened to the lightness with which he inflated his words. He brought me a present – the loan of his personal stereo and a tape of U2. He was very proud of the sacrifice he made for the tape, telling me that he had had to trade a whole carton of cigars, but joking that he planned to steal them back when the patient went to the operating theatre. When he placed the earphones on me and pressed play, the volume was too high but I nodded my head in gratitude and gave as convincing a pretence of pleasure as I could. Eventually I had to tell him that it was too loud and as he adjusted it I thanked him again and tried to nod my head in time to the music. After he'd gone I pressed the stop button with my elbow but sat wearing the earphones, thinking of a people who need statues that move, plaster madonnas who cry tears.

It is Basif's step I hear now, his brief hesitation and then the confident continuation of his approach.

'Good morning, Basif.'

'Good morning, Naomi. How are you today?'

'Not so bad. Thank you for the tape. It was very kind of you.'

'It's nothing. I can always get more cigars.'

'You didn't manage to steal them back again?'

'No, he gave one to all the other patients in the ward. They smoked them at night when no one was watching, but in the morning the head nurse smelled it and he said the doctor gave them to him as part of his treatment and I got the blame.'

I laugh and I know my laughter pleases him. Then I ask him if there is any news of the Swiss doctor.

'There is still some fighting close to the airport, but I think it will soon be over and then it will be safe for planes. Very top doctor. I think he will be able to help. Then you will be able to see again, see how handsome I am.'

I laugh again and say I hope I will not be disappointed, and this too pleases him. 'As beautiful as Sophia Loren's eyes, you said, Basif.'

'Of course.'

'What colour are her eyes?'

'Miss Loren's? Brown, I think. Sometimes she wore glasses.'

'Do you know the story in the Bible about how the blind man was cured?'

'No, I don't think so. Tell me.'

'My father would sometimes read it in church. It was one of the miracles. Christ healed a man who had been blind all his life

269

by spitting on the ground and making a paste, then putting it on the man's eyes and telling him to go and bathe in a pool called Siloam. What do you think of that, Basif?'

'It's not a treatment I know, but I'll look up my old medical books. Maybe we should try it, tell the Swiss doctor he doesn't need to come.'

'In the story, too, the Pharisees, the holy men, were angry that the blind man had been healed on a Sunday.'

'These things are important in religion,' he laughs. 'Would you let me look at your eyes, Naomi?'

'Of course. You feel a miracle coming on.'

'No miracles and I'm not the expert, but I'd like to look.'

I feel his hand lightly tilting my head upwards and back, his breath on my face as he comes close. I hear the click of the light, feel its heat on my face as I look where he tells me, and his hand leads my face to the right position. In one of my eyes I see a circle of light. At first I think I'm imagining it but then I know it's there and as I tell Basif he chuckles and when I hear the off click I hold the light in my head until it blinks like a beacon. I want to shout to Nadra but I know she's taken the children for a walk in the grounds of the hospital. In my excitement, I start to talk too much, but Basif slips into his doctor's voice and urges caution, warns that it might not mean much, that we must be patient, not expect miracles. But I know he's pleased and a little excited himself. I thank him again for the tape and try to return it, but he tells me it is my present and I must keep it and that he hopes to get me more. Then he tells me that soon he is going on holiday and that he intends to visit Paris, look up some of the people he studied with, then maybe go on to London or Amsterdam. He has friends in all these cities and they will show him a good time. When he speaks of Paris I think of Martine, try to imagine her sitting in a café with some handsome young man to whom she gives all her love, but the image splinters and is replaced by stronger memories. When I shiver, Basif asks me if I am cold and would I like to go back inside, and I have to make a joke and distract him with questions he will like to answer.

He promises that he will send me postcards, and I ask if they make postcards in Braille and he thinks this is a good joke and says that I am crazy after all, and asks me again if I know Marty Sullivan and if perhaps I am his sister. When he stands up to go he leaves me with his doctor's voice, saying there is a good chance I will be able to read the cards for myself but I must be patient and wait for the Swiss doctor. I nod my head and thank him again, listen to his footsteps as he walks away, the high bounce of his voice as he calls out to someone. Even in the distance I pick out his laughter. It is light and buoyant, shining in the afternoon sun, but as I sit and listen to it float slowly back to me I hear only its loneliness, its desire to live in the moment. I think of Sinead's story, listening for her father's key in the door, the kettle filling for his supper, and the night she heard the woman screaming and the silence that was worse than screams. For Basif too, I think the silence is worse, and when in his dreams the killers come back for him, he will know their faces, and there is no escape from that. And when the footsteps come too close and he wakes with a scream, I hope there will be someone to hold him too, tell him that everything will be all right. Perhaps he will be lucky. I blink my eyes and try to recall the circle of light, listen to the final skims of his laughter.

Sometimes as I sit under the tree I think I catch a stirring of its scent, but perhaps I imagine it, perhaps it comes from somewhere else. I don't sit under the canopy so often now, preferring the shade of the branches with the slight flutter and play of the leaves. The tree creaks, as if some spasm of age rucks through its tired limbs, the way a house will suddenly stretch and crack before settling again. I think of the house I grew up in, and the silences which ebb and flow through it like the rhythm of the sea. It is empty now, with a 'For Sale' sign in the front garden which rattles with every flurry of wind and grows rusty and blanched of its colours. Perhaps when the sea is calm, other noises will seep into the silence: voices from a radio in the kitchen; my laughter joining with my mother's as it fountains into the spaces then falls back about our heads; the sound of my father's tread on the stairs as he comes to look at me while I sleep, his footsteps as he walks through the yellow fan of light. I remember the touch of his hand on my head, lighter than I have ever known it. I lift my hand and touch my face with the glove, but the touch is too heavy and the yellow light of memory slips into shadow.

I look up, turn my head to the sudden, loud footsteps in the corridor. At first I don't recognize them. He wears shoes as opposed to sandals, and his pace is businesslike, quickened by purpose. But then I hear his breathing, the slight breathlessness, the occasional thin wheeze as if there isn't enough oxygen in the air to fill his lungs, and I know it's Stanfield. When the footsteps stop I sense he's standing in the corridor watching me and I lift my hand in a little wave that tells him I know he's there. As he comes closer, his feet pressing the dust of the courtyard, I anticipate the smell of his after-shave, and before he speaks I catch the waver of its spicy, citrous scent.

'Hello, Naomi, how are things going?'

'Getting better, I think.'

'That's good, that's good. Basif says you're making good progress.'

'You've spoken with him?'

'Yes, just briefly on the way to find you.'

'Did he say anything to you about my eyes?'

'No, I don't think so, only to tell me that the Swiss doctor is delayed by the fighting round the airport. But the word from the UN people is that it will only take a few more days to mop up the remaining pockets of resistance, and then the airport will open again. So I suppose you just have to be patient.'

'You're the second person today who's told me to be patient. Don't worry, Mr Stanfield, I'm good at being patient.'

I hear him sit down on the chair opposite. 'Call me Charles, Naomi.'

'What's happening in Bakalla? What about Martine and the others?'

'The UN have made two food drops. There's no reason why anyone should starve. The Agency's given up responsibility for Bakalla – it's too big for the resources we have available now. It's being taken over by a Swedish relief agency which is mostly government-funded. They do a good job. Everyone from Bakalla is safe in the capital. As soon as the airport is clear, Wanneker and Rollins are flying to Europe and on to the States, and we've fixed up Martine and Veronica with a UN flight out. Some delegation or other is due to leave and we've managed to bag a couple of seats.'

'You'll be happy when you've got me on a plane and off your hands, Charles.'

'Yes, you're my responsibility now and I'd like to see you safely home. I can't deny it.'

'You still want to send me back to Ireland.'

'I don't want to send you back to Ireland. I really don't care where you decide to go.'

'So long as it's out of this place. Out of Africa.'

'Yes, that's right, Naomi. I hope you're going to be sensible about this and not make my job here any harder than it already is.' His tone is that of a friendly headmaster, someone who prides himself on being firm but fair. After what Wanneker has told him, I make him nervous. I hear it in the tightness of his breathing, the deliberate control he exerts over his words, the tight, clipped rhythm of his speech.

'I sometimes wonder about your job, Charles, about what it is you do here. You organize things, fix things, make arrangements, isn't that right?'

'I suppose so. Yes. Things like that. I suppose I make certain things possible.'

'When we first arrived you paid off the faction controlling the airport, didn't you?'

' 'Yes, that's right, we paid them landing rights and safe passage.'

'How much did it cost?'

'I don't remember exactly. I pay off a lot of people. At the airport? Probably about five thousand American dollars.'

'Do you always pay the price?'

'If it's necessary. I don't always give them exactly what they ask, of course. There's a bit of haggling involved.'

'But you always pay?'

There is a sound like a hand brushing wrinkles out of clothes, and a slight cough. 'When it's necessary, Naomi. We don't throw money away, but there are times in this work when to get things done you have to pay the right people. All the agencies do it. It's hardly an earth-shattering revelation. Do you have some moral scruples about it? Is that what you're saying?'

'No I don't have moral scruples. Despite what you think, I'm not a complete fool. But sometimes you must give money to people who are part of the problem, who use it to inflict suffering on the people you're supposed to be helping.'

'I can't deny that. I suppose it's a case of weighing up the real benefits that will result against the possible disadvantages. It's just the world we work in, it's always been like that, always will be. I can't say I even think about it very much.'

'And you, the Agency, never stand up to anything, just go on paying the price, making accommodations, giving in.'

'It's not a question of giving in.' His voice is rigidly patient, deliberate, trying to avoid irritation. 'It's a question of what has to be done, a matter of better bend than break.'

We sit in silence for a few moments, then make small talk. There is the sound of a helicopter taking off and veering into the distance.

'When will you go home, Charles?'

'At the end of this year. I'm retiring. Probably be home for Christmas. I'm getting too old for this work.' He suddenly sounds old, his weariness evident in the effort his speech costs him. 'I have a sister who lives on the South Coast. I'm going to live with her.'

I have a sudden picture of him in his linen jacket and white hat walking on a shingle beach, poking in the seaweed with his stick, giving occasional slide-shows to groups of women in church halls. 'That'll be nice for you, Charles.' I hear the faint laughter of children, the high squeals that they make when they're playing a game. Then there is a long silence, and at intervals it feels as if he's going to broach the matter of my departure but it slips away.

'I suppose nothing can happen now until we get the verdict from the Swiss specialist, so there's no point in talking about arrangements. Is there anything you need, anything I can get you?'

'No, I don't think so. Thanks anyway.'

'Well, I suppose I should let you get on with your rest.'

'Yes, I'm feeling a bit tired, perhaps I should sleep.' I listen to him stand, politely decline his offer to help me back to my room.

'I'm glad you're feeling better. I'm glad we understand each other. I'm sure everything will work out all right.'

I nod my head but say nothing. There is no point. His footsteps clatter in the corridor as he hurries away. In the speed of his steps I hear his relief at having negotiated another difficulty. When he has finally gone I make my way carefully towards the corridor and my room, touching the guiding landmarks I have memorized until I have slow-stepped my way back to the room, where I lie on the bed and listen to the whirr of the fan and the distant hum of the generator. I sleep for a while, and when I wake I have lost consciousness of time. Outside is quiet and still and the air feels cooler, the hum of the generator louder, and I realize the day has slipped into night. I say Nadra's name but there is no one there, and with a little pulse of panic I wonder where she is. I hope she will come soon. The only light in the darkness. There is no shame or guilt in it, and for what is taken, something is always given and the only world I make her part of is the one she chooses for herself. Her touch is more beautiful to me than anything I have ever known, and it reaches into the past, to a young girl who presses her lips to the mottled coldness of glass, who steps in the footprints of someone else's love until the sea swirls it all away.

The fan slows, stops, then starts again, and as it does so I hear the lightness of her steps and her voice.

'You're awake, Naomi. You slept a long time.'

'Stanfield must have worn me out. He came to visit me this afternoon.'

'What did he want?'

'To see if I needed anything, to see if I was feeling better, if I would be co-operative.'

'He wants to send you home?'

'Yes but he's not going to talk about arrangements until after I see the Swiss doctor.'

'Will that be soon?'

'Stanfield thinks the airport will be open in a few days.' She is silent, standing at the foot of the bed. I call her close, smell the sweetness of her scent. 'One of the few things I'm good at is not going where people want me to go.'

When I tell her I think my eyes are getting better she's excited, and when she hears that Basif said it would be my chance to see how handsome he is, she giggles and makes the bed shake so much that the chart at the foot of it vibrates against the metal bed ends. Then she tells me that she's found a copy of *National Geographic*, and if I am a good patient she will read it to me. She likes to read aloud, showing off her pronunciation and making me correct any mistakes, asking questions to check that I'm concentrating on what she's reading.

She asks if I've eaten, and when I tell her I haven't she goes off to prepare something for us both. As I listen to her walk away I wonder if the final stains of bruising have faded from her cheek. Sometimes as she sleeps beside me at night she whimpers in her dreams and in the slow hours when I lie awake, trapped by the sear of my skin, her whimper joins with the other voices, the voices which won't let me go and which I can't shut out, which threaten to curse me all my life if I turn my face away. They make me feel the way I did when we found the women in the church; I try to say that there is nothing I can give but they won't let me go. I try to appease them, tell them that I will let no man fire his emptiness into me again, that I will let my voice be their voice, but whatever is offered is never enough. They tell me too that forgiveness is the worst sin, the greatest weakness of all.

The fan stutters into stillness and from somewhere in the hospital comes the cry of a baby. I wonder if the shutters have been closed yet and if the rain will return, even briefly. The nurse who came last night and closed them said there would soon be peace, but I said nothing. There will be no peace, just another place, another flag. The young men who assume the will of God move their jihad on, for to die a martyr is to go to Heaven. They are driven by something I do not understand but which I know is always the same. In their wake the images flicker across screens then drift freeze-framed into some frozen darkness of space, recalled to the light only by the falter of memory, by the strength of a curse. A body on waste ground, Salah with her open eyes, a mother holding up the shrivelled bundle that is her child. I think of my father preaching on that Sunday all those years ago, the Sunday of the long way. And then I see my mother standing on a pavement with her foot on a ring and beside her are others – Nadra, women of Bakalla, Basif, many more. She holds her hand out to me but I look at the other faces which hate us and I am afraid. She still holds out her hand and, somewhere in the distance, Rollins is laughing, but then I take my mother's hand and stand beside her.

Suddenly the fan kicks into motion and I feel the layered coolness of the air slink against my face, hear the steady hum of the generator. Footsteps pass in the corridor. I lie back on the bed. My skin suddenly tightens with a flurry of pain, and as always I think of the sea, let it wash over me, a sea brushed by a glaze of moonlight, stirred by a rhythm we shall never understand. Perhaps this is the time, perhaps this is the very moment, and in the darkness the polyps contract, puff their beads of eggs into the water like pearls suddenly springing free from their thread. I try to stem the pain, imagine a pink slick of sperm trembling in the water, then some time in the darkness a glint of coral starting silently through the currents. Swimming through the dangers, swimming until it finds the safety of the reef where it grows and renews what has been destroyed. I think too, for a moment, of a city which petrifies on its own calcereous skeleton, but the memory fades and there is only this other world, fragile and strangely strong, full face to the ocean, a rampart against the ceaseless beat of the waves.

ALSO AVAILABLE BY DAVID PARK

THE POETS' WIVES

'Outstanding . . . Thoroughly enjoyable and much deeper even than the sum of
its excellent parts'
IRISH TIMES

Three women, each destined to play the role of a poet's wife: Catherine
Blake, the wife of William Blake – a poet, painter and engraver who struggles
for recognition in a society that dismisses him as a madman; Nadezhda
Mandelstam, wife of Russian poet Osip Mandelstam, whose work costs him
his life under Stalin's terror; and the wife of a fictional contemporary Irish poet,
who looks back on her marriage during the days after her husband's death as
she seeks to fulfil his final wish. Set across continents and centuries these three
women confront the contradictions between art and life, while struggling with
infidelities that involve not only the flesh, but ultimately poetry itself.

'A marvellous triptych: lyrical, respectful of creativity but also sharply sceptical'
SUNDAY TIMES

'Park's tour-de-force . . . The depth of character and emotion [. . .] are hallmarks
of his work as a novelist of enormous sensitivity ****'
Dermot Bolger, **IRISH MAIL ON SUNDAY**

BLOOMSBURY

THE LIGHT OF AMSTERDAM

Shortlisted for the Irish Novel of the Year Award

'Subtle, understated, not without a hint of menace and always courageous . . . An important book'
Eileen Battersby, IRISH TIMES

It is December in Belfast, Christmas is approaching and three sets of people are about to make their way to Amsterdam. Alan, a university art teacher, goes on a pilgrimage to the city of his youth with troubled teenage son Jack; middle-aged couple Marion and Richard take a break from running their garden centre to celebrate Marion's birthday; and Karen, a single mother struggling to make ends meet, joins her daughter's hen party. As these people brush against each other in the squares, museums and parks of Amsterdam, their lives are transfigured as they encounter the complexities of love in a city that challenges what has gone before.

'Marvellously compelling . . . Park takes that most difficult of subjects – recent history – and with graceful integrity explores the difficulties involved in coming to terms with the legacies of the past . . . beautifully described in Park's crystalline prose'
DAILY MAIL

'A stealthily affecting novel, this could well give more famous names a run for their Booker money'
GQ MAGAZINE

BLOOMSBURY

THE TRUTH COMMISSIONER

Shortlisted for the Irish Novel of the Year Award
Winner of the Christopher Ewart-Biggs Prize

'Edgy and compelling ... yields moments of heart-shivering beauty ... A magnificent and important book'
Joseph O'Connor, GUARDIAN

In a society trying to heal the scars of the past with the salve of truth and reconciliation, four men's lives become linked in a way they could never have imagined. Henry Stanfield, the newly arrived Truth Commissioner, Francis Gilroy, recently appointed government minister, retired detective James Fenton and father-to-be Danny share a secret from their past that threatens to destroy the lives they have painstakingly built in the present.

'A fine, crafted novel, but it is also an important book . . . He sets out to examine what it means to be alive – and does so in fictions that are subtle, understated, not without a hint of menace and always courageous'
Eileen Battersby, IRISH TIMES

'We're reminded that with writers like David Park, the novel can itself be a kind of truth commission'
NEW YORK TIMES

ORDER BY PHONE: +44 (0)1256 302 699; BY EMAIL: DIRECT@MACMILLAN.CO.UK

DELIVERY IS USUALLY 3–5 WORKING DAYS. FREE POSTAGE AND PACKAGING FOR ORDERS OVER £20.

ONLINE: WWW.BLOOMSBURY.COM/BOOKSHOP

PRICES AND AVAILABILITY SUBJECT TO CHANGE WITHOUT NOTICE.

WWW.BLOOMSBURY.COM/DAVIDPARK

BLOOMSBURY